THE GUY NEXT DOOR

DEVON McCORMACK

THE GUY NEXT DOOR

ALSO BY DEVON McCORMACK

TWISTED RIVALRY

BFF: BEST FRIEND'S FATHER

BETWEEN THESE SHEETS

TIGHT END

TROUBLE

CONTENT WARNING

One of the main characters featured in *The Guy Next Door* struggles with bipolar I disorder. While the author has done his best to represent the lived experience of people with bipolar I, there are times when the character should consult mental-health professionals and law enforcement but chooses not to. The author has done his best to show why this is the case within the context of the narrative, but in real life, anyone who believes they are potentially having a mental-health crisis should reach out to appropriate resources for help.

This book also includes the following content, which may be triggering for some readers:

- Discussions about serial murders, sexual assault (no on-page SA) at the hands of a serial killer, suicidal ideation and attempts, and mental-health crises.

- Moments where a character with a psychiatric disorder questions his reality because of his condition.

- Depictions of stalking and surveillance.

- Violence and threats of physical and sexual harm.

1

LEIF

I RECOGNIZE THE guy taking his time at the bread aisle.

Like, a weird amount of time.

His complexion is something between ghostly and sickly pale, like he doesn't spend too much time outside.

Probably around my age—late teens, early twenties.

Short, dirty-blond hair, nearly brown, and spiked in the front.

Guy can't be over five-five or so, and even that might be a generous guesstimate.

I'm sure that's the same black hoodie I've already seen on him a few times.

What's his name again? Mom mentioned talking to the Rodgers about him, but for whatever reason, it's not coming to me.

Feel like it starts with a *Z*... Zack? No, something less familiar.

Zander?

That's not it either.

As he scans his bread options, I can't imagine he has to make a serious decision about white, wheat, or grain. Maybe he needs gluten-free alternatives. Or maybe he has a preferred brand they're out of, so now he must find an acceptable substitute.

With how he's fidgeting, rubbing his thumbs across his fingers, I can imagine him being the kind of guy to give too much thought to the type of bread he needs to buy.

Maybe he's not thinking about bread at all; my mind can drift off from time to time while I'm grocery-shopping.

Because of my previous interactions with him, part of me thinks it's a little creepy.

That's a shitty thing to think about someone.

Just because he's different doesn't make him creepy.

My parents live in a friendly neighborhood. Most everyone on our street has lived there for over a decade, so we all know each other. We're the kinds of neighbors who wave and stop on the sidewalk to catch up with each other. This guy has only been renting the Morgans' place next door for two weeks, so it's possible he hasn't had a chance to acclimate to the neighborhood yet. Although, I've made every effort to smile and wave if he's in his yard when I'm driving by. I'll even try to say hey when I pass him while I'm out for a jog or a walk.

And I get nothing, except maybe a glare.

It's possible he's an introvert—the quiet type who

spends time staring at bread for a few minutes as his mind wanders. Can't fault him for that.

He starts to turn, so I look back at the beef, picking up another packet to check the expiration date. I debate if I should try to approach him, maybe start a lighthearted conversation that will make him more receptive to my occasional waving to him in the neighborhood, but I'm not in the mood to get another glare, so I continue with my shopping.

After I finish, I return home. As I'm parking near the garage doors of my parents' place, my phone starts buzzing. I put the car in Park and check it. Mom.

"There you are," I answer.

Her voice comes through the Corolla's speakers: "Are you in the car?"

"Yeah, and you are too now. I wanted to make sure I didn't miss you again. Gimme a second."

I get out, and we go through a familiar dance until the car releases her back to my phone.

"How was today?" I practically sing out, pressing against what I know will be a sore subject.

She groans. "Can we start with your day?"

"I was on a jog when you called earlier. Then I swung by the store to pick up some beef for stroganoff tonight. And now I have some meals planned for the week."

"Please, Leif, don't tell me about the delicious meals I'm missing. I don't need any more reasons to miss being home right now."

I chuckle, though I can hear the sincere exhaustion and pain behind her words.

"Speaking of…how is my dear grandma doing?" I notice one of my reusable bags slipped to the back of the trunk, so I have to really get in there for it.

"Oh, the usual," Mom replies.

A.k.a. insults, demands, and just plain cruelty.

A little over a month ago, Grandma was diagnosed with stage four breast cancer. In most families, this is when everyone would eagerly join together to aid their fallen loved one. We don't have that kind of relationship with Linda, who I'm confident is a sociopath. And even with Mom's boundaries, being the compassionate woman she is, she wasn't about to let Linda go through this alone—not to mention helping her sister deal with their mother—even if it meant enduring Linda at her worst.

"You'd think she'd be appreciative that her daughter and son-in-law flew out to Indiana to help out," I say, unable to disguise my irritation.

As I lean into the trunk to grab the bag in the back, my elbow hits one of the overstuffed bags near the edge, and a can tumbles out, thumping as it hits the driveaway. "Great. Dropped the tomato sauce."

I'm determined to finish what I started, so I grab the bag, pull it out, and collect the others.

"I can call you back when you get the groceries in,"

Mom says.

"Are you kidding? If we do that, I might not get ahold of you for another five hours."

She laughs, and as I turn to find the fallen can, I don't see it where I heard it drop, so I check down the driveway.

"Weird," I mutter.

I start looking around when—

"Jesus," I say, freezing in place.

A guy is standing beside me, his face inches from mine.

I recognize that pale face.

The dirty-blond hair.

That black hoodie.

Goose bumps prick across my flesh as the hairs on my neck stand on end. The surprise has activated a primal response within me—heart racing, adrenaline coursing through my veins.

I'm not even breathing.

He must've gotten home right after me.

I wait for him to do or say something, but he just stands there, staring with these intense, steel-blue eyes.

Even though he's half a foot shorter than me, there's something frightening about the way he stares, as if he's putting a curse on me with a look.

"Leif?" Mom asks. "Am I back in the car?"

The guy moves his hand, and I pull away before I notice the can of tomato sauce he's holding out to me.

Oh, fuck.

Catching my breath, I say, "Sorry. You surprised me."

"Leif, what are you talking about?"

"One sec, Mom."

He places the can in one of my bags.

"Thank you," I say as he pulls his gaze away from mine. He offers a quick nod, then spins around and walks back to the Morgans' place, leaving my head spinning from the bizarre-as-fuck interaction.

What the hell?

I watch as he returns to the Morgans' before I close the trunk and head into the house. Once I'm inside, I consciously take a few breaths, physically and mentally recovering from the surprise. Mom waits patiently, and as I enter the kitchen, I say, "Sorry. I ran into that guy who's renting the place next door. What's his name?"

"Zane, I think."

There it is!

"Zane, yes. I saw him at the grocery store and was thinking Zander or something."

"What did he want?"

"He must've seen me drop the can, and he picked it up for me."

"That was nice of him."

"Yeah, I guess," I say, which is an odd comment since it was nice, but it was done in the strangest way possible. "Sorry, it was a weird interaction. He stood there, just looking at me. Didn't say anything. Kind of creeped me out."

There's that word again. I shouldn't say that, especially about a guy who just did me a solid.

"Anyway," I go on, "what were we talking about? Oh. Linda. Never mind. Can we keep talking about the neighbor being weird?"

I'm pleased when my playful remark earns a laugh.

"It's only been some nasty comments here and there. But I have to say, I'm glad you didn't come this trip."

Tension rises within me as I think about my previous interactions with Linda.

"With everything I've got going on, I think my therapist was right about setting a boundary here."

Mom's quiet for a moment, then says, "I'm so sorry about what she said last time she was over. That was so insensitive. And heartless."

After learning about my depression and stint in the psych unit, Linda didn't mind sharing her thoughts:

"Must be nice staying with your parents instead of going to school."

"I think a lot of these...what is it, Gen Z...use their mental health to cover up for how goddamn lazy they are."

"Sometimes the parent has to learn to give the kid a good kick out of the nest."

Which truly, for her, are relatively harmless comments.

I'm glad I don't have to put up with her, but I feel

guilty for not being there for my parents, especially when I know how vicious Linda can be to Mom.

"Speaking of Linda," Mom says, "she apparently saw your Instagram post. She's made some comments about your 'secret admirer' in that pointed way she has, like she wanted me to know she's keeping an eye on what you're up to."

Fuck. My. Life.

"I didn't post that I had a secret admirer," I snap. "I posted that to let whoever sent it know I was onto what they were doing and that it wasn't cool. And hoping that if one of my ex-friends knew who it was, they'd tell them to lay off."

The whole subject brings up a series of painful events: The psych unit. My fallout with my friends on social media. The subsequent harassment I went through.

And I'd rather not think about any of it right now.

The conversation shifts to what Mom, her sister, and Dad are navigating between Grandma's health and her home, and we catch up some more before she says, "And how is everything going with you?"

I hear the concern in her voice. I know she means well, but I don't love being the reason she's worried. I'm intensely aware that she would prefer to get ahead of it this time, rather than getting another call at three in the morning where I explain to her why I'm at the police station.

"It's fine, Mom. Really."

"So you feel like the antidepressants are working?"

A knot twists in my chest. I hate talking about this.

It reminds me of my pain. It reminds me of how bad things got. And it makes me feel like there's something wrong with me. I know Mom doesn't feel that way, but I can't help it.

"Yeah, they're fine," I force out when she says, "Oh, *she's* calling."

Great timing, since I didn't want to go down this route with Mom.

"I'm glad you're still feeling better," she adds. "Make sure you call me if you need anything. Now go make that stroganoff, and I'll pretend I can smell it from here."

I laugh. "When you get back, I'll make a special meal…you can name the dish. It'll be your treat for being far too good a daughter."

"I like the sound of that."

"I'll call you tomorrow. Love you, and tell Dad I love him too."

"I will. Love you too."

After I hang up, I finish putting away groceries before getting started on dinner. Then I get some chores done around the house before scrolling through social media on my iPad while watching TV on the big screen in the living room, an activity I don't regret losing the rest of my evening to.

It's around ten thirty when I head up to my room,

where my phone is charging. At least, I thought it was. Fuck. I head downstairs and grab Mom's charger from her office, and when I plug it in, I realize my cheap-ass one from Amazon must've stopped working.

Great start to my night.

I set the busted cord on my nightstand—figure I'll see if I can exchange it on Amazon—before checking on Kyra.

"Hey, beautiful. How you holding up?" I ask her as I open the door to her cage.

On a jog the other day, I discovered the Rennings' cat attacking a sparrow and, fortunately, managed to intervene before it was too late. My first stop was to animal rescue, where they checked her out, but already overcrowded with patients, they asked if I could watch her until her wings healed up, a task I was more than up for.

I assess her as I pour a spoonful of seed into her feeder.

"Oh, you're doing much better," I tell her, pleased she's not nearly as anxiety ridden as when I'd first taken her in. Her feathers look full and healthy, and she seems to be in good spirits, bouncing onto the feeder to finish off the last of the seeds.

"Good girl," I say as I inspect her left wing. The feathers are coming back in, but I figure it'll take a week or two until they're functional again—at least that's what the vet and articles I checked online suggested.

I close the door and latch it. Then I strip out of my thermal and jeans and head into my en suite bathroom. I wash my hands before pulling open the top drawer under the sink, tensing up at the sight of the pills in the orange bottle. Seeing them reminds me of my struggles, but I can't deny I've been feeling better since I switched to this new antidepressant two months ago.

I brush my teeth before hopping into the shower. The warm water splashes against my skin, soothing my muscles, relaxing me.

I grab the loofah and massage some liquid soap into it when I hear a loud *thud*.

Instinctively, I pull back the curtain, peeking into the bedroom.

Sounded like something might've fallen. But there's this fear in the back of my mind telling me someone broke down the door.

It's a ridiculous thought. We've lived in this house most of my life, and there's maybe been a handful of burglaries in our neighborhood. But of course, when you hear a noise like that, are you really ever worried about it just being a burglar?

It's only my overactive imagination, I tell myself. Some evolved trait to help my ancestors survive in the wild, but which doesn't do much more than make me anxious tonight. Although, anxiety is a welcome relief since I'd rather feel the twist in my chest from anxiety than the hollowness of depression.

I wait in silence, and when I'm about to return to enjoying my shower, another sound comes from downstairs.

Fuck.

I won't be able to finish my shower without imagining becoming the victim of a slasher-movie-worthy attack, so I turn off the water and grab my towel, drying off quickly. Tying the towel around my waist, I search around for something I could use as a weapon.

If I were downstairs, I could get the baseball bat from the front closet in the foyer. Or grab a knife from the kitchen. Or check to see if Mom still keeps pepper spray in her office drawer. But I make do with a can of disinfectant spray. As I step out of the bathroom, holding the spray out before me—noticing the floral print design across the can—I feel like a fucking moron. I expect I'm gonna search the house only to find an overturned plant or a book that's fallen in the dining room, but my imagination tortures me with different scenarios, tailoring a horror movie where this scene could easily fit in.

A bead of sweat runs down my forehead, but as I reach the door, I force myself to turn the knob, then pull it open and peer into the hallway.

Another sound catches my attention.

This time it's not coming from inside. Sounds like the backyard.

I hurry to the window and force the blinds apart.

My room light refracts off the windowpane, making it difficult to see, but I notice a moving silhouette on the inside of the fence.

The hell?

Is someone back there?

But that first sound was in the house, for sure. Was someone trying to get in and gave up?

I start to spin around when I'm shoved from behind, something pushing against my back. I jump from the scare, reaching back, and my elbow hits something.

"Ow, fuck!" I hear as I realize there's an arm around my waist.

The blood drains from my face.

My heart races.

My throat dries.

The fuck is going on?

"Hey, hey," the man who's got me whispers, "I'm armed."

I feel something at my cheek and turn to see a gun.

A fucking gun!

I freeze, and I realize that at some point when my attacker grabbed me, I dropped the damn disinfectant. Not that it would have done me much good, but it was all I had.

"Keep quiet," he whispers in a low, deep voice. "Nod so I know you heard me."

I obey, noticing how much my body's trembling.

"Put your hands up by your head."

Again, I follow his instructions, hoping to spare myself a bullet to the head.

"I'm not gonna hurt you, but you need to do what I say, got it?"

I'm sure that's what any psychopath would tell his victim, but I nod anyway.

He keeps his arm tight around me as he guides me back toward my closet.

Really wish I'd signed up for a self-defense class at some point in my not terribly long life, but the best I could do now is maybe try some moves I've seen on TV and in movies and wind up getting myself killed.

As he opens my closet, I catch a glimpse of him in the full-length mirror.

About half a foot shorter than me.

Pale face.

Dirty-blond hair.

Steel-blue eyes.

That creep from next door?

What. The. Fuck?

I've barely had the thought before he drags me into the closet, leaving the door ajar, so some of the room light spills in.

It's just the two of us, breathing intensely.

I'm still shaking. Or is he shaking? Are we both shaking?

He tugs me close to his body.

I don't feel the gun, but I imagine he's got it aimed

at my head, maybe planning to finish me off now.

My mind runs through scenarios of what he's gonna do to me.

Maybe kill me.

Maybe do some other terrible things to me before killing me.

That's what he has to do now that I've seen him, right?

Why the fuck did he pull me into a closet? No one's here. He could just as easily do whatever he wants to me in the bedroom.

"Stay in here." His hot breath hits my ear, and I gulp and nod. "I'm gonna go check and see if they're still here."

I barely process the words before he rushes out, quietly closing the door behind him.

Well, that wasn't what I was expecting…

I figured he would beat the shit out of me, sexually assault me…do something vile that I hadn't had time to consider…

But he left me in here…for reasons I can't imagine.

My heartbeat is in a frenzy, my nerves on edge, all my survival impulses telling me: *get out of this alive.*

It takes a few moments, but his words come back to me: *"I'm gonna go check and see if they're still here."*

The shadow in the backyard. Was someone else here? Did Zane come by to make sure I was okay?

No, this isn't how someone reacts to their neighbor

having a burglar in their house.

Not even a little.

I press my ear against the door, listening out for him. A few moments pass before I hear a familiar *creak* down the hall. I recognize that creak; it's from inside my parents' bedroom.

Just stay in here like he told you.

But my phone is still charging on my nightstand, and maybe if I can get to it, I can call the police. This could be my only chance to make a break for it.

Still shaking, I turn the doorknob slowly, hoping I won't make too much noise. I'm equally cautious about opening the door.

My phone's still on my nightstand, but he's left the bedroom door open, so if I go for it and he comes back down the hall, he'll see me. And if he sees me, knowing I disobeyed him, he might fucking kill me.

He might kill you anyway.

But if that's what he wanted, why leave me in this closet alone? And who was that in the backyard?

I don't have time to figure it out. I need to get the phone and get help.

Kyra chirps as I take a few steps out of the closet. I'm careful not to disturb the floorboards as I start around the bed, on the side opposite my phone, then crawl over the mattress to keep out of view from the doorway.

My phone's almost within reach. If I could only snatch it, I might get out of this.

Go, go, go!

I grab it off the nightstand, and as I turn to the doorway, I see Zane at the other end of the hall, that intense gaze on me.

I'm. A. Dead. Man.

He starts for me, his jaw tensing, and I sprint into action, racing for the door. My towel drops, and I let it fall as I manage to get to the door just in time to slam it shut and turn the lock.

Thank fuck.

As I start to dial, my hands are shaking so much, I figure I might drop the phone.

9-1-

"Hey! You! Upstairs!" a booming voice echoes through the house. "Sir, I need you to put your hands where I can see them!"

The voice has an authoritative ring to it. A cop? Is this some kind of miracle? Oh fuck, please be a miracle.

"Hey, hey, it's all good. Calm down." That must be Zane.

"Hands where we can see them, and drop to the floor," the officer commands, her voice booming as she directs Zane where to place his hands and asks him about weapons.

I'm about to call out that I'm up here and he's got a gun when Zane says, "There's someone else up here in a bedroom."

"Anyone else, come out where we can see you!"

You're safe, I tell myself. I grab my towel off the floor and wrap it around my waist, heading out the door.

Warn them about the fucking gun! is my first thought, but I've seen the goddamn news. What if they start shooting indiscriminately and I get caught in the line of fire?

But I notice Zane's on the floor, his hands spread out, though I don't see his gun on him. What did he do with it?

Keeping my hands up—since I don't want to have survived him only to get shot by a cop—I head into the hall.

Zane's a few feet from me, the two officers downstairs, both with their guns out.

"He fucking lives here," Zane says.

"Kid, you have ID?" one of the officers asks, and I nod.

"Yes, ma'am."

"Get down like your friend there, and tell us where it is."

Friend?

I'm in shock as I get into the same position as my attacker.

The first officer sends up the guy with her to retrieve my driver's license from my bedroom, and once they've checked it, they let me stand up.

"Someone reported a break-in," she says, "and the front door was open when we got here."

"That was me," Zane says. "I'm the one who called you. You can check my phone in my back pocket."

He called the cops? Another weird-ass part of this that's not making any sense.

But one of the cops checks his ID and phone, turning to the other. "He's telling the truth. Zane Grayson. This is you?"

"Yes, that's me."

"This your friend, Leif?" the female officer asks.

"Yes," Zane says.

"I didn't ask you. Kid, is Zane your friend?"

Zane closes his eyes, like he knows he's gonna be in deep shit for what he's just done.

"Is this your friend?" she asks again.

"No."

He hits his forehead on the floor.

But my mind's still spinning.

Yes, he had a gun and he grabbed me, but he didn't hurt me.

And he told me he was going to look for someone.

And now I find out *he* called the cops?

He looks at me, that determined expression gone. His eyes are wide, desperate, pleading.

He lied about being my friend. For some reason, he doesn't want me to tell them the truth. Maybe because it'll get him in trouble. Now that my senses are coming back to me, it's clear this wasn't what I thought initially, but it's still confusing as fuck. If someone else was here and he was trying to help, what if turning him in might get him in trouble?

Then again, what if I'm not in the right frame of mind from the trauma of everything that just happened?

This is a shit idea. I know it to my core.

Whatever the reason, I say, "Sorry, he's not a friend, but someone I know."

The cop's brow creases. "You kidding me right now?"

"Sorry. I was nervous. This was a shock to me. I've never been around cops with guns out before."

I notice Zane's only a foot away from the hall console. A gun could fit under there.

"Okay, kids," she says before introducing herself as Kendrick and her partner as Diaz. "I'd appreciate if one of you could explain to me what's going on."

Zane rises to his feet. "We were hanging out, and someone came in from the back door. I called the cops because Leif was taking a shower—"

"You were taking a shower while the two of you were hanging?" she asks, glancing between us. "You know it's fine to tell me the truth. We won't judge. I have a wonderful wife of thirteen years. It's not a big deal."

"We were hanging out," he insists. "I was watching a movie in his room while he showered. I heard a sound in the house and called. And it was taking forever for you guys to come, so I went to see if there was someone here. That's why I was in the hall."

Zane doesn't struggle to come up with a plausible lie, that's for sure. But why does he need to lie? If he saw a burglar from his place, couldn't he have told the cops that?

No, there's definitely more to this. And only my weird-ass neighbor knows what that is.

"Is that what happened?" Kendrick asks me, casually, not like she's waiting for me to shout, *"No, this guy had a fucking gun to my head, and I thought he might kill me."*

But he doesn't seem nearly as intimidating now.

"Yeah, that's right," I say. "When Zane was looking around, I saw someone head out through the back door."

The officers let me change into sweats and a tee, and I meet them downstairs with Zane. Kendrick inspects the front door, getting down on her knees with a flashlight as she takes a look at the lock. "Did you leave it unlocked?"

"I don't think so, but I really can't remember."

Zane and I exchange an awkward look, and I try to read his expression, as though all the answers I need for what's going on will be encoded somewhere on his face.

"I don't see any signs of forced entry," Kendrick says, pushing to her feet. When we head into the kitchen, the back door's open too. Kendrick performs a similar inspection, aiming her flashlight at the lock before saying, "There are some markings here. Could've been picked by whoever broke in."

"Should we change the lock?" I ask.

"Maybe get one with a different locking mechanism,

since whoever came in has clearly figured out how to crack this one, but it seems like you scared them off. I wouldn't be too worried about it."

After the scare I've had, I think I'll go for changing the lock.

Kendrick and Diaz take some more notes.

"We'll check around the neighborhood for anyone suspicious," Kendrick says as she leads Diaz to the front door, "but keep your alarm on, and you should be fine."

Are they about to leave me with Zane?

As if sensing my fear, he pipes up. "I'll see you tomorrow, Leif."

The goose bumps return.

Tomorrow? Am I really going to see him then?

I mean, he does owe me an explanation.

Or maybe he wants his gun back.

For now, he leaves with the cops, and I hurry around, locking the doors and turning on the security system before taking a deep breath.

You're alive. You're fucking alive.

But what the hell just happened?

2

ZANE

A S I APPROACH the door, I wonder what the hell I'm doing.

This is a mistake.

He could call the cops; he *should* call the cops. Hell, he should have told the cops I'd broken into his house and pulled him into a closet with a gun like a fucking monster.

Standing on his front porch, glancing around, I remind myself what a shit idea this is, but I need to talk to him.

And I need my gun back.

After I ring the doorbell, a few moments pass before I notice Leif through the sidelight windows.

This house has too many damn windows. Anyone can see right through. Watch him, the way I've watched him for the past couple of weeks. However, to the credit of this voyeur's paradise, it works both ways, and he spots me through the window, the eyes on his sexy face widening before he hides behind the door.

I wait to hear his phone trilling as he calls the police. Or for him to tell me to leave him the fuck alone, but as I'm trying to imagine what I could possibly say to navigate this, I hear, "Can I help you?"

There's a tremble in his voice, and I'm pleased to detect his innate, primal fear.

He *should* be afraid. That's what's going to keep him safe, alive.

I try to shake those kinds of thoughts away—they're like shit Dad would have said.

"I think you know why I'm here." Did that sound creepy? Fuck.

I wait for a response, but nothing for a few moments before he says, "You wanna tell me why you were over the other night?"

"I do, but not out here. Not like this."

Silence.

"How do I know you won't hurt me?"

"Did I hurt you when I had the chance?" That fucking sounds creepy too. Shit, I'm bad at this.

Nothing from the other side. Okay, maybe this isn't happening, and I'm probably scaring the shit out of the poor guy, so I start toward the steps when I hear a *click* behind me. I turn to find him standing inside the cracked-open doorway, pepper spray in hand. In sweats, and he's wearing one of his beanies…why does he have to wear beanies? I love a man in a beanie. And his tank top is tight around his chest, his lean, muscly arms on full display.

I maintain eye contact to keep from ogling him, but fuck, he's hot.

Stop being a creeper!

Too late, I guess.

"What? You're not gonna Lysol me to death, are you?" I say to cut through our awkward stare-off.

But he just keeps staring at me.

Doesn't get my humor. Fair enough. Maybe not all that funny, given what happened the last time I saw him.

"I mean, I'm the one who should be mad," I add. "You really nailed my nose."

He assesses my face before looking me over. Maybe trying to figure out if I have any other weapons on me. But he won't see the knife in my ankle sheath. I'm not a fucking amateur.

"I guess." He starts to turn back to the house, but then quickly pulls his attention back to me. "Just so you know, you try anything—before opening the door, I sent an email to a friend to let them know the last person I was with, Zane Grayson. And that officer who was here last night will—"

"I get it. Everyone will know I'm your psycho stalker killer. Can I come in or what?" I ask it like I'm some kind of vampire, waiting for his permission, and that's how he's eyeing me.

He's obviously struggling with it, his gaze shifting around before he says, "Fuck it. Come on. Close the door behind you."

He steps aside, facing me as I close the door.

"I assume you know where the kitchen is now," he says.

"Yup," I admit as I head in. "You want me to sit down? Or will this be like…give me my gun and then ask me to get the hell out of here?"

He follows me into the kitchen, keeping his pepper spray ready for me.

"I think it's ambitious for you to assume I'm gonna give you your gun," he says.

As I enter the kitchen, I have a little more time to appreciate the design. White tile floors. Dark-gray cabinets. Marble backsplash, counters, and island—all white with the occasional light-gray vein. A glass kitchen table with some clear ghost chairs around it. As appealing as the style is, my eyes are particularly drawn to a plate of jumbo chocolate-chip cookies on the kitchen island, which stir an intense growl in my stomach. Clearly some steel oats weren't cutting it for breakfast. Not for this greedy belly.

"Nice kitchen," I say.

"Is that sarcasm?"

"No, but don't worry. It's not only you. Apparently, everything I say sounds sarcastic, so my actual sarcasm gets lost in the mix."

"I promise, not being able to detect your sarcasm isn't what I'm worried about."

"Ha. Ha. Ha," I drag out. "He doesn't just tremble in fear; he tells jokes too." That one definitely doesn't hit. "Sorry, I'm trying to make this less awkward."

"I don't think there's a way you'll be able to do that." His deadly serious expression assures me of it.

"Um…I figure I can't really make this any worse, so would you mind if I had one of these cookies?" I can't help myself. They look so damn good; they're distracting me from the reason I'm here.

"Sure. You want it heated up?"

"Is that sarcasm? Because I wouldn't mind, if you're seriously offering."

His eyes narrow, and he smirks. "I mean, I'll heat it up for you. But sit at the table. You're making me nervous standing there."

I make myself comfy in one of the ghost chairs. "These are more comfortable than they look," I observe, which earns another look from Leif as he fetches a pair of tongs from a glass of kitchenware and a small plate from the cabinet.

"Guess this isn't the conversation you figured we'd be having?" I ask.

"That's an understatement." He grabs one of the cookies with the tongs and plates it before placing it in the microwave.

"So…are you gonna tell me what happened last night?" he asks.

"What do you mean?"

"The part where you broke into my parents' house and pulled me into a closet with a gun—"

"See? Didn't catch the sarcasm. But at least you're pretty."

Too fucking pretty. I need to stop looking at him. He's freaked out enough as it is.

"Now would be a good time to start explaining shit," he says as the microwave buzzes to life.

"Where do I even start?"

"I've seen you the past couple of weeks around here. You're living at the Morgans' place? Renting?"

"Yeah."

"You've looked at me weirdly more than a few times. Are you a stalker?"

"Not in the sense you might think."

His brow creases. "You can understand why that's a concerning answer, right?"

"I'm not gonna pretend I haven't been watching you. I have. Since a little before you first noticed me."

"Why did you rent the Morgans' house?"

"To watch you." I don't have any reason to lie to him. Not about this. I stare him down, surely unable to disguise my determination, my obsession.

He glances around uneasily. The microwave pings, startling him.

"I think you're asking the wrong questions," I tell him as he retrieves the cookie.

"And I figured you wouldn't beat around the bush

like this."

He's right. I'm stalling. But the truth will freak him out more than thinking I'm some fucked-up stalker. Still, I gotta get it out. "You gonna believe me if I say I was trying to protect you?"

He approaches with my cookie, moving cautiously, watching me as though waiting for any sudden movements. Then he places the plate on the table and steps away, his pepper spray's security lifted, his finger ready to hit the trigger.

I pick at the cookie, testing the heat as I lick the chocolate off my thumb. Damn, that's good. I wonder if it's delicious or if I think that because I haven't had enough to eat today.

"You make these?"

"Yeah," he says, his expression twisting up.

Of course he did. The guy's always in the kitchen, making one thing or another.

"You said protect me. Someone else was here last night, weren't they?"

"Yeah."

"I knew it."

I brave a bigger bite of my cookie, thinking it might be too hot, but it's just right—a perfect chunky/gooey combination.

"Fuck," I mutter. "Damn, you can bake."

"Thank you...?" he says, but the way he inflects, it sounds more like a question. "So who was it?" he presses.

"Okay," I say around a fresh mouthful of cookie, "if I knew who it was, obviously I would have gone to the police, and we could have ended it right there."

"How could you possibly have known someone was going to break into my house if you don't know who it is?"

Put this kid out of his damn misery. "You familiar with the Jason Kilbourne disappearance? Guy who went to Wyachet Community College. Went missing from town last year."

Leif nods. "I didn't remember his name, but I remember seeing the story."

"And last March, another WCC student went missing."

"Yeah…"

"You don't happen to have any water, do you?"

He glares at me.

"Fair enough. A little over a month ago, you remember posting a note on Instagram? About someone you thought was bullying you by pretending to be a secret admirer?"

His face flushes red. "I remember."

"I have a hard time figuring why you'd imagine that was a joke. You're a hot guy. I would think you'd be used to the attention."

His gaze shifts around uneasily. "I've had a rough year, and since I came back home, some of the people I knew haven't been all that welcoming because of…reasons."

"You don't have to be cryptic with me. I know about your meltdown in Atlanta and the stint in the psych unit."

For the first time, he avoids my gaze, turning away from me. "We're not talking about that."

I immediately regret bringing it up. "Sorry. Fuck. No. I don't want you to think I'm being insensitive. Shit. I guess I was anyway, but trust me, whatever you've been through, I've had my share of crap too. No judgment. I'm so used to that shit that clearly it seems like a nonissue. I meant, I researched you after I saw the post."

Just keep on digging that hole, Z.

I eat another chunk of cookie, sticking as much in my mouth as I can manage. Maybe that'll keep me from saying any other dumb shit.

He heads to the fridge and fetches a bottle of water. As he approaches me with it, he doesn't struggle like he did with the cookie. Just passes it to me. I take the bottle and down a quarter of it, washing down the cookie, which feels like it's moving in clumps down my throat.

My stomach forgives me for my neglect, and I breathe a sigh of relief, happy this whole bit has prevented me from saying anything else to hurt Leif.

"So why would you care about some dumb post I made?"

"There are these subreddits where you can speculate about different crimes. A bunch of podcasters and social media sleuths gravitate to it. While I was trying to figure out what happened to the second guy who disappeared, I ran across a comment from a user who claimed he knew him and that he'd received a letter from an admirer about a month before he went missing. I tried to reach out to the Reddit user to see what he was talking about, but he didn't respond to my DM. Then I mentioned it to the cops, but they didn't give a fuck about some random Reddit user who could have been bullshitting. I followed the subreddit, and sometime later, I got pinged, and suddenly I see a reply to that previous comment from one of these Reddit sleuths—a link to your Insta post. Never underestimate the power of geeks with too much time on their hands." As I reveal this, his shoulders relax, along with the arm holding the pepper spray, so that now he seems a little less ready to temporarily blind me.

"So you found my Insta. And then…"

"I searched through your other posts, saw you'd tagged your mom in a picture together. She had some posts up for her financial consultant business. There was only a PO Box on the website, but her LLC paperwork on the Georgia Corporations Division site listed this address for her contact information…which…I assume you get where this is going."

Damn, I'm really begging him to just call the cops on me again, aren't I?

I shift uneasily in the chair. "You know, it sounds

much worse when I say it out loud like that."

Leif stares at me for a few moments. I'm waiting for him to flip out over that, but it doesn't seem to affect him—maybe because he's already pieced together that I must've done something like that to be here in the first place.

Finally, he says, "And then you decided to rent a house near me, so…what? You can watch and wait for this serial kidnapper?"

"So that I can get this fucker myself," I say through gritted teeth. "Hence the gun."

"And you think that's who was in my house?"

"Someone was creeping around the back. Looked like a guy. Average height, slender build. I have night-vision cameras to keep an eye on your yard, and—"

"You what?"

Shit.

"I've set up some stuff around your yard to keep an eye on things. I'm not doing it to violate your privacy."

"But you are violating it. You know that, right?"

He's not wrong.

"Yes," I confess.

He takes a breath. That's fair. He has a lot to consider. This is all new information, and if I were in his shoes and didn't know anything about this shit, I'd be wigging out too.

"Assuming it was a guy you saw last night and he is this serial abductor, why would he be after me?" he asks, and it's not even a question directed at me. Be a great time to keep my damn mouth shut, but I can't help myself.

"Let's just say you're his type."

"What does that mean?"

"You have a certain similarity with the two other guys who went missing. Around the same age—eighteen to early twenties. College kid. Dark hair, pale skin. Little muscular. Attractive. Very attractive."

That makes him wince. And if I haven't given myself away already, I sure as fuck did just then.

3

LEIF

THIS GUY IS so strange.

Why does he keep looking at me like that? And why did he lick his bottom lip when he called me attractive…no—*very* attractive?

He was probably getting a smudge of a chocolate morsel off his lip.

It's the last thing I should be fixated on, especially after he's revealed that he believes I'm the target of someone who kidnaps men who are "my type" and that he was over here intervening in what could have been my kidnapping. Not to mention what he's been doing—cameras watching my parents' yard? What the hell? Where else does he have cameras?

He finishes off the cookie.

That was pretty damn fast, like the guy hasn't eaten in days. I'm tempted to offer him leftover stroganoff from last night, but no, this guy's not my friend. I don't even know if I can trust what he's saying. He could be bullshitting. Yes, someone else was in the backyard last night, but how do I know they're not friends?

"Anyway," he says, licking his fingers, "when I saw that guy lurking, I thought I might have had him, and then of course, as you'll remember, things didn't go according to plan. I wasn't gonna put you in any danger, so I called the cops right when I saw him. I just didn't expect them to be as quick as they were."

Yes, that lined up with everything that happened. If he's making this shit up, he's doing an impressive job.

He takes a swig of water before his gaze returns to me. It's hard to tell if he's eyeing me in a strange way or if it's just how it feels, like he's undressing me with those wide, steel-blue eyes.

But I still have questions.

"If he came in through the back, why was the front door open?"

"I couldn't be sure where he was in the house, and I figured if I opened the front door, which is right by the stairs, he'd have a hard time getting you out from your room without the whole neighborhood seeing. Figured it might stall him for a minute. Give me a chance to get to him first."

Again, it makes enough sense, but barely.

And if everything he's saying is true, I have a whole other world of concerns. "So what am I supposed to do now that you've told me I might have a guy stalking me? Go to the cops?"

He chuckles. "Yeah. Let them know I was here, and

I'm sure they'll usher you on in to the right person to talk to, believe everything you're saying, and have an armed guard watching you until this psycho moves on to his next victim."

"Even I can tell that's sarcasm."

I couldn't help myself, and my remark makes a smirk slip across what's predominately been a fairly stoic face.

"Sorry," he says. "I'm a little bitter with the Wyachet PD. Yeah, you need to contact them." He pulls a flash drive out of his pocket and sets it on the table.

"What's that?"

"Surveillance video of the guy who was in your yard. Shows him breaking in and leaving the same way he came."

From the cameras he has on our yard…

"Show it to them and tell them about the break-in. And I don't know, if you could somehow find an explanation for why I was at your place other than me following your ass, that would be helpful."

"What?"

"I figured I was gonna nail that guy last night, wrap this up, but then he fucking got away, and that cop saw me and took down my name, so now I'm in a bit of a jam because you need to let the police know what's going on, but if they find out what I've been doing living next door, they're gonna be up my ass about it."

"If they find out you've been stalking me, you mean?"

"Yeah…"

I don't know why the idea is kind of exciting. Maybe it's just one of the intriguing aspects I'm learning about this man who was watching me. Stalking me. And who's now making me wonder if I'm still here because of it.

But as much as he's soothing my concerns around him, he sure as fuck isn't soothing me around what might be the real threat: whoever sent me that letter.

"Can't you show them that post about that letter?" I ask. "Or get them to find the guy who posted it and ask what was in the other letter?"

"He posted about the similarities. The cops didn't think much of it. For instance, in your letter, the admirer says you're like a marble statue. He'd written something similar in the one I was told about, but it compared him to a Grecian statue, and it's my understanding that a lot of those were sculpted from marble."

Goose bumps prick across my flesh, but I remind myself he could be making this up. He's already seen mine on Insta.

"Told the cops to talk to that guy who posted on Reddit, but last I checked, they still hadn't bothered. The detective in charge of the case didn't seem enthusiastic about it either. Since I don't know how or if Jason Kilbourne knew the second guy who disappeared, she said I didn't really have anything for them to go off of. That it could've been a troll trying to cause trouble. Said they don't get into wild goose chases over the shit people post on subreddits."

"So the cops aren't gonna buy any of this?" And really, I don't know that I am.

"They won't take it seriously. On top of all that, there's another issue. When you walk in with this video and bring up this shit about the letter, they're gonna find my name attached to the incident report, and I can guarantee you they'll think this is all bullshit."

"Why?"

Not for the first time since he came here, he hesitates. I don't get this guy. It's been like pulling teeth to get out what he was doing last night. He keeps holding back, but given everything he's shared with me so far, I don't get why he has to be so goddamn cryptic.

"Listen, dude, if you want to protect me, then I need to know what's up."

"Oh, I'm sure Detective Roth will let you know. She'll be the one you need to ask for when you go to the station."

"So you want me to go to the cops and tell the truth? I thought you said you were in a jam."

"Yeah, that's where it's tricky. You're free to do whatever you want, but if you want to be believed, tell them you got that note and that a friend told you about seeing the post on a subreddit related to the previous disappearances. I reached out to you about it, and we became chummy. We're friends, and that's why I was over."

"Why would I say that?"

"Because that's your best chance to be taken seriously."

"What if I find out I'm protecting the wrong person?" I'd have to be a moron not to ask.

"That's where you're gonna have to trust me. Trust that I already know you're in danger, and that I'm gonna protect you better than any cop. You can go in there with this stuff, and I know what Detective Roth is gonna say: *It's all circumstantial. None of this means anything. This kid Zane's gotten in your head. You're reading into things.* So when you get done talking to them, you're still only going to have one guy who's interested in protecting you."

What if what he's saying is true? What if there really is somebody trying to kidnap me? Or…what if it's not true? What if the cops are right to think the issue is in Zane's head? Hell, what if he never even talked to the cops?

"And I'm supposed to take your word for all this?"

Those steel-blue eyes shift back to his plate, only a few crumbs left now. "There's a lot I'm not explaining. Some of it you're not gonna get answers to; other parts, I'm sure Detective Roth will illuminate, and then, well, the moment I walk out the door, you're free to google the fuck out of everything I just said."

"You think I didn't google the fuck out of Zane Grayson already?"

Of course I looked up the guy who pulled a gun on me. Tried to find social media accounts. Any info I could. The most I came up with was that he was in the AV club in high school.

He smirks. "Looks like you're gonna have to get more creative with your web searches. You're a smart guy. You'll figure it out. Now about my gun…"

"I should've already given that to the cops."

"Shoulda, woulda, coulda."

I don't know that it's a smart idea to give it back to him, but I also don't want that gun sitting around my house any longer. Makes me think of all the articles I've read about people getting hurt by the guns in their homes, especially since I don't have a safe to lock it in.

"Maybe I don't want to give it back," I confess. "Guns are dangerous. You could hurt yourself or someone innocent."

"I'm very good with a gun, Leif."

He sounds confident, but that doesn't make me feel much better. "If I give it back to you, are you still going to be watching me? Like you have been? With the cameras and being a creeper next door?"

He closes his eyes, rubbing his hand over his face. "I've thought a lot about that after blowing my cover like that, but if you tell me right now to stop, I'll pack my bags and be out of your hair." He purses his lips, his hand balling into a fist. "But, Leif, I really don't think that would be a good idea. And I don't want the next time I see your face to be on some cheap Wyachet online news story."

It's hard not to believe a guy when he says something like that with such intensity.

I take a moment to consider all the shit he's told me.

About last night.

The subreddit.

The letter.

The video.

The cops.

"I guess if you're gonna be my personal bodyguard, you need a gun," I say, and he looks taken aback.

Despite how wild this all is, in a fucked-up way, it makes some sense. Or maybe our chat has left me spinning to the point where the absurd suddenly sounds reasonable.

One thing seems apparent: Zane believes what he's telling me. That doesn't mean it's true. He could be having a mental breakdown. Maybe that's why the cops don't believe this shit he's talking about, but either way, someone was actually in my place, and he scared them off. Surely, even if he was suffering from a delusion, he could have happened to intercept a burglar.

And there are other possible explanations. He could know exactly what he's doing. Maybe this is all some elaborate con worthy of a true-crime podcast. He wants to manipulate me with this story so he can rob shit from my parents' house. Had a friend break in the other night to make these outrageous claims seem more plausible. Although, that seems like a lot of work when he could have just worn a stocking over his head, put that gun to me, and gotten me to do anything he and his friend wanted while they packed up shit from the house. Or use this con on a wealthier family.

On the flip side, everything he's saying could be true.

Whatever the truth may be, I'm willing to take a chance on Zane's version. At least until I've had some time to think it over, maybe come to my fucking senses.

I make him wait outside as I head upstairs and fetch the shoebox I stashed the gun in. When I return it to him, he says, "Thanks. Love Converse. Hope they're my size."

He glances around awkwardly, and I can't help but laugh.

"Oh, see? You like my humor after all," he teases.

"I think you're very charming for being awkward as fuck." As soon as I say the words, I regret them because his eyes are on me again.

There's something about the way he looks at me. And he called me very attractive. Is he bi or gay? Or is he so damn awkward these kinds of looks and comments could mean anything?

"Okay," he finally says as he looks to the porch. "I'm gonna head back to my place…watch some footage from last night. Kidding. That would be weird."

"Yeah, that comment was more in the creeper

realm."

"I'll quit while I'm ahead."

He turns to start off the porch, but an idea springs to mind. "Wait!" I say. "Stay right there."

I don't even wait to see if he heard me. Just close and lock the door. I head back to the kitchen and grab the leftover stroganoff. When I return to the door, I hand it to him.

"I made it last night, so it's still good. Not everyone likes stroganoff, but give it a chance. I have a pretty awesome spice combo for it."

He stares at the Tupperware as if he doesn't know what he's holding before saying, "Um…thank you…I guess."

"Yes, *thank you* is the correct response, creeper," I tease with a wink.

"Thank you," he says, smiling as he turns and, without another word, heads back along the walkway to the driveway, then to the sidewalk, glancing my way briefly as he returns to the Morgans' place.

I close and lock the door. I take a deep breath, almost a gasp, as though some part of me is surprised I survived that encounter. Mom and Dad would freak out if they ever found out what I'd just done.

Hell, if they heard the wild shit he told me, they would already be on the phone with the cops. And I'm trying to figure out if that's what I should be doing, but instead follow another of his suggestions.

Sitting at my desk, I run Google searches while Kyra hops about her cage, which I've set nearby to keep her company. She chirps, her head bobbing about like she's trying to figure out what's captured my attention.

"Zane Grayson" "disappearance"

"Zane Grayson"

"Z Grayson" + "disappearance"

This isn't going anywhere...

"Disappearance" + "Jason Kilbourne"

I'm inundated with headlines and posts.

I see what I'd expect—information about the day he went missing, interviews conducted with family members, pleas for information from the public.

Zane knew the person he believed was the second victim of this mystery abductor, and he saw a response on a subreddit about my Instagram post, which gives me an idea.

"Reddit" + "disappearances" + "Jason Kilbourne" + "victims"

The first result looks promising: serial abductions in Wyachet, Georgia.

I follow the link to a forum about Jason and see a comment from Dman281. A quick scan reveals this is the post Zane read about the second victim, Michael Grayson.

Zane Grayson...

They're related.

Now I get why he was so cryptic.

"Well, Kyra, I found a little something about our new friend."

I read the post:

Dman281

4 mo. ago

Hey everyone. Lurker on this sub, first-time poster. Wanted to see if anyone knows anything about JK receiving a letter from a secret admirer before his disappearance. I know Michael Grayson, and he contacted me about a letter from a supposed admirer about a month before his disappearance. He was trying to figure out who sent it. I didn't think anything of it at the time, and I've tried to give the cops this information, but they don't seem interested or think there's a connection.

From what he read to me, the letter was very ornate—like poetic language, not the way people talk. A lot about his appearance. Had some weird shit about how he was like a Grecian statue. No signature. Will provide more specifics to any serious inquiries, but please, no bs.

If anyone knows of something like this with JK, please reach out. I'm not on here much, but I'll get a notification for PMs.

EDIT: If you run a blog or podcast, please do not contact me. I've shared all I'm comfortable with, but any help is appreciated.

The guy posted this four months ago, so everything Zane told me about the post and my letter checks out.

I pull up on my phone the pic of my letter:

Leif,

I see you.

> *Heart and soul that you wear on your sleeve.*

> *The beauty of this form—a marble statue in a world of drooping clay.*

> *An heir to the beauty of your ancestors.*

> *I hope, when you look in the mirror, you see yourself as I do—*

> *A divine gift to the mortals who have the privilege of finding you in their gaze.*

> *Maybe one day I can find the courage to share these feelings with you face-to-face.*

> *Or maybe it's best to let them remain untainted by the disappointments that come once a dream has been realized.*

> *Just know, you are seen.*

> *You are adored.*

Sincerely,
Yours and only yours

Marble stone instead of a Grecian statue, exactly like Zane said. A lot about looks. Unusual, poetic language. Not signed.

But Dman281's description is so vague, couldn't a

lot of love notes fit this description?

Still, it's more ominous now that I know it might not be some cruel prank from my ex-friends or their asshole buddies.

As I put my phone on the desk, Kyra approaches the edge of her cage and tilts her head, like she's watching me as I continue my investigation on my laptop, this time for "Michael Grayson."

While Zane didn't have any social media accounts I could find, Michael does. An Instagram with plenty of pics…

He and Zane have similar eyes, and their hair color's about the same. I suspect brothers, which is confirmed when I see a pic of them together, the caption reading: "Just chillin' with my bro."

Fuck.

Knowing they're brothers is bad enough, but as I review the photos of them together, it's clear how close they were—*are*…we don't know that he's dead, I remind myself. Although, given how long it's been, it's hard not to be skeptical.

There's plenty about what Zane shared with me that doesn't make sense, but this adds a layer of clarity, confirming that, even if he is delusional, he's got a good reason to be.

But am I really about to trust the guy who broke into my house and pulled a fucking gun on me?

Fuck, I guess I am…

4

ZANE

S ITTING AT MY laptop, I watch the surveillance footage around Leif's place.

Five cameras, one for each side of the house and an extra one in the back, since as I anticipated, that seems like the most likely point of entry for an abductor if he doesn't want to be seen by any of Leif's neighbors.

"See how we can keep an eye on the perimeter?" Dad said, displaying the different viewing screens on his laptop. "That way, we can see anyone coming."

One of the cameras allows me to see into Leif's bedroom, but he's kept his blinds closed since our chat, and I understand why. Despite turning away whenever he's changed or stripped down, that doesn't change that what I'm doing is wrong, especially with where my mind goes whenever I see him grab the hem of his shirt and pull it up to his chest, revealing that tight body. Although, I feel less guilty about all this now that I know it's all been worth it. That I actually intercepted someone's fucked-up plan to carry him off for whatever sick reason this monster has in mind.

It's a little after seven. That's about three hours before Leif usually heads to bed, and he's in the kitchen. He just finished cooking his dinner. Feel like I can still taste the kick of that stroganoff he gave me earlier.

I didn't waste time after he gave it to me. I hurried home and warmed it up on the stove before cherishing the kick of paprika and Dijon mustard.

It's hard to make out what he's cooking tonight; he's got it in a clay pot that's been cooling on top of the stove. He glances around uneasily. He's done that a few times since our talk. Figure it freaks him out knowing I'm watching, which I feel like shit about. He's packing some of it up in Tupperware, even before eating, which isn't the norm. And he's made more food than usual, maybe to have some throughout the week.

He packs the Tupperware into a backpack on the counter. He slings the backpack over his shoulder, then grabs the clay pot with two pot holders before heading for the door.

What is he doing?

Soon, he's out the front door, on the move.

I can tell from Camera 1 that he's making his way through the yard toward my place.

"Fuck," I mutter. I hurry to the bathroom and check myself in the mirror. Glad I fucking took a shower earlier. I throw on some extra deodorant, and the doorbell rings.

What is wrong with this guy?

I hurry downstairs and open the door, and I'm sure my confusion is written all over my expression.

"Care for some spaghetti squash chili?"

"Uh…sure," I say with a shrug.

I step aside and let him into my place. For the guy who kept pepper spray on me throughout the morning, he sure as hell doesn't seem afraid of me now.

That's a mistake.

He leads me into my own kitchen.

"What are you doing here?" I ask as he sets the pot on the stove.

"Figured I'd give you an update after my visit with the cops."

"Yeah, I sort of…"

"Followed me to the station? Yeah. I'm more aware since our chat."

After our visit earlier, I'd tailed him to the station, parking nearby while he met with them. But I thought I was doing a good job keeping my distance.

"I was half expecting them to raid this place," I say, "but all I got was a voice mail from Detective Roth, asking me to call her back."

"Funny 'cause no one's contacted me." He doesn't sound happy about that. Like he's having to come to terms with the fact that the cops aren't going to take this as seriously as they should.

"What happened?"

He smiles, and I can't imagine what he has to smile about with everything he has going on. "I hope you like corn bread. I also brought over some coleslaw I made the other day."

"It's like getting a visit from Jamie Oliver. Are you avoiding my question because the cops are about to bust down the door?"

I'm joking. I assume they wouldn't send him into danger if they thought I was a threat, but why isn't he just getting to what went down?

"I'm only doing what you did to me this morning," he says. "I wanted answers, and you were…less than forthcoming."

"Yeah, I was there," I remind him.

"So why don't you sit at the table, and I'll fix us some plates?"

"Okay…"

I take a seat at the table, anxious as fuck. His vengeance is cruel but just. Probably doesn't hold a candle to what I did to him, so I need to take it on the chin. I'm sure I can safely assume he didn't tell Roth the truth about last night; otherwise, there'd already be a police vehicle outside my door, not a voice mail. But the details of what he shared matter. If he didn't say the right thing and the cops interfere, he could fuck this up for both of us. For himself because I won't be able to keep him safe, and they won't either. For me because this is my only chance to save my brother.

If he's even still alive…

"How did you like the stroganoff?" He makes himself at home, searching through the cabinets.

"It was very good," I confess. "My stomach is incredibly appreciative."

As he pulls out plates and bowls, he glances over his shoulder, smiling. God, that's a fucking smile. Between what happened last night and what I told him today, how can he still have such a killer smile?

And that fucking beanie. There's a shift in my pants. Oh fuck, now's not the time for a boner. That'll really freak him out.

"You're not even gonna give me a hint about what happened?" I ask as he continues prepping.

"Well, I told my parents about the break-in, alerted the Neighborhood Watch, and then got a locksmith to change the lock."

"You know that's not what I'm asking about. And that I already saw the locksmith drop by earlier in the day."

"Which drawer is silverware?"

Fucker.

I direct him, then lean back in my chair, taking advantage of a meal being served to me. Been a long fucking time since I've had that.

He fishes some pepper and salt from his backpack and seasons our chili bowls before bringing his concoction over to me, the bowls and silverware set on the plates. He's not as standoffish as he was this morning, setting my plate and bowl right in front of me. Then he places his on the opposite side of the table and takes a seat.

"This is good timing," I say. "I wasn't sure what I was gonna do for dinner. Wanted to order a pizza, but kind of got to save up my money to stay here. My rent before this was only six hundred, and this is a little under two thousand."

"You like pizza? What kind?"

His head jerks subtly and his face twists up, like he realized what a weird question that was. Almost seemed instinctual, like something he would have asked anyone. Then he realized he was asking the creep next door.

"I usually go for something pretty basic, like pepperoni. If I'm real adventurous, I'll do chicken Alfredo. Really very basic guy. I mean, I have my steel oats for breakfast, and then I'll make a roast beef sandwich for lunch. Maybe eat some canned soup or chili for dinner."

He stares at me, looking serious, as he did when I was telling him all that messed-up shit earlier.

"What?"

"I can't imagine eating like that."

"This is how we ate as kids, so I guess it's normal to me."

He's still staring at me, like he's trying to make sense of why kids would eat like that, so I try to get him off it.

"Bon appétit," I say, and he watches me take a bite of

the chili.

I close my eyes as a piece of spaghetti squash hits the roof of my mouth, the bottom of the spoon sliding over my tongue. There's a hint of spice; I've only had two meals from him, and I can tell he likes spices.

"Fuck," I say. "This is even better than the stroganoff. Not that it wasn't good. It was amazing."

"If you're real good, I packed another cookie."

"Then I guess I'll be real good."

He chuckles, and I'm wondering how the hell this is happening. What's going on? Maybe this was how he was feeling all through our chat this morning.

I lick my lips and take a drink of the bottle of water he set out.

After we've both taken a few bites, I'm still on edge. Want him to put me out of my misery. "Am I gonna have to finish before you tell me?"

He swallows some coleslaw, then says, "I went to the station like you told me to. Talked to an officer who added some notes to the incident report and took the flash drive. They said they'd pass it all on to Detective Roth."

"And you haven't heard from her?"

"Nothing yet."

"Interesting because she called me earlier. I didn't answer because I wanted to wait and see what you said before I start lying my ass off."

"I found a happy middle ground between the story

you suggested and something closer to the truth. Said I met you, and you told me about the post. That we got to talking and you moved in next door before this thing happened."

"That was clever."

"Figured no reason to commit a felony by lying to a cop."

"Yeah, that's how I play it."

It's a relief to hear. Not that Detective Roth isn't going to give me hell about this, but at least we don't have to get into the specifics of how we actually met…and they have some reliable evidence that could help them get their act together and do something to make sure Leif's safe.

"I don't know what was in my head," he goes on. "I guess from watching so much TV, I had this thought that they were gonna swoop me into an interrogation room and try to get as much information as they could, but they just gave me Detective Roth's card. Told me she *might* give me a call."

"Like I said before, it's so little to go off of, and Roth isn't convinced the two disappearances are connected. Young guys, they go missing sometimes, that's what she told me. If we had that fucking letter, I think we'd have something, but—"

"You didn't mention Michael was your brother."

I'm quiet.

Very quiet.

I take my first bite of the coleslaw. The shift in conversation has sucked some of the joy out of the flavor, but it's still good.

"Yeah," I say after swallowing. "I knew you were gonna find out sooner or later. I preferred for it to be later, and not to have to be the one to talk about it. It does…get me emotional."

I'm waiting for him to make a comment, like others have, about the fact that I don't appear very emotional, but he wears a warm expression as he says, "I'm sorry. I don't have any siblings, but that must have been hard."

"You have to take care of Mike," Dad said, his eyes wild and wide as he hands me the gun. "You have to always be there if anything happens to me. It's all on you, bud."

I nod. "As you probably already saw, we're very close. When I heard about this letter, I was surprised he hadn't mentioned it because we spoke on the phone pretty much every day. I guess he thought it was nothing, but God, if he knew how big this was going to get, I'm sure he would have taken a pic or something."

"So you've looked for the letter?"

"I checked his room at the apartment he was staying in. Nothing."

"It's eerie hearing you say that mine is similar to your brother's. It sounds like this person is trying to make someone feel special but then gives the same bizarre compliments to different people."

"Definitely sounds like a creeper. Not that all

creepers are bad."

I immediately regret making the tasteless joke at an insensitive time, but Leif snickers, and it's nice that, despite not knowing each other long, he seems to get my weird sense of humor.

But just as quickly, he quiets, surely freaked out about the possibility of being a serial abductor's next victim.

"I should probably go," he finally says.

"You haven't really eaten."

"I put some in the fridge at my place, and I'm not really hungry right now. You can store the rest of the chili and bring back my clay pot when you're finished."

"Okay," I say as he starts to grab his plate.

"I'll do the dishes, since you made the meal."

"Oh, thanks." He grabs his backpack off the chair.

I hop up, and we head for the door. "Keep me posted if you hear anything from Roth," I tell him, mostly because I don't know how to make his exit less awkward.

"For sure. And you…keep me posted if…I guess if someone's trying to kidnap me."

Silence stretches between us.

Another fucking awkward moment, and he tugs at his beanie before heading on his way.

5

LEIF

I SIT ON a bench in the reception area of the Wyachet Police Department, scrolling through my phone. There's a text from Mom, letting me know Grandma's faring well through the chemo.

I wish I could update her and Dad about everything that's going on, but I can imagine what that series of texts would look like:

Yeah, there's a guy who claims he's protecting me from a serial abductor.

Oh, and I made that guy dinner the other night.

At the police department now because a detective called yesterday.

Kyra's doing fine, btw.

I obviously told them about the break-in last week. And about the cops coming over and the broken lock on the back door.

But I haven't brought up Zane.

I was still trying to figure out how to bring him up, even before that story he pitched me about possibly being stalked by a killer. But if I mentioned that, they'd rush back home and be worried…maybe for nothing.

Or maybe I need to believe it could be for nothing.

I don't know what to think of Zane. He intrigues me.

Not just the wild things he's told me, but the way he looks at me.

Something exciting about when his gaze is on me—and even thinking that his gaze might be on me when I'm not looking.

What the fuck is that about?

And then there's his personality—his strange behaviors, his awkward sense of humor.

It's…adorable, which isn't something I've ever thought about another dude.

Since the last time I saw him, it's been a rough week, especially trying to get to sleep at night. Although, knowing he's watching me, that if anything happens, he'll be over to help, sets me at ease. I don't know if I should feel safe knowing he's watching, but for whatever reason, it's comforting. Probably the only reason I'm able to doze off eventually, even though I can stay up as late as one in the morning.

"Leif Anderson," a woman says as she comes from a nearby hallway. Straight dark hair, and a warm smile pulls across her face as she approaches. It's the sort of friendly face I wouldn't expect to see on a lieutenant detective. Not that I know what a lieutenant detective would look like, aside from the ones I've seen on TV.

I push to my feet and approach her.

"I'm Detective Roth." She offers a handshake, then asks if we can take the stairs so she can get some exercise in, and discusses the chilly weather as we head up to the second floor, her heels clicking against the cement steps. As we're heading down the hall, she says, "Thank you for coming in today. I'm sorry I wasn't able to meet with you sooner, but I was at a cabin in Jasper with my family when I was sent an email about your visit."

"It's not a problem."

Although, I must admit, given the seriousness of what Zane told me, I figured it wouldn't take nearly five days before someone contacted me.

She leads me into an office—tidy, only a few stray papers on her desk and a couple of dinged-up boxes stacked by a file cabinet. She invites me to sit in front of her desk, and as she settles behind it, I take in the view through the wall-length window behind her, overlooking the homes and mid-rises of downtown Wyachet.

"Before we went to Jasper, I knew something like this would come up. Always does. But *this*...I was not expecting."

"It's been a surprise for me too," I confess.

"I'm sure. Now, I reviewed what you told Officer Kendrick, and from what I can make out, there was a break-in at your parents' home on October seventeen, and while that took place, you were with Zane Grayson, who called the police."

"That's correct." Correct-*ish*.

"I don't know if you told Kendrick, but she didn't note it—how do you know Zane?"

No trace now of that friendly expression she'd first offered in the reception area. Her stare and the tension in her jaw convey uneasiness, which I'm guessing has something to do with Zane. It's a look that suggests he wasn't bullshitting me about them not taking this seriously because of his involvement.

"He approached me after coming across something online…on a subreddit."

She nods, waiting for me to divulge more, but I leave it there. Still, she waits some more, and I'm wondering if her silence is a police tactic to get people to disclose more details because I'm tempted. But if I start rambling, I'm gonna slip up and say something that'll put Zane in a spot. And maybe have Detective Roth not taking this seriously, which considering there was someone in my home, it's fucking serious.

When I don't go on, she says, "Right. So you were never aware of Jason Kilbourne or Michael Grayson until you met Zane. Is that right?"

"I heard about the disappearances, around town."

She purses her lips, nodding, her gaze shifting around her desk. "Yeah. As I said, this call was a surprise, but I wish it were more surprising."

"You expected me to call?"

"Not necessarily you. It's complicated."

It reminds me of how goddamn cryptic Zane was when he first came over. *Get to the fucking point!*

"I want to start off by saying that Zane's a good kid," she tells me, a clear disclaimer to something that's going to leave me wondering if that's really the case. "When his brother went missing, I was placed in charge of the case. Zane was very helpful and, like any family of someone who went missing, he wanted updates and to be involved in the process. All those things I respected.

"I will say, however, that I listened to him more than I should have. Let him come by to follow up because he was grieving, and having lost a sister when I was younger, his case resonated with me. But he became too involved."

"What do you mean?"

"Zane became convinced that a professor at WCC was involved in Michael's disappearance. Since there was no credible evidence to support his suspicions, I couldn't do much more than chat with this professor. Nothing came of that chat, but one day, Zane came in with a blog post that seemed to link this professor to his brother. It seemed credible enough for me to follow up on the lead."

This was what Zane was telling me about—the bad call he'd made. The reason I must be careful about what I say.

"And I did follow that lead. The blog was linked to a

VPN, which means we couldn't trace it to an IP address, but we could trace it to a VPN provider. With that much, I felt confident talking with this professor. He was very cooperative. Let us use his laptop, no questions asked, and I didn't see any evidence of the VPN provider on there. But knowing Zane's background, what he does for work, I started to have my doubts. I asked Zane if I could meet him at his home. I told him what I'd done to follow up on his lead, then asked if I could check his laptop to see if *he* used the VPN provider linked to the blog. He came clean, which was reassuring in some ways, disappointing in others."

"He made that whole thing up so you'd look into the guy?"

"Yes, that's right. Unfortunately, what Zane did is a crime, so it was an involved process, ensuring this professor and the department wouldn't try to pursue anything legally. I bent over backward to keep Zane out of trouble. It was a very unfortunate mess."

Yeah, I can definitely get why they wouldn't take him seriously if that's how things went down.

"So now that you know about that incident, you can see why an acquaintance of Zane's showing up with this new information could be concerning to me?"

"I can see that." There's a knot in my stomach.

"Don't get me wrong—like I said, he's a good guy. A little socially awkward. A little timorous, as I'm sure you've noticed."

As much doubt as she's raised in me, I'm still struggling to make sense of some things.

"But there was someone breaking into my house in that video on the flash drive. Did you have a chance to look at that?" After Zane left, I watched it—it looked like a man in all black and a ski mask had been trying to get into the house.

"Could be a friend he talked into helping him. Or maybe just someone trying to burglarize the place."

"A friend? Like he got someone to do that?" I'd considered this, but not that seriously. What kind of fucked-up person would he be to do that?

"Well, if something happens that connects to his brother's disappearance in some way, maybe Zane believes we'll continue pursuing the case. Not that we aren't still looking into it, but it's clear Zane doesn't think we're doing our job. I don't know what else there is to do. I've exhausted all my resources. Even when he brought in that subreddit post linking to your Insta, I did my due diligence. Checked the Reddit account it came from."

"What did you find?"

"A dead end."

She has this knowing look, and I must admit, hearing these things is sobering. They make more sense than the bizarre reality Zane tried to convince me of: that some maniac is trying to kidnap me along with his other victims.

"Even the connection on that subreddit, this imagined link between Jason Kilbourne's or Michael Grayson's disappearances, doesn't ring true. Yes, the guys are around the same age. Young men, which is probably why they got any media attention—this stuff happens all the time in this town to people of other ages and demographics, and no one bats an eye. But some bloggers and podcasters have linked them, probably because they need to create more monetized content and because the true-crime media they consume leads them to thinking any connection—even just attending the same community college—is enough to persuade us to get search warrants and bust down doors. But I think you can see why it's a stretch to assume they're connected outside of this Reddit thread. The letter sent to you could have easily been written by someone who had already seen the Reddit post. Maybe even someone who had a vested interest in stirring up more interest in this case. Maybe even Zane."

More fair points.

More reasons to make me doubt him.

"Do you consider yourself Zane Grayson's friend?" she asks, and I wonder what sparked the question.

"Not friends. I haven't known him very long."

Her gaze shifts to her computer monitor before trailing back to me. "I didn't plan to share this, but maybe this will help you wrap your head around what's going on. Mike Grayson suffered from a lot of mental-health challenges, just like Zane."

"Meaning?"

"His brother's made several suicide attempts before he went missing. He and Zane have both been 10-13ed." She hesitates before explaining, "That's the Georgia code for a psych hold."

I'm tempted to tell her I know what a 10-13 is from experience, but she doesn't need to know that.

"So you can understand that it's not unreasonable to believe that Mike didn't need any help disappearing. Any number of things could have happened. And as far as Zane's interest in his brother's case, that's understandable, and I'd rather not get into his story, but I do want to mention that, during that time when he was framing that professor for being involved in Mike's disappearance, Zane wasn't taking his medication, and I do think that contributed to his erratic behavior."

"What does he take medication for?"

"I'd rather not disclose more than that," she says, not blinking as she issues the boundary. "I want to tell you enough to help you understand that you need to go no-contact with Zane Grayson. I'm worried he's trying to use you to persuade us to investigate his brother's disappearance further. And that won't be healthy for either of you."

10-13s.

Medication.

Zane also has a mental-health issue. Could that be

what this is all about, rather than me being in serious danger from a psychopath?

"Do you mind if I ask how he approached you?" she asks.

Fuck.

"Met him in my house when he scared the shit out of me and dragged me into my closet. And he's been living next door to me all this time."

Sure, that would go over well.

"He came to my parents' place, where I'm living right now. He wanted to talk to me about the post."

That stays within the realm of misleading, but not an outright lie. Not my fault she didn't ask a more specific question.

"Well, let me know if telling him to leave you alone isn't enough. There are other options."

"Other options?"

"Like a TRO." At my look, she explains, "A restraining order."

A restraining order? For someone who thought he was harmless, now she's suggesting I might need a restraining order?

She wraps up our meeting, and I return to my car. As I slide into the driver's seat, I'm still trying to make sense of everything she told me. Her explanations sounded fairly reasonable. Much more than anything Zane told me. What if he's using me to bolster his fixation with his missing brother? But what if he also believes I'm in danger?

I figure most people, after talking with Detective Roth, might want nothing to do with Zane Grayson, but our conversation has made me that much more interested in him.

What if he's having a mental-health crisis?

I've been there. I know what it's like to lose touch with reality.

And after what he's been through with his brother, would that be such a terrible thing?

I don't have the feeling he would hurt me.

And maybe I'm just that fucking gullible, but I don't think he would be deceiving me like she suggests.

Yes, Detective Roth has given me plenty of things to consider about the night I found Zane in my house. It should be enough to scare a normal person off.

But maybe I'm not a normal person.

6

ZANE

"So you like your new place?" Jesse asks.

I sit at my desk, Zoom on one of my two computer monitors, chatting with my therapist.

"It's fine. I like the area," I say, which is true enough.

"That's good. Have you made any new friends?"

Does the guy I'm stalking count?

Of course, I haven't mentioned anything about Leif to her or my psych.

For obvious reasons.

Jesse doesn't know why I moved here. Or what I've been up to for the past few weeks. Or that I've got surveillance footage up on my second monitor, watching Leif's house. If she did, that'd be a different conversation, involving the cops, upping our therapy sessions, and getting Dr. Byce to reassess my current doses.

"No new friends, but I'm still keeping in touch with Alex and René."

Friends I met during my 10-13.

"And work? Are you keeping busy there?"

"Yup. Enough to get by, at least."

I used to work in IT at a company in Macon, but since I started watching Leif, I've been living off my savings and online tech gigs that allow me to make my own weird-ass schedule.

"And how are you managing with your meds?"

"Still taking them, if that's what you're asking." She knows all about my fiasco with the Wyachet PD. And even a few of the times before that, when I foolishly convinced myself I could just drop the meds altogether. Needless to say, I've learned my lesson. "Dr. Byce changed my antipsychotic dosage, and the new mood stabilizer is working better than the last one."

"So the mood swings are better?"

"Yes, that's what I meant by better," I snap before catching myself. "Sorry. I'm stressed. And annoyed that I had to get up early."

I schedule these sessions at six a.m., knowing Leif won't be up yet. To make this lifestyle functional, I try to build my schedule around watching him. But it's been more than that. The past few days, since he's visited with Detective Roth, I've been even more on edge than usual.

What did she tell him? What does he know about me?

"You can't trust that guy," I imagine her saying. *"He had a horrible manic episode that led to him trying to get an innocent man implicated in a crime he didn't commit."*

Shitty that if she told him that, he might never want

to speak to me again. Even shittier that it's the truth.

"Do you feel you're having issues with your sleep cycle?" Jesse asks.

Oh, you have no idea. The only thing that's made it all tolerable is that the security cameras have AI monitoring, so I can create a notification alarm in my app to know when Leif's on the move or someone's outside the house. Unfortunately, there's also a squirrel who really enjoys hanging around his place, who'll sometimes set off the same alarm, and fuck, that's annoying.

"Eh, I'll live."

I interpret her head tilt as disapproval, and I intercept her comment. "It's fine. I'm doing all the right things, and I've been eating better recently."

"That's good to hear."

The chili he brought over is likely the last meal I'll ever get from Leif Anderson, but it was sweet of him while he didn't think I was going to murder him in his sleep. At least I got a few days of leftovers out of it.

We chat about other everyday stuff, and I keep evading what I've really been up to before she asks, "So is there anything you wanted to discuss today? Maybe your brother?"

"What's there to talk about? The cops are done with him. Now he's fucking gone, and I'll never know why."

"I hear a lot of anger and resentment."

"Those seem like tame words for what I'm feeling. Hard to get over the loss of the only guy in this world who's ever really understood what I've been through."

"Is that what you expect? To get over it?"

"I just wish I had answers. It's the uncertainty. Thinking that he could walk through the door tomorrow, or I might never see him again. It's a fucked-up world. And a lot of times it felt like it was the two of us versus it, and now he's gone."

At least there are some things I can still be transparent about.

"Especially with your childhood together, I can understand why you would feel that way. It was only the two of you with your father."

I flash back to a moment with Dad, his eyes wide in that way that made me uncomfortable as he adjusted a gun in my hand. *"You did better that time. Now again. Come on. Only two kinds of men in the world: those who know guns and those who don't."*

"Dad, you're scaring me."

"You need to be scared, Zane. It's the only thing that'll keep you alive in this messed-up world. I might not always be around to protect you guys, so I need you to be my strong one."

But I don't want to be strong.

I tense up.

"Can we not talk about that?"

"We've discussed this before. Is there a reason you're uncomfortable with it today?"

"I just don't want to go there."

Jesse never pushes. I've seen enough therapists to know it's her job to only talk about shit I feel like talking about, but damn, she sure knows how to pick at a tender wound.

After we finish our session, I get some shut-eye.

I'm in and out through Leif's morning routine. I'm lucky he's mostly a homebody—aside from trips to the store, the gym, or around the neighborhood or the park for a jog. Today he doesn't get out of the house until four in the afternoon, when I tail him to Kroger. I keep at the far end of the parking lot, and I have no doubt he's seen me already. I'm sure he's noticed me whenever he's run an errand after I told him what I was up to, but he hasn't called the cops on me, so maybe it's ridiculous to assume that Detective Roth disclosed all my dirty secrets.

Or maybe she's got people tailing me right now?

Am I being paranoid?

Maybe these meds aren't working.

No, stop it! It's not my fault. It's how Dad trained Mike and me—that's what Jesse'd say.

When he's finished shopping, I tail him back to his place, but when we get to his house, he pulls into my driveway, parking by the garage doors.

The hell?

I pull in beside him, and as we get out of our cars, he heads to his trunk. "Will you give me a hand with these?"

I stand there, watching him as he pops the trunk and

collects his recyclable bags from the back.

"Or are you gonna make me do it myself?" he asks.

I join him, grabbing a few bags, noticing a rather eclectic combination of meats, veggies, and cheeses.

"What is all this for?"

"Oh, some of it is stuff I picked up while I was at the store. We only need some of it."

"For?"

"You said you liked pizza, so I was gonna make one for dinner."

My jaw drops, and a sound escapes like I meant to say something, but I'm speechless, so I obey his orders and help him get the groceries inside.

Like the first time he came over, he makes himself at home, storing some bags in the fridge and others on the counter. While he's searching through my drawers, I ask, "What do you need me to do?"

He pulls a cheese grater from the drawer. "Here we go. Grate the mozzarella. I already made the dough, sauce, and some chicken earlier. I'll get the spinach ready and then swing by my place and grab those."

I grab the mozzarella, the grater, and a plate and start my work at the table while Leif rinses the spinach.

Despite everything that's happened, he's got this laid-back attitude as he makes his way around the kitchen, but I'm still on edge.

"So how did that chat with Detective Roth go?" I can't wait in suspense any longer.

What did she tell you?

The truth?

Surely, she hadn't told him the worst of it if he's in my kitchen making me fucking pizza.

"It went about as you expected." He holds the spinach in one hand and finds a cutting board under the sink with the other. "She was pretty direct about everything. Said she didn't have any reason to believe the break-in at my place had anything to do with the disappearances. Told me we probably shouldn't be talking anymore." As he chats, he takes the spinach and the cutting board to the kitchen island and takes a knife from the knife block.

"That sounds about right."

He chops the spinach as I grate, and when he's finished, he says, "Okay, when you're done, I've laid out the other cheeses. I'll be back in a flash."

He takes the grocery bags we brought in back to his place as I continue my work. He returns with some kind of pan or cookie sheet covered in a towel and a container of cooked chicken. He's brought another grater, and he helps me with the cheese, sitting in the chair adjacent to mine at the table.

"I'm guessing you made the crust and sauce from scratch."

"Is there another way?"

"Shut up. You're just showing off. You could have easily picked up a crust and sauce from the store."

"It's no beef Wellington."

"I'm gonna assume I understand the context of that statement."

He chuckles before he turns to me. A tuft of his curly brown hair slips out from under his beanie as he flashes that beautiful, cocked smile. My gaze travels around his face, inspecting his features. It's nice seeing him up close like this. Unlike the first times we were around each other, he doesn't even seem to be thinking about his safety when he's next to me. I like that he doesn't consider me a threat anymore—at least, I can't imagine why he'd be over here if he did.

It contrasts sharply with seeing him under far more strenuous circumstances, when I was dragging his half-naked body into the closet.

His hot breath hits my lips, and I study his mouth. What would it feel like?

He winces as he seems to catch on to what I'm doing, and I look away. I wonder what he feels, having some creeper this close to him, watching him, studying him.

"So you really do enjoy cooking," I say. "Like, more than most people."

"My grammy used to cook and bake with me a lot when I was younger and I'd go visit her."

"Is that the one your parents are with now?"

He huffs. "No. That's Grandma Linda. She's an asshole. Grammy was wonderful. Loving. Kind. Passed away a few years ago from a heart attack. Her cooking puts me to shame."

"I'm sorry for your loss."

My words seem to catch him by surprise. "It's okay. It's been five years now. And we had some great times together—including finally getting her approval for my pecan pie—so that was nice." He smirks, but I can see there's sadness there too. That mixture of joy and pain that comes from losing those we love.

It quiets him for a bit as we finish grating. Then he places the toppings on his crust.

"Now we'll leave it to rise," he says, setting the oven timer. We wash our hands in the kitchen sink, and I grab us bottles of water from the fridge and join him at the table, where he's made himself comfortable.

"So…" he says, "I have some new questions for you, now that I've had time to reflect on everything."

"Yeah?" I sit in the chair adjacent to him, watching, waiting for him to get uneasy about how close we're sitting together, but he seems unfazed.

Nice as that is, I'm tense again, wondering what questions he has for me.

7

LEIF

CONSIDERING HOW MUCH he surprised me in our first encounter, it's nice to surprise him for a change. Is it terrible that I think he's adorable when he's all awkward and uncomfortable, which seems even more the case now that we're sitting so close? Since I mentioned having more questions for him, he's started digging his thumbnail into the side of his opposite hand. Am I wicked to leave him hanging for a bit longer?

But I go easy on him to start. "What sort of work do you do? To pay to rent this place…your car…your security system around my parents' place?"

"Oh." He chuckles. Clearly, that wasn't what he figured I'd ask.

"I freelance online, mostly IT-type gigs—anything to do with coding or SEO, I'm pretty good at those. It's not a lot of money, but I get by. And it lets me choose my hours."

"That must make watching me easier," I tease, and his gaze narrows like he's wondering how I can joke about that.

Although, feels like that's the only way to get through any of this.

"Did you go to college?" I ask. "Are you in college?"

He shakes his head. "No. I would like to at some point, but I've been able to get work just fine without it."

He keeps it short and to the point; he's not making this any easier than when I was trying to figure out what the hell he was doing in the house.

I try another question. "Where did you learn how to use a gun?"

"My dad taught Mike and me."

Again, it's a short reply. Makes me worry that this line of questioning isn't going anywhere, but worst he can do is be as cryptic about everything. "The other night, when you mentioned you knew I'd been in a psych unit, you said you understood, but I was so hung up on not going there, I never asked what you meant."

"I knew she'd fucking blab," he says through his teeth. He pushes his hands against the table as he gets up, like all he wants is to get the hell away from this conversation, and instinctually, I reach out and take him by his wrist, which makes him freeze in place.

His skin's so soft. So warm.

His gaze shifts to my hand, then meets mine again.

Did I make a mistake? God, what if he doesn't like being touched?

I immediately release him. "Sorry, I shouldn't have

done that."

"No, it's fine," he says, a smile tugging across his face. "Just…nothing."

One second he's frustrated, maybe even pissed, and now he's smiling. I can never get a read on this guy.

"If you don't want to talk about it, I'll understand," I say, hoping to set him at ease, and he sits back in his chair.

"What's there to talk about if she already told you?"

I figure the best thing to do is be honest with him. "She didn't tell me specifics, but she brought it up when she warned me to stay away from you."

"Maybe you should listen to her."

"Should I?"

He's quiet, like he's thinking it over.

"You made it sound like my time in the psych unit wasn't a big deal," I add, "so why don't you want to talk about this with me?"

"It's easy to say about someone else's shit, isn't it?"

His gaze settles on the table as he seems to struggle with the thought of sharing with me. I'm racking my brain, trying to think of a way to get him to open up, and fuck it, I go for it. "Freshman year of college, I was staying at the dorms at Georgia State. I'd never had any major issues. Life was pretty chill. Supportive parents and friends. Good grades throughout high school. Felt like I was gonna get my bachelor's in culinary arts, hopefully work as a chef, and get on with a pretty normal life.

Then all of a sudden, seemingly out of nowhere, something shifted in me. I shut down. Started sleeping all day. Not going to class. Telling my friends I was busy. Calling in sick to work. I've never had anything like that happen before. Mom and Dad would call, and I'd act like everything was all right. Lie to them about attending class because I didn't want them to know something was wrong. And then more days went by."

Zane wears a sympathetic expression as he listens. And despite the tension that knots in my chest, there's something nice about having someone to share this with.

"On one level," I go on, "I knew I was gonna fail my classes if I didn't go, but it was hard enough to go out just to get food. It was like being a zombie, walking around to exist but not feeling anything. The next thing I know, I'm having thoughts about jumping out of the window in my room. Somehow that got me on a website where I could chat with someone. And I can't even remember what I said, but it was apparently enough for them to call the cops. They showed up and took me to the hospital."

Zane reaches for me but stops himself. "I'm sorry you went through that."

"I assumed something like that would only happen if I had some fucked-up trauma, but this was out of the blue…and so fucking heavy."

His hand slides across the tabletop, even closer. I wish he would take my hand, but why would he? We're fucking strangers. Maybe not strangers, but he definitely doesn't know me well enough for that.

"How has it been since?" he presses in a gentle voice.

"After the hold, I stayed with Mom and Dad and worked with a therapist and psychiatrist to get my head on straight. Zoloft wasn't much help. That still felt like a fog. Then Lexapro was better, and for the first time, the fog lifted, but it didn't magically make everything go back to the way it was. I'm still not that person I was before…whatever the hell happened in my head. I don't know that I ever will be again."

When I decided to share this, I figured it was to get him to talk, but after going further than I thought I would, I'm wondering if some part of me wanted to share that with someone other than a therapist. Whatever my motive, there was something cathartic about getting it out, and the sympathy in his expression soothing.

Maybe I told him for the same reason I came over here today. Because whatever he's been through, maybe he understands what I'm talking about.

His hand rests on the table, halfway between us. If he won't take my hand, I could take his. Tell him that, whatever his shit is, I'm not gonna judge him. But after how he reacted to me taking his wrist, I'm not gonna risk it.

"Thank you for sharing that," he finally says. "It's a wicked thing when a mind turns on itself, isn't it?"

His remark speaks to what I already knew: that he

would understand.

"I guess it's my turn now," he goes on.

"You don't have to share anything you're uncomfortable with. I just thought it might make it easier."

"I'm worried the moment I say it, you won't believe any of this other stuff. Then I'm like, fuck it, you probably already don't believe me. But I know that whole back-and-forth in my head is covering up the fact that I really don't want to share that stuff with anyone." He takes a breath, his gaze shifting about as he seems to grapple with this internal struggle.

I wish he knew how much I understood.

"Maybe a different question," I say.

"No." That comes out harsh. Given how compassionate he's been throughout our conversation, it takes me by surprise. "It's not fair to put you through all this and then keep it from you." He takes another breath, a final moment to sit with his secret.

"Bipolar I," he says, almost a whisper through his teeth, like it was a strain to share. "Mine manifests as manic episodes with a healthy dose of psychosis. I'd always had issues with my moods, but it got much worse when I got out on my own. Particularly paranoia. I take a mood stabilizer and an antipsychotic to regulate. Mike had his shit too. He was studying psych at WCC because he wanted to help people who dealt with the same shit. That's the kind of guy he was."

I can hear his admiration in the way he speaks about

his brother…as well as the pain of his loss.

"Not sure if Roth mentioned it," he goes on, "but after my bro disappeared, I started slipping with taking my meds. Just distracted, and then that turned into me telling myself I was fine now and didn't need them. And that was a mistake. I made a huge mistake."

"She mentioned one of Mike's professors…"

He shakes his head. "No, he's a professor at the school Mike attends, but not his professor. When he went missing, his landlord told me he needed the rent money, which I could cover for a month, and he let me in to search his things. I was hoping to find some explanation. Mike kept a planner, and he mentioned 'Meet with Tolle' twice the month before he disappeared, once on a Tuesday and once on a Thursday. No time on it. Just that note. When I was trying to make sense of it, I discovered that one of the professors in the English department at WCC was named Isaac Tolle. I mentioned this to Roth, who asked him if he knew my brother. He claimed he was helping him with some essays."

He huffs. "My brother never needed any help with an essay. I know that sounds like a wild claim, but I fucking knew him. He was the reader and writer in the family. He's the one who helped me with my essays growing up. I got the science and math, and he got that. That's the way it was, so that was a red flag for me. I showed Roth his transcripts, how he didn't need any help there, but Roth didn't think much of it." He eyes me suspiciously. "You don't buy that either. I get that it might not make sense to someone who didn't know Mike, but I know with everything in me that he was the kind of guy who figured out shit on his own. Just like me. That's part of how we grew up. So even if he had been struggling, he wouldn't have found someone…and for this, definitely not."

"I wasn't doubting it," I assure him. "I'm just listening."

His expression relaxes. "Yeah. Sorry. I was remembering how Roth pushed back when I told her that was my reason for being suspicious. Was frustrating trying to explain Mike to someone who'd never met him. But after that, long story short, I had some experiences that led me to think he could have been involved with my bro's disappearance. And since I wasn't taking my meds, it got bad. Even thought I was seeing the guy around town. Like total strangers would look like him for fractions of a second. I convinced myself I was right. But I didn't have enough to convince Roth, so as I figure she probably already told you, I made up this blog to make it look like Tolle was obsessed with Mike. I wrote journal entries about my brother, as though I were Tolle. I even borrowed pieces of his profile and website to make it seem legit. I found this quote: 'I think the devil doesn't exist, but man has created him, he has created him in his own image and likeness.' It's from the author of *Crime and Punishment.* I don't remember his name, something Russian…"

It's Dostoevsky, but I don't want to interrupt him.

"I know it's fucked up," he says, "but I was so fucking manic, it seemed like the right thing to do, and you know, part of being manic is some ideas you'd know are total crap when you're fine seem real fucking brilliant. I thought I'd cracked the code. They'd look into it and find my brother…or find out what happened to him, at least."

I know what he means. To find out if his brother was murdered. I can't imagine what it must be like for him to even express that…to have to entertain the possibility.

"Then maybe I could have some peace of mind," he adds. "Not sure that's true, but it's what my fucked-up brain convinced me of."

Even without his confession, since I spoke with Detective Roth, there's been plenty of doubt in my mind. But now that he's shared the truth with me, I can see why that's not something he could've led with when trying to convince me I was in danger. Although, I have to keep in mind that, regardless of my doubt, someone did break into my parents' house that night.

A coincidence? Possibly.

Or as Detective Roth suggested, someone Zane hired to cause a stir and persuade them to reopen the investigation? I'm not buying it.

Zane closes his eyes. "And now you don't believe any

of this shit, do you?"

"Would it be difficult for you to understand why I have doubts?"

"Yeah. I think there'd be something really wrong with you if you just took my word for it."

It's a relief to hear him say that—assures me he's at least being reasonable. We're quiet for a few moments as I process everything he shared.

Doing that a lot lately…

Finally, he asks, "What are you thinking?"

"A lot of things."

"I'm on my meds now," he tells me, as if to keep me from worrying. "I'm not going to let that happen again."

I gaze into those steel-blue eyes. Is it strange to trust this guy? Even when I don't really know him?

There's something else there too. I *like* looking at his eyes.

"It's still on the table, though." I'm not sure what he's referring to until he goes on, "Say the word, and I'll be gone."

If this is all a delusion he's suffering from, it's because he's grieving the loss of his brother. And if he wants the cops to take him seriously, it might be shitty to be using me, but I'd actually get that too.

The way he looks at me, I can tell he's waiting for me to tell him to get lost.

Maybe that's what I should say, but instead I say, "I don't really know what to think, but I'd rather you stay for now, and we play it by ear."

His expression relaxes and he takes a breath, like he's been holding it until my response.

"Thank you, Leif. I know you're in a real spot here."

"It's okay. I'm becoming increasingly intrigued by you."

That seems to catch his attention, and I notice him glancing at my mouth in that way that reminds me of how he looked when he first came to chat with me.

When he called me *very attractive.*

"Anything else you wanted to ask me about?"

I wonder if I should go there, but it might lighten the mood, so I just go for it. "You've made some comments in the short time we've known each other…about me being attractive, and then the way you look at me, you have this very determined expression on your face."

"That's not a question."

"Do you need me to make it one to give me an explanation?"

He smirks, and for the first time in this whole fucked-up mess, his fair cheeks pinken.

God, he's cute when he blushes.

Where the hell did that thought come from?

"I'm queer—gay," he explains. "And you're a very attractive guy, Leif…obviously, since that's what I said."

A pulse of excitement radiates through me. What is happening?

I've never been into guys. I've jerked off once or twice thinking about Timothée Chalamet, but that taste never translated into real life. And I imagine plenty of other straight guys have jerked off thinking about Chalamet.

But as Zane looks at me and tells me he finds me attractive, I'm…curious.

Maybe this is some kind of wild trauma response to how we first met that I'm mistaking for something else.

"Don't worry, Leif. I know you're straight. I've seen all the photos of your exes on Insta and Facebook, so I'm not creeping on you. And I can keep it professional when I'm watching you. Though sometimes that can be difficult, honestly. I mean, you're pretty hot, and that ass…"

This eagerness in me pulses up once again, but he stops there.

Why does his mention of my ass make my cock shift in my pants?

"What do you like about my ass?" I press.

He stares at me, licks his lips. He hesitates before saying, "It's firm. Notice it when you jog, how it jiggles. I imagine if I could…" He stops himself but licks his lips again. And I don't know why my cock is so damn hard over that.

"Well, there it fucking is," he adds. "Guess you really don't want me being the one to watch you now."

"I didn't say that."

His head jerks as he does a double take—maybe he's as surprised by my response as I am. Or the way I can't take my eyes off him.

His eyes narrow. "What do you mean?"

"I don't know. As I said, you intrigue me, Zane."

His lips curl into a smirk. "If after all that you aren't telling me to fuck off, then I guess I'm not the only one who's fucked up."

"Isn't that what we've been determining in this conversation? That we're both a little fucked up?"

His smirk spreads into a smile, and damn, he's got a gorgeous smile.

I don't know what's going on. I've been curious about the guy since I first met him…since he first made weird comments about me being attractive, but now that he's laid everything out on the table, I'm starting to realize it's not only this complicated shit that brought him here that interests me.

What the fuck are you doing to me, Zane Grayson?

8

ZANE

SILENCE STRETCHES BETWEEN us.

It was such an epic conversation—from him confessing that shit about his past and then me confessing my shit.

And then he said he was intrigued by me…

What does that mean?

The looks he gives me, the fact that he hasn't freaked out… Some straight guys enjoy attention, even if it's from a queer guy. I had a friend—Tau—who had one straight guy torture him for years. They did everything together, and the guy lapped up his attention, but he always had a girlfriend, never made a move. Just loved basking in my friend's interest.

I don't have too much time to consider it because our pizza's ready. Leif pulls it out of the oven, and we let it cool a bit before enjoying slices.

"God, that's good," I say, reveling in the mix of the cheeses, spinach, and chicken. With my eyes closed, I fully embrace it, since these meals are a treat. "You're spoiling me."

"Watching you enjoy it makes it worth it." As he says that, I notice him watching me eat before taking another healthy bite.

I gaze into his eyes, maybe longer than I should. But that's become something of a bad habit.

There's a question in my mind, a place I don't want to let myself go to, but a vibrating sound catches my attention before Leif pulls his phone out of his pocket. "Ah, that's my parents," he says around a mouthful. "Probably calling to update me about Linda. Think I'm gonna head back."

He sounds so cool, so unfazed by everything we've just discussed as he shoves the rest of his pizza in his mouth and hops up, starting for the door.

"Wait," I say, and he stops and spins toward me. "You're not gonna take some with you? I can't eat all this."

"I insist. You said you don't cook much, and I have leftovers from lunch yesterday."

But I don't want him to stay just for pizza. I've enjoyed getting to know Leif beyond what I've learned from stalking him.

"Oh, before I go." He approaches and hands me his phone.

Maybe since I'm in stalker mode, my first thought is, does he want me to put a tracker in it?

"Your number," he says. "Put it in."

I chuckle. "Oh. Right. That's what normal people do."

I input my number, then hand him his phone.

"See you later, creeper," he says with a wink.

It's disappointing that he's going already. It's nice to have some company, or maybe I like that he's the company. I assume the latter. But he heads on his way, and before I know it, he's gone.

SITTING AT MY desk, I take another bite of the chicken Alfredo pizza. I close my eyes and savor it.

Fuck, that guy knows how to make a pizza.

I'm appreciative he insisted I keep the leftovers since, outside of what he's brought me, the homemade meals I typically encounter come in the form of frozen dinners, sandwiches, and cans.

I just wish he'd been able to stay longer. Beyond the attraction I can't deny, it was nice to talk to someone who knows what it's like to lose control of his mind. Who knows things some people in this world won't ever understand…at least, I hope most people don't have to live like this.

I check the time on my computer monitor, and it's a little past eleven. After Leif left, I got in a good bit of work, since I have to pay the bills. And if what I've learned in my stalking is any indication, Leif should be finishing up his shower right about now.

I set my slice on a plate on my desk, watching the surveillance footage on my monitor as a shadow moves around Leif's bedroom, behind the blinds. Having seen him in only a towel, it's easy for me to imagine what he looks like behind those blinds at this time of night. It's the sort of thing that makes my dick perk right up.

I want to slap at my crotch. I shouldn't enjoy this; although, maybe this is the way my mind tries to make the best of a shitty situation.

Or maybe I'm just creeping on him.

"Hey, Dr. Byce. I wanted to check in with you about my doses. If you could give me a call when you get a chance, that'd be great."

Shortly after our discussion, I called my psych. I've had a few discussions with her since I became Leif Anderson's neighbor. I'm not so oblivious that I don't realize all this could be a cause for concern. Despite taking my meds, it wouldn't be the first time I'd ever experienced symptoms and needed to have my doses adjusted. Of course, I won't tell her how I'm spending my days. Just mention some feelings of paranoia. Make it sound less concerning than maybe I should; although shouldn't you be honest about this shit with your goddamn psychiatrist? But if I told her the truth, I'd definitely wind up in a psych unit. Not that that would be so terrible if I needed help, but if that happens, I won't be able to protect Leif.

It's a struggle because I do believe I'm right, but I believed I was right about Isaac Tolle, the professor from Mike's school. This is different, though, since I actually have evidence and rational reasons for thinking Leif's in danger. But what if it's all a lie I'm telling myself? Part of this delusion I'm suffering from?

I didn't tell Leif, but when he said he wasn't sure what to think…well, I'm not sure either.

I take another bite, practically sucking too much of my slice into my mouth.

As I set it back on the plate, the blinds at Leif's window pull up.

What is he doing? Doesn't he know someone other than me could be watching right now?

But the blinds steadily reveal sweatpants, then his nude torso. He stands at the window, looking out, searching. Has he heard something outside?

I check the other cameras, wondering if there's something I'm missing, when I see him texting on his phone. As a text comes through on mine, I snatch it quickly to check.

LEIF: You watching? ;)

I gasp with relief. As I look up from my phone, he's at the window, offering a gentle wave.

Instinctively, I raise my hand at my monitor, then feel like a fucking idiot.

"Isn't that what we've been determining in this conversation? That we're both a little fucked up?"

I smile at the thought. If *I'm* messed up for doing this, then *he* definitely is for knowing all that he does and letting me continue.

"You intrigue me, Zane."

I'm intrigued too. For obvious reasons. I don't imagine Leif's a stranger to some queer guy lusting over him. I tell myself it's his abs and his beautiful face, but having chatted with him, I must admit it's more than that now.

He's charming and sensitive. God, what it did to me when he told me that shit about what he went through in college; the bravery it must've taken for him to share something so deeply personal. Not enough people understand what it's like when a mind becomes its own enemy. Maybe that's why he felt safe sharing it with me. It's the only reason I was willing to give him my secrets. But that conversation has bound me to him even more than I already was. Given me a new determination to protect him.

ME: Of course.

ME: You already know I find you attractive. This feels like a cruel tease.

I regret the moment I hit Send, but damned if it isn't true.

LEIF: I thought you said VERY attractive. Have I

already been demoted?

My cheeks are hot as I study his image on my monitor, trying to read his expression.

ME: No, you haven't been demoted.

God, why am I fucking answering like this? Even more importantly, why is *he* texting *me* like this? But I have bigger concerns.

ME: But someone else could be watching.
ME: Close the blinds.

A selfish part of me doesn't want him to, while the protective part wants to head over and close them myself. But if I were in his bedroom right now, with him in only sweats, fuck, he'd really think I was a creeper.

My phone buzzes again.

LEIF: Just thought you might enjoy the view. ;)

I lick my lips, like the creeper I fucking am.

LEIF: Night. x
ME: Good night, Leif.

As he closes his blinds, I'm relieved no one else can watch him but devastated that I can't either.

Too quickly, my memory of that body fades, and my creeper instincts kick in.

The surveillance images are pulled up on my right-hand monitor, so I open another screen on the left. I scroll back through the footage that's downloaded to my hard drive and grab the little-over-a-minute of footage of him at the window, waving. I upload the footage into another app and play it on a loop.

Biting my bottom lip, my hand gravitates under my boxers, stroking.

My eyes are fixed on his expression. Why did he fucking tease me like this, knowing I'm gay, knowing I'm lusting after him?

Maybe he's like Tau's friend, a straight guy wanting to soak up all my attention because he doesn't get it in other parts of his life.

To think of how much hell I used to give Tau, but now I fucking get it.

Fuck…those abs.

That face.

Those eyes. Those damn eyes.

Isn't it weird enough that he knows I'm watching him, but now he must know I'm about to cream to his image?

Memories of that night when I pulled him into the closet flash through my head. We were so fucking close. At the time, I was concerned with keeping him safe, but now I just remember his ass being pushed up against me, my hand against his abs to keep him tight against my body.

That's probably the only time I'll ever get to touch his magnificent body.

As I'm jerking off, I'm staring at his face, imagining what he'd look like with my cock in him. Imagining him writhing beneath me, begging for more, those lips wide as he calls out my name.

Guilt flashes through me.

Enjoy the view.

He wants me to enjoy this—or am I telling myself that to get myself to the end?

My palm's too dry, and I can tell I'm rubbing myself raw, but it doesn't matter because a few moments later my cock pulses in my grip as I shoot into my boxers, my body lurching forward in my seat, still looking at Leif's face.

I take my wet hand out of my boxers, feeling the warmth of me against my crotch as I catch my breath.

"Why did you do that to me?" I whisper to this image of him.

And now I really feel like a fucking creeper.

9

LEIF

AFTER I CLOSE my blinds, I strip down and get into the shower.

Enjoy the view.

Why am I hoping he did enjoy it?

Is it cruel to taunt him when I know he's attracted to me? Maybe, but it was such a thrill thinking about the way he looks at me. That he doesn't even look like he could hide his attraction if he wanted to.

I've never messed around with a guy before, but while I'm showering off, I notice I'm spending extra time scrubbing between my ass cheeks, even though I've already washed there. This isn't about washing, though.

It's curiosity.

He likes my ass. What would he want to do with it?

Obviously, I know the answer.

I've never been interested in anal before, but all of a sudden I'm thinking about gay sex and what it'd be like to have a guy in me.

I've heard great things about the prostate. It would

supposedly feel good.

I run my middle finger around the rim, pushing the tip in, but my ass is pretty tight. How do guys get a fucking dick up there? I push a little farther, but it weirds me out.

Stop it! What the fuck are you doing?

This is all Zane's fault. He has my brain doing wild things.

I finish washing up, but I can't let go of my curiosity.

With my towel around my waist, I sit at my desk, performing a quick online search for anal toys. I've heard of butt plugs, but some of these are way too big. I check out a few that seem reasonable sizes, and as I'm looking, think about Mom and Dad getting home and finding one of these in my room.

But they won't be home for another week or two, so now would be the time to experiment...

"WE SHOULD BE home Monday," Mom says.

"That's great. I'm glad Grandma's letting you claw your way from her clutches." Keeping the phone to my ear, I open the front door and lean down, picking up a package off the porch.

"We'll see," Mom continues as I head back inside. "She's able to get around, and I think Cathy can handle this better on her own." Cathy is Mom's sister, a.k.a.

another of Linda's favorite victims. "And if we need to come back, it's an easy flight. I can't imagine if we'd tried to do this before the pandemic, but your dad and I've had a pretty easy time working virtually."

While we chat, I set my box on the kitchen table.

"So what have you been up to?" she asks.

"Um…not much."

Kind of true. It's been a few days since I made pizza for Zane, and since then, I've mostly been watching TV or making meals for my neighbor/stalker. Whenever I take them over, he acts so appreciative and tells me how much he's enjoyed whatever I last made him, and it's enough to encourage me to keep doing it. It also feels like the least I can do for him since he's dedicating so much of his time to watching me.

After the break-in, it's comforting knowing someone's keeping an eye on things because since that night, I've been nervous, fearing that intruder might return to finish what he started.

But it's quiet. Maybe this is the calm before the storm?

Or is it an indication that this is all in Zane's mind and that really was a burglar whose timing lined up with Zane's paranoia?

Whatever's going on, I enjoy having Zane watching me, and not exclusively for my safety. I must admit that since the pizza, I've become more apt to walk around my room without a shirt on, playing with the blinds so he can see me, even if only for a minute. It's made me more than a little curious about some things about myself that I hadn't previously considered.

I chat with Dad too, and by the time I hang up, I'm in my room with the package that arrived earlier. I was following the tracking, so I'm not surprised when I open it and see a postcard with a graphic of my product along with a variety of others this adult store offers. I set the card and paper packaging beside the box, then retrieve the funky, black, S-shaped toy that was one of the less intimidating shapes and sizes on the site. Still, the thought of putting this thing in my ass makes me cringe. But if that's such a strange thing to me, why am I considering it?

I never considered things like this before I met Zane. And it's not like he's mentioned anything other than finding me attractive and that little bit about my ass, so why would that get me thinking about sticking things up it?

Okay…maybe I get that one.

I tuck the little fella into my nightstand and toss out the packaging and product info in the trash bin by my desk before sliding my phone out of my back pocket and texting Zane:

ME: My parents are coming back next Monday.

I'll feel safer once they're home. If someone *is* trying

to abduct me, that'll be much more difficult with them around. And make Zane's work a lot easier. But that's not the only reason I'm texting him.

ME: So...since I know you're not doing anything on Friday, how about you swing by and I'll make you something?

I'd like to see him again. Not only stop by his place to drop off chicken tikka masala, but to chat with him.

I'm relieved he doesn't leave me waiting. Although, based on what he's said about watching me, I guess this shouldn't be a huge surprise.

ZANE: That'd be good. I finished off that last bit of the tikka masala, so it'll be nice to eat again. :)

The corners of my lips tug into a smile, and now he's got me thinking about what I should make for his visit.

When Zane arrives on Friday, he's looking healthier than when we first met. It was a couple of weeks ago, and maybe it's just in my head, but his cheeks look fuller, and the bags under his eyes aren't as severe. I take credit for some small part in that.

I invite him in, and he starts for the kitchen, but I say, "Actually, before we eat, I wanted to show you something."

His forehead wrinkles up. "What is it?"

"You'll see. Come on."

As we head upstairs, he tails behind me. I glance back

at him. He looks adorable in his jacket and jeans, his stoic expression frozen as he glances at the photos along the wall. When we reach my bedroom, we exchange a quick glance. It's electric. It's…surprising.

Stronger than the last time I saw him.

But he quickly turns away.

"This is my buddy Kyra," I say, guiding him to her cage. She's pecking at seeds in her feeder, but as I approach, she glances between us.

"I've seen her when you have her out."

"Yeah. I don't love keeping her cooped up in a cage, but I don't want her to hurt herself. And once she's better, I'm gonna let her go. Back to the wild, where she belongs."

"How did you get her?"

"I was jogging and happened to be coming back when the neighbors' cat had a go at her. Nipped her wing, but I managed to chase the cat off. Kyra was dinged up pretty bad. I've been nursing her back to health. But look how good she's doing. Her wings still aren't quite there, but I'm hoping in the next few weeks."

Zane is eyeing me strangely.

"What?" I ask.

"That was very kind of you. I doubt I would have interfered with a cat. Let alone taken her in."

"I figure you don't really know until you're in that situation. It's not like I had plans to do that."

"Did you buy the cage?"

"There's a thrift store over in the outlet with the grocery store. They had one for fifteen bucks, so I snatched it up. But she eats a lot, so I'm almost out of the bag of food I got her."

"You do like feeding things, don't you?"

I grin. "I guess so."

Our gazes meet again, and we stare at each other for a moment. Again, I'm having some very anal-centric thoughts I can't explain. It's clearly tied to him, though. He finally breaks our stare-down, saying, "You wanted to show me this?"

"Yeah. I don't know why. I don't get to show her to many people. And I think she could use some fresh company. I'm sure she's tired of seeing my face all day long."

"I sincerely doubt that," he says, not a trace of humor in his voice as he studies my expression.

The thrill of hearing him say that, and the way he's looking at me, makes my dick twitch.

Jesus, when did I become such a horny fuck?

"My parents haven't met her yet, but they're used to this. I used to do this as a kid. Take in an injured turtle or lizard or mouse."

He raises his finger to the cage and strokes between two of the bars. "Hey, Kyra. It's nice meeting you. I think you're in good hands."

I'm pleased he likes my little surprise, even if I don't entirely understand why I wanted to share that with him.

Maybe because I enjoyed the chat we had, sharing those other parts of myself I wouldn't want to share with someone else. Someone who wouldn't understand.

"Anyway, I'm sure you're hungry. Let's get you fed."

"That works for me," he says, starting for the door, and I follow. But he stops abruptly and I knock into him, would have probably knocked him down if I hadn't caught myself.

What the hell…?

I follow his gaze to the trash bin by my desk. Now I see what he sees.

Fuck, it's that postcard for that fucking anal stimulator. I didn't think I needed to shove it to the bottom of the trash.

"What is *that?*"

"Nothing," I lie, which is senseless since he approaches the trash and snatches the postcard, assessing it before turning to me. "Is this a sex toy?"

"It's something I got online. I was…I don't even know."

"Sorry, I guess it shouldn't surprise me that a straight guy would be into this. I know some guys are into pegging. Still, this was not what I was expecting to see."

God, my face must be red right now.

As he places the postcard back in the trash, I say, "It's something I've been thinking about. I've never done anything back there before, and I was playing with my fingers, and…it seems too tight to really do much of anything. I mean, I know you can get something in there and have heard things about the prostate feeling amazing, so just thought I might try to get something to warm me up."

I've said too much, but even more, it's clear by the way it came spilling out that it's something I wanted to share.

With him.

"Anyway, as I said, something I've been thinking about recently."

"How recently?"

Fuck.

Don't answer that. Don't fucking answer that.

"Just a weird thought, and I'm in my early twenties; I'm supposed to be experimenting with that kind of stuff, right?"

I expect a chuckle or something, but he's staring at me with that determined expression. God, it's fucking sexy.

Silence stretches between us. We're good at awkward silences.

I don't even know what to do now, but he finally shakes his head and says, "I feel like saying something cheesy about how you don't need one of these when you have a guy who's perfectly willing to help you." He doesn't make eye contact when he says it.

"Yeah, that would be cheesy."

"Yeah…" He looks away.

But I could tell, even as he made the comment, it wasn't a joke. And I wouldn't have wanted it to be a joke.

"So, Zane…why don't you just tell me what you really want to do?" My words come out like I can't hold them in, like they're telling on some secret desire that lingers within me that I haven't quite come to terms with. Judging by the way his eyes widen, they clearly surprise him too.

"Wh—what?"

"Why make a joke out of it like that when you obviously want something?"

Maybe I want it too.

What the fuck am I thinking?

Although, I don't know that thinking has much to do with any of this.

This is primal.

I didn't consider this when I brought him to my bedroom, but now that he's here, something curious within me wants to get to the bottom of what I've been thinking about since our chat.

Get to the bottom. Fucking apt.

"What do you actually want?" I ask, like I'm demanding a confession.

He flinches, then studies me for a moment, as if he's considering the consequences of what he wants to say.

"Stop thinking about it, Zane. Just say it."

We've already seen so much of each other—when we

shared that shit about our mental health. That was a hell of a lot harder to share than what I want now.

His jaw tenses. I'm convinced he'd tell me this is a shit idea, but his gaze is right on mine as he says, "I'm thinking I don't want you having some half-ass experience the first time. You don't know what you're doing back there. That I'd be better at showing you what it feels like than your fingers or some fucking toy." He sounds like he has a personal grudge against it. "And that I want to watch your expressions for your first time, see how much it gets to you…how out of control it makes you as your body bows to my touch."

My face is hot again, but it's not from embarrassment.

He approaches me slowly. "Is that what you want?"

"Yes," I spit out. Once again, it's like I don't have control over my own fucking mouth. It's fucking telling on me, but I don't want it to stop. Not when he's looking at me like that.

"Take off your clothes," he says, and a jolt of excitement races through me.

I like Zane bossing me around. Saying what he really wants rather than keeping it bottled up.

He moves toward me. It's wild to think how terrified I was of him those first few times we met, especially considering how hard my dick's getting in my pants right now, and he clearly notices. A smile slips across his face as he looks at me. "Take off your clothes, and get on the bed," he says, much softer this time.

I hesitate for a moment, but then fearing I might overthink it and talk myself out of it, I toss my beanie on the bed. Then I remove my shirt before tucking my thumbs in the waistband on either side of my jeans, pulling them down with my boxers, revealing how hard I am at the mere thought of doing this with him. I step out of them and stand before him. His gaze trails up and down me, drinking me in…and God, if that doesn't make my stiff dick twitch even more.

He winces. "I thought you said you were straight."

"No. You kept insisting I was straight."

Not that I'd ever considered myself anything else, but my interest in him? That sure as hell isn't straight.

He smirks, God, like he's enjoying knowing how hard he's made me.

I pull back my comforter and slide into bed.

I'm so out of my element. Here's a guy who knows what he's doing. Who wants to show me what he knows, and I'm fucking clueless, and nervous as fuck.

Without a word, Zane spins around and heads toward my desk.

I wonder where the hell he's going when he grabs my swivel chair and pulls it over beside the bed.

"Lube?" he asks without looking at me.

"In the nightstand."

He digs through it, and I can hardly judge him, considering how I rifled through the drawers in his kitchen when we first met. When he finds the bottle, he sits in the chair, then looks me over. "Lie back, relax."

"The relaxing part's more difficult."

He smiles. "It's okay. We won't do anything you're not comfortable with. And you say the word, and we stop."

His words help me settle in as he squirts a few pumps of lube onto his fingers. Setting the lube back on the nightstand, he reaches his left hand over my leg, watching my face as his fingers slide between my cheeks. "I'm only gonna play around it. Not going to go in yet."

"Yeah, of course."

"You're shaking." He rests his other hand on my torso, his warmth soothing me some more, but making my dick firm too.

"This wasn't how I was expecting to spend this evening."

"Well, me neither, but here we are. And don't worry. It'll be good. Think of it as me helping you jerk off."

As clinical as he makes it seem, even by sitting in the chair beside the bed, it's hot as fuck.

While I'm nervous, he's at ease. Like a man who knows what he's doing.

His fingers run up and down my hole, then in a circle as he strokes my side with his other hand.

"I'm glad I cut my fingernails before I came over," he says, and I laugh.

"You ready for a finger?"

I nod, and he slides his index finger—just the tip— in. This is much more exciting than when I was trying to do it to myself.

I close my eyes, relaxing into the sensation as he massages back and forth, subtle movements, lulling me into the experience.

I take deep breaths. It's not a terrible feeling, but it's not like the best feeling in the world either.

"I think I can do another," I say.

Zane presses what I assume is his middle finger against the edge, making room.

I was expecting discomfort or uneasiness, but Zane is cautious, taking his time for my hole to make space for him. He's able to get farther back, when a ripple of sensation shoots through me, a wave of heat and nerves radiating outward. "Whoa," I say.

"There it is," he whispers, watching my expression as he massages what I definitely know is my prostate, each stroke sending bursts of energy through me. Now I'm shaking, but not from nerves.

I close my eyes, rolling my head back against my pillow, letting Zane have his way with my hole as I get lost in the sensations rushing through me, Zane in total control of this experience.

"Another," I beg. I just want more.

I hear him snicker. He must love how hungry I am for this, and fuck, he should enjoy it.

There's the pressure of a third finger, and as he slips

back to that spot, I find myself enjoying the combination of the pressure and those sensations as he teases my prostate.

Fuck. Fuck. Fuck.

I put my hand to my nipple, massaging like I sometimes do when I'm on my own.

"Do you like your nipples played with?" he asks.

"What? Oh, yeah."

As I open my eyes, he says, "Here, let me."

He licks the fingers on his free hand and then pinches them gently around my nipple, stimulating it and my prostate at the same time, working my body like he's playing an instrument.

My dick is so hard, it's fucking throbbing, and a bead of precum leaks onto my belly.

As another series of sensations takes me higher, I lock eyes with him as he tortures my body with his touch, driving my nerves wild as they spark all around. I grab my cock and stroke.

"Hey, no, no," he says, almost as if panicking, which makes me stop. "Do you mind if I play with it for a bit?"

"You're not gonna stop what you're doing?" Now I'm the one panicking, not wanting him to stop his work that's got my hips shifting with his movements as my fingertips buzz with sensation.

"I don't have to," he says with a smile. "Scoot closer to the edge."

I obey, and he leans forward until his head's at my crotch. His tongue runs up and down my cock.

"Holy fuck," I say as he offers a steady, rhythmic series of strokes inside me.

I figure he might try to blow me, but he just keeps on like that as he applies more pressure to my prostate and nipple.

My body twitches and jerks in his hold, and he presses his lips against the base of my shaft, sucking along the edge, applying pressure with it between my belly and his mouth.

I can feel a familiar urgency pushing through me…

Right on the edge…

Every nerve in my body fucking activated…

"I'm gonna come, Zane." He speeds up his mouth against my shaft and gives my prostate the extra caress it needs to send me over the edge, shooting across my stomach as I'm lost in a sea of bursts and jolts, twisting and contorting as I lose control of my body until I finally regain some of my senses again.

I feel more warmth on my belly and realize Zane's licking up the mess I made, sucking until it's all cleaned up.

With his fingers still inside me, he looks up, a trail of cum dripping from his bottom lip back onto me. He beams, wearing a cocky smirk, surely because he knows everything that just happened was his doing.

And I'm suddenly aware of what this interest in my ass was all about.

And why I was right to let Zane be the man who showed me exactly how good it could feel.

10

ZANE

I CAN FEEL him dripping down my chin.

It felt so good to have my lips against his cock, my fingers deep in him as I teased his nipple with my other hand, feeling his body vibrating with pleasure as he shot.

And tasting him… I almost feel guilty that, of all the meals he's made me, this one was the best.

I started off in his chair, feeling so in control, but now I'm hunched over, like a monster devouring his cum; although, he doesn't seem to mind. He watches me as I thumb my chin and slide it into my mouth, savoring the last drop.

"No. You kept insisting I was straight."

I've never been so happy to be so fucking wrong.

My mind's spinning, my cock stiff as a brick.

"Did you want to get off?" he asks.

Of course he would ask. So fucking considerate. So fucking kind. So fucking Leif.

"I'm glad I didn't bust my nut while I was doing that." Because I was getting close. "You don't mind?" I ask.

He's the one who suggested it, so why am I asking for permission?

Maybe I'm waiting for him to realize we made a horrible mistake and tell me to get the fuck out of his house.

"Do I look like I mind?" he asks with a chuckle.

I rise back up, unfastening my belt, when I realize I'm still wearing my jacket. That's probably why I'm sweating like a motherfucker. I unzip it and tear it off, discarding it on the chair before dropping my pants and my underwear.

He sits up, his eyes fixed on my cock.

"And here I thought you were asking selflessly," I say, "but you only wanted to see my dick."

"Can't I want both?" he asks with an adorable laugh, before adding, "That's very big."

"You surprised that a guy who's five-four can have a cock like this?"

He chuckles again, his face turning red.

"Really? I just had three fingers in you and that's what makes you blush?"

But, fuck, I love that I made him blush.

For once, I'm not the most awkward guy in the room.

I lean over to the nightstand and snatch the lube. I'm about to squirt some for my cock, but I hesitate. "Unless you wanted to try something else new? See what it feels like between those beautiful lips?"

There's a flash of something I haven't seen when we started messing around: worry.

"Forget I said that."

"No, maybe."

"Nope." And I already have lube on my cock, stroking. "If you want to do something with my dick, there's not gonna be any hesitation. You gotta beg for it."

"You get very bossy when you're horny."

"So I've been told." He watches me jerk my cock. "God, that's such a tight hole. Thank you for letting me have it."

"You're welcome."

Thinking about sticking my dick in there is enough to make my hips rock, and a jolt of energy rushes through my pelvis.

"Do you want to come on me?" he asks, his expression full of curiosity.

"What did I say?"

"Please come on me, Zane," he says quickly, like he thinks I'll take the offer off the table as fast as when he was too uneasy to tell me he wanted my cock in his mouth.

I snicker. "That's much better. Where do you want me?"

"Where do *you* want it?"

"On that pretty face."

And now he's wearing a big grin. I feel like we want

the same thing.

"Close your eyes. I don't want to get any in them."

He relaxes on his side, propping himself up on his elbow and closing his eyes.

I walk, my jeans still locked around my ankles as my knees hit the side of his mattress.

Seeing him so eager to have me on him sends another ripple of energy shooting through me, and I growl as my cum bursts out in ropes across his cheek, a little shooting onto his nose.

"Yes, just like that. Just like that," I say as my hips rock and I release the last bit of cum on him.

"Fuck yes," he whispers, and as I come down, sensations bursting through me in waves, he opens his eyes, gazing at me with a satisfied expression.

"Thank you," I tell him.

"Thank *you*."

"Now that was hot, but let's get that off your face," I say.

I walk with my jeans still around my ankles to the bathroom for a towel. After we clean up, Leif slides back into his jeans. Doesn't even go for his shirt, which suits me fine.

"I think you definitely gave Kyra something new to look at," I tease.

He glances at her cage. "Oh fuck. I could have at least covered her." He plops down at the foot of his bed.

"Why are you sitting down? I came over here under

the impression I was getting fed."

"And I fed you." Oh, the way he's smiling, he fucking loves how clever that was, and I'm living for it.

He must be able to tell that now that I'm coming down from my climax, I'm ten times hungrier than when I arrived because he hops up and heads for the door. We go downstairs and he preps plates for us, still shirtless as he serves me a bowl with salad.

"Once we're done with this, I've got spaghetti with meatballs, fresh parmesan, and garlic bread."

"If you tell me there's dessert, I'm gonna have to marry you." I regret the words as soon as they escape my dumb mouth. "Sorry. I didn't… That's a weird joke."

"I'm starting to get that that's kind of your thing," he says as he finally settles in the seat on the other side of the table. "I'll try to keep from picking out rings prematurely."

This is another thing I like about being around this guy. Makes me feel like my brand of weird is a nonissue.

"But yes," he goes on, "of course there's dessert."

Yes. Of fucking course there would be.

I start on the salad, struggling to recall the last time I had a meal with courses in it.

"So…I'm an asshole for assuming you're straight. Cis white gay male privilege, I suppose."

"If you'd asked me a few weeks ago, that's what I would have told you." He digs his fork into his bowl and takes a bite of salad.

I enjoy a bite too, realizing quickly there's no way this guy got this dressing from a bottle.

After a few bites, I notice he's smirking and watching me again. It reminds me of the way he looked at me after I lapped his cum off his abs.

"What? Do I have dressing on my face?"

"No. I was just thinking how you're all awkward regularly, and then we get to messing around, and suddenly you're all bossy and telling me I have to beg for it."

"Oh…that. Yeah. I get caught up in the moment."

"I can tell. I like it."

Is it just me, or did his eyes sparkle under the room light? That had to have been in my head.

"That is a very big dick, though. I was anxious enough about fingers, and then I see that… It makes a guy nervous."

"I don't think nervous is what any of the guys I've been with would say."

He chuckles, but I can see that same curiosity in his expression, like he had before I was standing by his desk, stunned by the image of the sex toy in his trash bin.

"But enough about my cock. I want to hear about your hole," I say before taking a bite.

"It's very happy," he reports. "I'm pleased to say I didn't have any reason to be worried about trying to get something in there, and also, when you touched my prostate, I was like, oh my fucking God, I can't believe I never tried this before. Reminds me of the first time I ever jerked off, like, how hot my face got and the way it activated every nerve in my body."

"That would be why people are into it."

"Definitely not gonna have a problem trying that toy out now."

Or you could try my fucking dick next.

No, I'm not saying that. *Just be cool…so the total opposite of everything you know.*

"I'm glad you let me play with it first. Think you need to know the difference between a toy and the human touch."

"Clearly, you know what you're doing. I assume you've messed around with a lot of guys."

"I guess that's subjective. But there were some periods of time before I was on meds where I'd have manic episodes and didn't know what was happening, and my sex drive felt out of my control. I had this compulsion, and I'd get on apps. Don't really regret any of it, but just felt like I was on autopilot, doing what my body needed me to do. So I put in my hours, if you know what I mean."

"Sorry, I didn't mean to make you share something that personal."

"I wouldn't have shared it if I didn't want to." I like sharing things with him.

He takes another bite of salad, then asks, "Have you been with girls?"

"No. Never. I pretty much knew when I was younger that I liked guys. But I'm guessing that's not true for you."

"First crush I had in school was a girl, and it was like, painful. Didn't know what to do with my feelings, they were so intense. Really, it's a very new thing for me."

Why do I love that as much as hearing that I got to be the first to play with his virgin hole?

"So I'm basically responsible for making you bi-curious?"

That catches his attention. "You like knowing that?"

"Yeah. Strokes my ego," I say before taking another bite.

"Well, maybe when my parents come home, we can try something like that again, but at your place because we won't be able to get away with that here."

I'm staring at him again, and he notices. "That'd be nice," I say. "I have plenty of other things I'd be happy to show your hole."

He's practically glowing as he chews some of his salad, and given we came not ten minutes ago, I'm shocked at how hard I am again.

"Also makes my job watching you that much easier." I figure I might as well put it out there, since he must be thinking it.

"You are a strange one, Zane." The way he says it, with that smile across his face, I can tell he fucking loves it.

After we finish our salads, I offer to get my own plate, but he insists, so I let him serve me again. His meatballs are as good as everything else he's made me so far, and I practically lap up the meal like I did his cum. And when we're finished with dinner, he pulls out a tiramisu from the fridge. Not even that hungry after everything we've eaten, but I don't want him to think for a second that I don't appreciate this, so I don't leave a trace of it on my plate.

"That was all…incredible," I tell him, licking my spoon.

"Thank you. Was the tiramisu over the top? I considered something simple, like cookies."

"You already know I love your cookies, but this tiramisu was pretty spectacular."

"I love a compliment, so thank you."

"Is that a way of fishing for more compliments about your glorious hole?"

"I mean, it wasn't, but I'll accept that too."

I laugh. "This has been nice."

"To get a break from watching me for a change?"

"Maybe finding a new way to watch you."

But there's something else on my mind, a burning question I can't shake. "Speaking of watching you, you haven't posted on social media in a while. Used to put a lot up about the culinary program you were in, and on Insta you'd have the dishes up. You were clearly very proud."

"Yeah…"

"Did that stop after things started going downhill?"

He nods.

For the first time since we messed around, his expression turns serious. And just like that, I sucked all the fun out of the room. It wasn't my intention, but I want to know him…really know him, the good and the bad.

"Yeah. That was before…" He hesitates. "The psych unit."

"But you still love cooking. Obviously."

"Yeah. Even when I was at Georgia State, I was making stuff. I'd get through with classes and then I'd hit the gym, then the grocery store, and head back to the dorms to get to work. I shared a dorm apartment with three guys, and they had plenty of friends. They'd chip in to cover the food, and it kept me busy, but I was happy doing that. Then…it got rough, and before I knew it, I was struggling to get out of bed. Nothing felt exciting anymore, especially not that. Really hard to know that the one thing I could always count on just…felt empty."

It reminds me of our conversation about our mental health, about those moments when our minds turned on themselves. Knowing what a struggle it was, I hate that anyone else had to go through shit like that too.

"I'm glad to see it's not that way anymore."

"Me too. I used to be a lot more active, and not only with that either. I'd go out to parties with friends. I was in a few clubs. Then I came home after the mental-health facility, and I was in such a fog. I remember going to the library and looking at book covers just to do something…anything."

There's a rush of adrenaline, my body alerting me I need to probe. "Which library?"

"Chelsby Hill, over near Hamlet Mill."

"Really?" It's the first connection I've made to Mike since Leif and I started chatting.

Could be nothing. It's a small city. There were likely plenty of places Mike and Leif could have frequented, and I wouldn't know it. No need to make a big deal.

But now that he'd said it, my gut instinct can't disregard it, even if the connection was only in my head. I don't bring it up to Leif, though. No need to freak him out over what's probably nothing.

I quiet that voice inside me, fearing it's the same one that wanted me to hound Mike's poor teacher.

Although, a creeping fear tells me it isn't.

And that I have work to do.

11

LEIF

I PACE AROUND the house in my sweatpants and socks. Last night was fucking everything!

I'm still reeling from the high of having Zane's fingers in me, working my body like I was his fucking sex puppet. There's no way he can realize what he did to me by showing me that. And being so patient. So considerate. Dedicated to ensuring it was a mind-blowing orgasm.

I can't believe he was the guy to introduce me to that part of myself.

Even as we shared dinner after, all I wanted was for him to show me what else he could do with his hands. His mouth. Even that cock.

Imagining the things he'd do to me has got me leaking in my sweatpants.

I pull my phone out of my back pocket for what must be the dozenth time since I woke up, reading his last text from the night before.

ZANE: Thanks again for filling my belly.

A smile tugs at the corners of my lips as I start to text again: **So…you wanna hang toni—**

No. It's too soon.

Keep your cool.

Although, I don't know how the hell I'm supposed to play cool now that I'm so fucking curious, and Zane's the only one I want to help me figure this out.

I try to distract myself by making a quiche for breakfast, making it bigger than I normally would so there'll be plenty for Zane for the next few days.

As I'm stirring the egg and veggie mixture, my phone buzzes on the counter.

I'm already smiling as I pick up my phone, frowning when I see it's a message from Dad: **Your mom and I can come home early! Should be there this evening. We're free! *crying emoji***

I should be thrilled, not just to see them, but knowing they'll get a break from Linda. But the excited wave that pulled me to the phone collapses into a pit of disappointment. Looks like I'm gonna have to put the whole sexual-exploration thing on hold.

Accepting my fate, I finish the quiche and then pick up around the house throughout the day, and when Zane messages, I tell him the news…but don't mention how desperate I am to get together with him again.

That evening, when I hear Mom and Dad pull into

the driveway, I grab a hoodie from the front closet and throw it on, then open the door. Even with the hoodie on, I can feel my nipples hardening as a cool breeze rushes inside. I slide my crocs on and hurry to help them with their bags.

As I offer them hugs, I say, "I'm surprised you guys made it. Figured Linda might have found a way to get you on a return flight."

"We're surprised too," Dad says, wide-eyed, his expression hinting at the hell the past couple of weeks have been for them.

"Even if they call," Mom says, "we're not going back for at least a week. God, it's cold out here. I think it was warmer in Indiana."

"It was lovely before y'all got here," I say, "so I think you brought this weather with you."

"Back for less than five minutes, and we're responsible for the weather already," Mom says with a smile.

I help them pull their bags inside. Dad checks the back door the locksmith fixed, then joins us at the kitchen table, where Mom's catching me up about their trip and how Linda, my aunt Cathy, and my cousins are.

I should be eager to see them, but I'm tense. On edge. And not just about being deprived of sex.

I'm worried they might be in danger here, but if Zane's right and someone was trying to abduct me, it's possible they were doing it when my parents were gone because they don't want to make a production of it. And if that's their MO, then I doubt they'll do something that will keep them from being able to hunt again. Of course, I don't dismiss the reality that my parents might be more creeped out by finding out there's a guy next door watching our house, keeping an eye on their son…and who just so happened to get off with him last night.

Yeah…lots of things they're probably better off not knowing.

"So tell us what you've been up to," Mom says once she finishes showing me pics of the cousins and their new cat. "And while you're telling me, if you broiled a roast, I could eat about half of one right about now."

I laugh, heading to the fridge. "I don't have a roast, but I have some meatballs I can heat up." I pull the container out and start heating them up in a pan.

"How have you been feeling?" Dad asks. "All right?"

I remind myself they mean well, but I can hear much more behind their words when they ask how I'm doing, which makes sense given how bad it got, but I wish I could just shake them and get them to stop worrying about me.

Although, sometimes I worry too, so I can't blame them.

"I'm feeling good," I say, stirring the meatballs.

"You see anybody while we were gone?" Mom asks, which makes me nearly do a double take, her words catching me off guard. "Any of your friends?" she presses.

Of course that's what she means, dumbass. "Oh, no. Everyone's in school right now. Studying, finishing up projects."

"Have you talked to Steven?"

Steven's one of my buddies I roomed with at the dorms. He always tries to reach out to catch up, but I haven't talked to him recently.

"No, he's texted me a bit about this new pickleball league he joined, but I need to give him a call."

She and Dad are quiet for a few moments before she says, "I wish you had some company and not be cooped up in this house all day long."

I consider what I should share, but I think this is a safe way to bring up Zane. "I actually met the guy who's renting the place next door."

"The one you said was creepy?"

"One and the same." I chuckle. That wasn't so long ago, and it's wild to think how much has happened in the short time since I thought he was trying to kill me. "After he grabbed that can I dropped, we started talking. He's a pretty friendly guy. Well, *friendly* might not be the word. He has a *friendlier* side to him than I thought."

"When did you talk to him?"

"He came by, actually." Like when I talked to that detective, it's probably better to be as honest as I can and skirt around the truth.

"Came by?" Dad asks. "Why?"

Hmm. Finding a half-truth for this bit isn't going to

be as easy… "He wanted to make sure I was okay after the burglary." That's reasonably close to the truth.

The meatballs sizzle in the pan, and I stir them around as Dad asks, "But everything's been fine since?"

"Yeah," I lie, since I'm leaving out the part that this burglar might not have been here to burgle. "Lock's changed. Neighborhood Watch on alert. I've been keeping the alarm on, and nothing's come up since."

"That's good," Dad says. "Just strange since this has always been a good neighborhood. But I guess it's what happens when the economy's like this. You weren't hurt. That's all that really matters."

"No, and I need to give you back your pepper spray, Mom. Been carrying it around since then."

"Did you get the one from the office?" When I confirm, she says, "Keep that one. I have another. So tell me more about that guy…Zane."

"What?" I ask, which makes her expression twist up.

"You talked. I assume you know more about him than that he's friendlier than he looks."

"Oh, yeah." I meant for that to come out casually, but as the words escape my lips, they sound suggestive. I check my parents' reactions, but they didn't seem to pick up on it. "He's nice. I think he just has a hard time warming up to people."

"What does he do over there?" Dad asks.

"IT work, online." I take the pan off the heat, turn off the burner.

"Yeah, but why does he live in that house? At his age, he should be going to college or staying somewhere he can go out and party."

"From what I've made out, he doesn't seem the partying kind."

I wonder if Dad notices how I evaded answering his question, and I figure now's my chance to get them off this subject. I talk about Kyra's health while I fix their plates, and after we finish our little catch-up and the meatballs, I head up to my room and plop down on my bed.

My ass feels so fucking needy right now, but it's gonna have to wait.

Still...just because we can't do anything tonight doesn't mean we can't make other plans.

ME: So...my parents just got home.

ZANE: I noticed.

ZANE: Obviously.

God, that should be disturbing, not making me laugh.

ZANE: Now maybe I can get some sleep.

I laugh again. Seriously, this shit is fucked up. I shouldn't be laughing.

ME: I was a little bummed. My ass misses you.

ZANE: Funny 'cause my fingers are missing your

ass. *squirt emoji*

Now I'm beaming. And my ass cheeks clench slightly, as if in anticipation of the next chance we'll get.

ZANE: Don't worry. They'll still be here for you when you're free.

Something naughty rises up within me. And maybe I'm feeling bold because everything he's texting suggests he doesn't regret what we did and that he's looking forward to it again. So I go for it.

ME: I think you know those aren't the appendages I'm interested in next time.

ME: Not that I would mind being reintroduced.

ME: But you've got something else I'm real curious about.

He doesn't respond as quickly as he did to the other texts, and for a moment, I'm like, seriously? He can't show me what he can do to my ass and that fat cock and expect me not to be curious. Finally, a response comes through.

ZANE: This doesn't sound like begging...

I'm getting hard again.

He's such a dirty motherfucker. I love that as apprehensive and tentative as he can be, there's this sex-fiend side to him, unashamed of what he wants or how he wants it.

ME: Gives me something to work on before I see you again. ;) x

ZANE: Looking forward to it.

A naughty idea springs to mind, and I head to the window and open it.

ZANE: What are you doing?

ME: Can you see my bed from there?

ZANE: Yes. But so could someone else.

ME: Who's got their own camera set up or on a ladder?

I get why he's concerned, and he's not entirely wrong. It's a possibility. But I'm so damn horny, I need to do something.

ME: I'm calling.

ZANE: The hell?

ME: Just pick up, okay?

After closing the blinds, I hurry by Kyra's cage and toss the cover over it, then remove my phone mount from the desk. I roll my swivel chair over to beside my bed and attach the mount to the arm of the chair, positioning the camera so he'll have a good view.

A part of me is wondering what the hell I'm thinking, but another is so damn excited, I can't help myself. I pull back the sheets, sliding onto the mattress. Then I retrieve some lube and my new toy from the nightstand.

As I'm sitting up, about to place the call, I hesitate. Should I be doing this?

But the fact that Zane doesn't want me hesitant, wants me begging for it, encourages me to make the call, and I'm relieved when his face pops up on the app.

"What are you doing?" he asks, squinting.

I turn down the volume on the phone. Mom and Dad are watching TV downstairs, so I doubt they'll hear, but better safe than sorry.

I display the toy for Zane, and his eyes widen, his lips curling up.

I feel so fucking naughty—wicked, even—as I whisper, "We'll see who's begging for it the next time I see you."

12

ZANE

I WAS SO on edge when he was at his window like that. I might be overly cautious, and fuck if I don't want to look at him all the goddamn time, but I want to protect him more.

And now I'm fucking hypnotized as Leif lies back in bed.

God, I miss that body already.

I lean back in my chair as he squirts lube onto his fingers and spreads it between his cheeks. With his toy beside him, I know where this is going, and *fuck*.

I shouldn't be so damn jealous of a fucking toy, but that ass is mine.

No, that's not right. It's not mine. He let me finger him once, and now he's torturing me with the promise of giving it to my cock.

Fuck…he's driving me wild. Is this some kind of punishment for not letting him put it in his mouth?

Don't torture me like this, Leif. Don't fucking torture me.

It's been hard enough with his parents arriving home this evening, though I should be happy about it. He's safer with them around, but I'll admit, I was hoping Leif would want to meet up again for the reasons he just texted me about.

He's curious about my cock, which works great since I'm curious about his ass.

I should be fine. I've gone for how long without any hole, and it hasn't been fun, but it hasn't been as excruciating as it is now.

Something about the tease I got from Leif—feeling him up, knowing the dimensions of his hole, knowing where his goddamn prostate is. The way his brows shift when he's coming.

And he's about to make it so much worse.

He takes the toy and starts exploring around his ass.

"I'm gonna grab some lube," I tell him, rushing, fumbling around.

I hurry to my nightstand and grab some. No need to burn my flesh with my dry hand like the last time I desperately caved to him.

When I return to my chair, he's still working that thing into him, rocking his hips gently. It makes it easy to imagine how he'd take me.

"You're not gonna be able to take my cock that fast," I say.

"No?"

I shake my head. "I'll have to ease into you. You'll

tense up; they always do. And I'll have to wait for you to relax again, like I had to wait for you with my fingers. And then I'll slip the head in…wait for you to adjust to me before inching in farther."

He pushes the toy deeper. "Yeah? You'll be good to it."

"Of fucking course I will."

He's got me salivating.

I pull off my boxers and wet my hand, then begin stroking myself, matching the rhythm he's already worked up.

As he pushes the toy back, he's gotta be getting close to his prostate. Again, there's a sting of jealousy, like some guy is fucking him. I can tell when he's hit the spot by the way his body shifts in his bed. With his other hand, he plays with his nipple.

"It'll feel better when *I'm* the one playing with that nipple. I'll make you shoot harder than you've ever shot in your damn life."

It's becoming a mission—an obsession.

As his head rolls back against his pillow, a radiating sensation pulses in my hips.

"God, that sounds so good," he says.

I think about my raw cock inside him—not that I'd do that in real life, but I'm not gonna lie to myself about what I want. I want to watch him adjusting to my size. See how happy he looks when he's finally filled up. See how that ass matches my thrusts.

I lick my lips as my strokes become less controlled, more frenzied and desperate, my body seizing control, determined to get me to climax.

I can feel I'm getting too close, so I force myself to slow down.

I need to let him come first. Need to train my body to service his needs.

His body jerks and twists before he blasts across himself—this toy's good, so I'm gonna have to be better, a challenge I accept willingly.

"Can I come?" I whisper.

"Please do it," he begs. Fucking begs.

And it hits my ear just right. I growl and call out as warm cum covers the side of my hand.

"Fuck yes. Fuck yes, Leif…"

I gasp as I catch my breath, coming down from the intensity of my climax.

I think about the fucking mess we've made, and how I want to make this mess with him in real life. And as grateful as I am that he gave this to me, I'm also pissed as hell because it's a cruel reminder that I can't have his ass tonight. And that every hour that passes until that moment is an hour I'll resent.

That pretty smile rushes across his face as his gaze is on the camera. "That was nice," he whispers. "Thank you."

"Thank *you*."

A quake rushes through my body, and I wipe my

boxers across the mess to clean up until I have a chance to get in the shower.

Leif sits up and gazes into the camera. "Night, Zane."

"Good night, Leif."

He ends the FaceTime, and I figure he's heading for the shower, so I toss my boxers into my laundry hamper, take a shower, and as I get out, I glance around my room, noticing what a fucking mess it is.

I head back to my desk and pull up the screen I'd been on before Leif distracted me with that delicious video call.

I'm even more fixated on it after the call. Like some primal part of me sees Leif as my mate whom I must protect.

My screen shows a live view of the Chelsby Hill Public Library.

Since Leif mentioned going there, it's become a bit of an obsession.

"You at the library again?" I ask Mike.

"You bet. Been reading some Proust and Faulkner."

"You have not!"

"Okay, maybe just some King and Robb, but hey, it's better than nothing."

I can't help but laugh. "That's more like it."

Mike spent a lot of time there, and now I know Leif did too, both when they were going through a rough patch. What if this was where whoever's behind Mike's disappearance picked out his victims? Saw these vulnerable men, and something about that turned them on?

What if Jason Kilbourne frequented this same library?

Not that this abductor's pattern needs to be anything so obvious. And there's the possibility that this is all some random connection I've made, like I did with Isaac Tolle.

It's probably nothing. Don't know how many times I've had to keep telling myself that, but I know by how it's rattling around my brain that I won't be able to let it go.

Now that Leif's parents are home, this is the perfect time.

I return my attention to the surveillance footage.

I don't want him out of my reach, but if there's a chance I can get a lead that can help take me to Mike—and maybe preemptively save Leif—wouldn't that be worth it?

As I ENTER the Chelsby Hill Public Library, I'm already feeling like this is such a stupid idea. But I'm so fixated on it, I knew I'd regret if I didn't. I didn't tell Leif what I was up to, just asked that he stay home with his parents while I ran an errand for a few hours.

I've been in plenty of bookstores, but I've maybe been inside a library twice in my life.

It's about the size I would've expected for the area—not massive. There are two rows of maybe a dozen computers, with only three kids who look like they're either students at the community college or the high school down the street. Mike used to say he preferred coming here over the library on campus because it wasn't as crowded.

Mike never liked being around too many people.

Beyond the computers are several aisles of books, and a sign indicates there's another story above us, where their fiction section can be found. As I take a lap around the place, I notice various seating areas throughout. It'd be easy for some stalker to sit at any of these and get a view of whomever they might be watching around here.

This dumb idea's rolling around in my head that I'll see some mysterious figure. Maybe a guy in a hoodie, tucked away, acting shady enough that I'll just know he must be the guy.

I know that's not how shit works in real life.

And as I'm looking around, I'm struggling to figure out why I'm really here. Is this like with Tolle? No, I feel lucid and clearheaded. And I have a reasonable amount of suspicion in my theories, which wasn't the case when I was chasing that lead.

Not knowing what the hell to do next, I head upstairs to the fiction section and wander the aisles. There aren't many people on this floor, and there's something eerie about heading through the aisles—it'd be easy for someone to hide up here, maybe watch someone through the openings over the books. A stalker could spend weeks in here, waiting for someone and finding a place to settle and keep an eye on Mike or Leif.

I don't know where I'm going, but I wind up by two shelves' worth of JD Robb's books. I settle with this feeling in me, knowing I'm standing in the same spot where Mike must've stood.

A warmth comes over me as I embrace that familiar sense, but nearly as quickly, it flees, leaving me hollow. I'm glad I opened up to the moment while it lasted because it's not the sort of thing I can recreate.

I meander through the aisles, in no hurry, making my way to the King section.

I round the corner to the next aisle, and as I start down it, I catch a glimpse of someone on the other side of the library. Beyond the aisle on the opposite side, they're sitting at a table-chair setup by a window, but I can only see their back. As I move closer, they come into view, and I freeze.

I recognize that profile.

The hair.

The jawline.

The five-o'clock shadow.

My hands shake as goose bumps prick across my flesh.

Isaac Tolle.

I step back, slowly, cautiously, and head back around the bookcase.

He doesn't turn, so he must not notice me. Thank God. If he did, he'd call Detective Roth and tell her I was stalking him again.

Fuck. Fuck. Fuck. I can barely think straight.

I followed him for about two weeks, but never in that time had he come by this library. It's near the college, so of course it's not a huge surprise that he would be here.

This doesn't mean what I think it means…does it?

A rush of panic sweeps through me, part of me fearing that maybe I was onto something. Another part of me fears that, even if I wasn't, now I'm going to start working down the path that led me to fucking nowhere.

My hands are cold, but I'm sweating. And breathing heavily.

Flashes come back to me: watching him through the window of his house; following him around the grocery store; hacking into his email account.

It races through my mind—not only the realities, but how I felt in my heightened emotional state, this otherworldly feeling that seized control of me, had me taking photos of him and collecting a fucking scrapbook's worth of information about this guy.

And then finally, fabricating evidence against him to get Detective Roth to check him out—an epic fail.

I don't even know how I get out to the parking lot and to my car. I need to get away from here. Get away from him before he spots me and calls Roth.

I slip into the driver's seat of my car and take deep breaths, collecting myself. Part of me wants to believe there's no way I saw whom I just saw.

He could be here, though. He's a teacher who works nearby. It means nothing.

But another part of me knows better, fears what it might actually mean.

And fearing that I already know what this is going to mean for me.

13

LEIF

ZANE'S BEEN QUIET the past few days. Unusually quiet, and it started after I FaceTimed him so he could see me playing with my sex toy. Was that too much? I know I'm not playing it cool, but fuck playing it cool.

Zane gave me a taste, and now I'm greedy for more.

But I have other concerns at the moment. I struggle with what to tell Mom and Dad about the subreddit and Zane's theories. On the one hand, I want them to take the necessary precautions for our family's safety. On the other hand, if I tell them too much, they could get in touch with Roth, and she'd make them really concerned about the guy next door.

I want to talk to Zane about it, but now he's suddenly less available than before. When I reach out on Monday and Tuesday, I get back quick responses about how he's catching up on work.

On Wednesday, he gives me a similar BS excuse: **Still gotta get some things in. Bills to pay, ya know?**

He's giving weird vibes.

Is he uncomfortable after what we shared, or is it something else? Something more concerning?

I make carbonara for dinner, and as much as I want my parents to enjoy the meal, I really made it for *him*. When we finish eating, I pack some into a container and head on over to his place, mashing my thumb on the doorbell; I'm not meaning to, but I'm sure the ring conveys my frustration.

It takes Zane a minute before he opens the door. "Yeah?"

"This is really starting to remind me of the time I hooked up with a girl and she immediately treated me like I didn't exist anymore."

"Can you not do this on the front porch?" he asks, his eyes widening as he searches around me, like he's worried someone might overhear me. He steps aside, letting me in, and closes the door behind me. He still doesn't look at me, acting more like he did when we first started chatting after the break-in.

I figured with my parents home, he'd get more sleep, be more together, but he seems agitated.

I head to the kitchen and set the container with my carbonara on the counter. "I've needed to talk to you the past few days, and suddenly you've been mysteriously busy."

"I do have to make a living."

"Just stop. I can tell it's more than that."

He still won't look at me, and I can't keep on trying to act like everything's normal. I notice the bags under his eyes are more severe than when I saw him the other night. Tension rises in me as my real fear intensifies—that he's struggling again.

"What's wrong?" I ask.

"Why does something have to be wrong?"

"Nothing *has* to be wrong, but you're not acting like yourself."

"You don't know me well enough to say that." He sounds annoyed.

"Something's wrong," I insist, standing by my gut instinct.

He finally looks at me.

"Dude, come on. What is it?"

"Oh, now I'm *dude*? Are we fighting?"

I have to stop myself from rolling my eyes. "Yes, that's what this is, if I didn't make that clear when I showed up at your door and started getting onto you."

"I have a lot on my mind recently."

"Hey," I say, approaching him and resting my hand on his shoulder. "Talk to me."

He looks at my hand on him, and then his gaze meets mine again, though it's warmer now. His shoulders relax like he's letting his guard down a bit. But this whole thing leaves me wondering what the hell could have changed so much in the past few days.

The tension in me intensifies, and as much as I worry

about his mental health, there's another fear I can't shake, and it's something that's easier to discuss, so I just say it. "Is it last week? Do you regret it? That would explain why you haven't texted as much. That's probably why you didn't want me to come over today."

Fuck.

"I'm sorry," I add. "I shouldn't have asked you to show me that. It was inappropriate, and…" The next words are hard to force out, but I somehow manage. "We don't have to do anything like that again, if it's made you uneasy."

He chuckles. Is he relieved I said it so he didn't have to? "You think that's what's on my mind?"

Okay, maybe I'm totally wrong, then.

"Leif, the only way I would regret any of that is if *you* regretted it, so I want you to get that out of your pretty head." He flicks his thumb through my bangs. "Why didn't you wear a beanie tonight? It's cold out."

"You don't deserve the beanie," I tease.

"Now you're just being mean."

His gaze meets mine again, but briefly.

I can tell something's still bothering him, but at least this exchange assures me it's not about what we've done together, which on the one hand is a relief, but on the other, concerns me that it could be much worse.

He inspects my mouth like he's about to lurch forward and take it.

I'm tempted to take his, when he whispers, "Can I

show you something?"

"Of course."

"Just…please don't be weird about it."

I rub my thumb along the fabric of his sweater. "Zane, don't you get by now that you can trust me?"

He turns his head subtly either way, his gaze shifting as though he's still debating if he should even show me whatever the hell it is. Then he closes his eyes. "Fuck," he mutters as he retrieves his phone from his back pocket.

"You mentioned the Chelsby Hill Public Library the other day, and I haven't been able to let it go. So on Monday, when I told you I was gonna run some errands, I actually went there. I didn't even know what I was looking for, and then I saw…"

He shows me a photo of a man. It's an average-looking guy in his late thirties or early forties. Dark-brown hair. Wearing a button-down shirt, sporting a friendly smile for the camera.

"This face ring any bells?"

I shake my head. "Why? Should I know him?"

"He was at the library when I went on Monday."

"I'm not following. A lot of people go to that library."

He huffs like he doesn't want to tell me whatever he's thinking, but then he says, "He was the teacher Mike met up with. The one I tried to frame to get Roth to look into."

I turn back to the image, almost wishing I could

place it from somewhere to give Zane what he seems to need to hear. Of course, I can't do that. I have to be honest. As I open my mouth to assure him I don't know this man, he cuts me off, "Please, pretend I didn't ask."

He shoves his phone back into his pocket.

Nearly as quickly as he'd let his guard down, his jaw clenches and he looks mad enough to start pounding his fist into the wall.

Now he really won't look me in the eyes.

I want to soothe him. Want to chase away whatever worry he has. "Zane," I say, moving closer to him. "Please talk to me about this."

"You're gonna think it's in my head."

"You don't know that."

It's a concern, but I don't give a flying fuck if it is. I know how hard it can be, and I want to be here for him. Doesn't he fucking get that?

Makes me feel like a real dick for all those times when my parents ask how I am, and I just want to push them away. Surely, they care about my well-being the way I care for his.

His eyes well with tears. "Well, maybe I'm worried if I say it out loud, then *I'll* realize it's all in my head."

"Come here," I say, guiding him to the kitchen table. "Sit down."

As he does, I sit in the adjacent seat.

"I'm not gonna pretend to understand the hell you've been through, but from my own shit, I can say the worst thing is to keep all that bottled up. Haven't I proven that I can handle some pretty wild shit? Let's say it's not in your head. Maybe talking it out will help you sort things out. And if it is in your head? You think you're gonna get rid of me that easily?"

"You'll think I'm the creep next door, who did all this for no reason. Not only a creep; this pervert who did all this to seduce you."

"Don't make it sound so sexy." At his glare, I quickly retract. "I'm sorry. I was just trying to make this conversation lighter. I know this is serious, and I don't want you to feel like I'm minimizing your feelings."

Given his tension and the way he can't bear to look at me, I can tell he's in so much fucking pain. I want to let him know he doesn't have to do this on his own, so I reach across the table and take his hand.

He looks at our hands before making eye contact again.

"Whatever's behind why you did this, there is a reason, Zane," I assure him. "And I don't care what that reason is. So why don't you tell me more about this teacher?"

He turns his hand, rubbing his thumb across mine. His warm skin feels so smooth. Despite how this conversation is stressing me out, his touch helps set me at ease.

"Please," I say. "Talk to me."

14

ZANE

AFTER WHAT I told him, he should have bolted out the door. He should have told me he wanted nothing to do with me when he first learned about my struggles with my mental health.

But he's here, holding my hand, wanting to hear more.

He has a kind spirit. Like Mike.

It makes me wonder if that's what whoever is behind the disappearances saw in them—this beautiful, rare quality. And if they did, why would they tear that from a world that's already filled with too much cruelty?

But maybe no one would want that because this whole idea of someone abducting Mike and Jason is just a creation of my own fucked-up mind.

"Please. Talk to me."

I struggle with his request, but now that I've dragged him into this, he has a right to know.

"I glossed over this when I was telling you about Isaac Tolle," I force out. "After seeing Tolle's name in

Mike's planner, I hacked Tolle's email and found out he volunteered at Habitat for Humanity. I showed up to a few builds, thinking I'd talk to people who knew him…see if they said anything about someone he was spending time with. And I didn't get anything, but on the third week, Isaac showed up."

Wyachet's not a small city, but it's not New York, so it's not shocking that I would run into a teacher who volunteered and who happened to have interacted with Mike and Jason.

Leif must realize this, which is why I still can't bring myself to look at him. "You're still not seeing it, are you?"

"Zane, it makes sense why seeing that would look suspicious. At the very least, it's noteworthy."

Despite what he says, I can hear his skepticism. Or maybe that's what I'm expecting to hear, so I keep going. "It wasn't only that he was on the build. He recognized me, but it was more than that. He looked guilty as sin, like he knew I was onto him. It's possible he checked social media after Mike disappeared, but if he recognized me, wouldn't he have mentioned it? That interaction is what started the real obsession. I could just feel this instinct. Something in my fucking bones that told me he did it…and I needed Roth to see." As I say that this was the most I had, I know how it must sound. "It seemed like something was there."

"When you were following him, did he ever go to the

Chelsby Hill Library?"

I look at Leif for the first time since I started getting into details. I was expecting him to look shocked or horrified, but he seems curious.

Is he really entertaining this when *I'm* having a hard time with it, and I'm the one who lived it?

"No," I admit. "And I don't want to sound weird, but I mean, I was on that guy's ass. I saw where he went to the gym. The restaurants he preferred to meet friends at. The Lowe's he buys his plants at."

"So it could be a coincidence?"

"You think I didn't fucking consider that?" I practically growl as heat rises in my chest, and Leif's eyes widen and he leans back like my reaction fucking scared him.

"I'm sorry," I say quickly. "I know you're trying to help. I'm defensive. That wasn't about you; that was about me. I just... I've thought this out from every possible angle. And back when I was following him, I did get in my head about it, and these connections, the way he reacted, were on my mind. The more I followed him, the more it consumed me. But I couldn't make anything else out of it. The guy was squeaky clean. And there was this tenuous connection, and I had this feeling that if there was a reason for the cops to look at him, they'd find something I couldn't. And then that blew up in my face."

I want to curl up into a ball, disappear so that he

won't see me while I'm like this.

I don't like feeling so vulnerable and exposed—that's why I keep all these damned secrets.

So I spit out what's left to share before I have a chance to chicken out. "Then I saw him at the library the other day. And I feel fine right now. I've taken my meds, yet I still have this instinct, and it makes me think there's something fucking *there*, and I wasn't wrong then. What if he stopped going to the library for a while after he took my brother because he figured the cops might be checking places he frequented, and he didn't want to look suspicious? What if he's looking for a new victim because he wasn't able to grab you?"

It's a wild speculation, he has to know that, more like something out of a Netflix movie than something that would happen in real life. But it's plagued my mind so much that I feel like I have to exorcise it from my being so that I can have a chance of letting it go. "There. Now you know exactly how crazy I'm being." I feel dirty for sharing it, like I need to take a shower.

Like now Leif won't be able to look at me without seeing that I'm fucked up.

In my mind, there's a video that keeps playing, different scenes of the moment it finally hits Leif exactly how messed up I am—his eyes widen, he races for the door, he screams for me to get away from him.

But he's still here.

Why is he still here?

"Zane," he says gently, "I imagine anyone who experienced the kind of loss you did would be grappling with the same things you are." Despite how exposed I feel for sharing that with him, his words make me feel safe. "I can't imagine what it's like to have this big question mark around why he's gone and trying to figure out how to make sense of it. I don't think that means there's something wrong. And if I were in your shoes and saw those connections, I could see me having a hard time not thinking there was something there." He quiets, then adds, "I'm sorry. I'm worried I'm fucking this all up. I'm trying to be careful about what I say, make sure I'm not making this worse, but…"

I look into his eyes again, shocked that with all the compassion he's shown me, he could think that. "Leif, you're not fucking this up. I'm fucking this up because I know I'm not going off much. And the past few days, I've pulled out all the notes I made about Isaac. Started stalking his social media. I'm spiraling right back into it. I didn't want to talk to you because I didn't want you to see me like this. I figured it would pass. I talked to my psych. I didn't tell her specifically what I was doing, but I told her that my paranoia has intensified and that I'm getting those feelings about that teacher again, so she's bumped up my dosages again. I have this feeling that I'm onto something, but then I'm also like, that's what I felt before and…"

I let my words trail off.

He must know what I mean by that. I don't want to have to speak it. Don't want to think about how hard it was when I had to spend those seventy-two hours getting my head back on straight.

"I shouldn't have told you any of that."

"But I'm glad you did." He firms his grip on my hand, and damn, it's so reassuring.

"I'm kind of glad I did too," I confess. "It's hard struggling with this just inside my head. There's a lot of shit in there like that."

I shake my head, wishing I could shake it all right out, but I've learned by now that no amount of struggling internally or externally can make those thoughts go away.

And with them, comes a torrent of memories.

"I was supposed to take care of Mike," I spit out. "That's what Dad always said. 'You're in charge of your brother. You make sure he's safe.' But I failed. So fucking miserably."

"I obviously don't know much about your dad, but do you think he would have expected you to stop him from going missing? How would you have been able to do that?"

I shoot him a look. I know he's trying to be helpful, and he couldn't have understood how far off he is. "Leif, trust me when I tell you, he would have expected me to keep Mike safe. *Always.*"

His gaze settles on the tabletop for a moment before

he releases my hand.

No, don't go.

Although, it's a premature fear since he pushes to his feet only to scoot his chair around the corner of the table, closer to me.

What the hell is he doing?

He sits back down and sets his hand on my thigh, stroking his thumb across my jeans. "I'm sorry," he says. "I shouldn't have made that assumption about your father. I, of all people, should've known better. I hate it when people assume I should have a great relationship with my grandma just because we're blood related. I don't know what you've been through. But I do know from everything you've shared with me that you're not responsible for your brother going missing."

As a tear falls from my eye, I wonder where the hell that crept up from, but I don't fight it. I don't mind Leif seeing me like this. "I should have done a better job keeping up with him. I should have called him more. I should have followed him everywhere…"

I'm not so unaware of myself that I don't realize that's why I'm doing this with Leif. Because I'm making up for what I couldn't do for Mike.

He raises his hand to my face and wipes the tear from my cheek.

Warmth pulses through me.

I feel so fucking safe right now. I can't remember a time when I ever felt so safe.

I turn my face into his hand and kiss his palm.

Our gazes meet again, and for the first time since we started our chat, I don't feel like I have to hide from his gaze. He's seen this dark shit in me, and he's still here.

Who are you, Leif Anderson?

Once again, I find myself staring at his lips, and an impulse rises within me. I lean toward him, waiting for him to jerk away, but he doesn't react the way I expect; he leans closer.

My gaze shifts to his eyes, those beautiful brown irises sparkling under the chandelier light.

Our lips graze against each other's, and as an electric charge moves through me, Leif's mouth opens, like he's inviting me in. I hook my arms around him, practically falling out of my chair as I slide my tongue into his mouth, my face pressed against his.

God, he tastes good.

And the kiss dissolves all my worries and fears.

Assures me that nothing I said has fucked anything up between us.

There's a moment when we're trying to figure out how to position our bodies, our lips parting only long enough for me to straddle his waist. And in our frenzy, we manage to butt heads.

We laugh before our lips mash against one another's again, our hands greedily groping each other's bodies. My limbs, my tongue, my cock are beyond my control as we work up an intense heat.

I figured it would feel good to kiss him, but how could I have ever imagined the sensations that surge through me?

Will I die like this, unable to drink or eat because my body refuses to let this experience escape my grasp?

Another sweep of his tongue in my mouth sends a wave of sensation through me, and my cock is so painfully hard that I growl.

Leif's hand slides from my waist to the front, down to my crotch, strokes my fly, my hips rocking.

I'm so fucking intoxicated that it's hard to even remember the specifics of what we were just talking about. There's only Leif and all the sensations he's worked up.

My kisses turn to nibbles against his jaw and neck, then a series of licks.

"Zane…" he whispers, and my name's never sounded so good, so erotic.

"Yes," I breathe into his flesh, not letting up my kisses.

"I want you." His hand presses more firmly against my cock. "I *need* you."

"I need you too, Leif. God, how I fucking need you."

15

LEIF

W E HAVE TO break apart briefly so I can put the carbonara in the fridge, but then Zane grips my hand and guides me up to his bedroom.

I'm in a bit of a daze from what happened downstairs.

One minute I was talking to him about so much pain and darkness, and the next, he was on me, his mouth devouring my fucking face.

I'm clinging to that experience—his tongue teasing mine, the weight of him on my thighs, his breath slamming against my cheeks between forceful, urgent kisses.

He has two monitors on his desk, dark screens on both. There are some stray clothes scattered across the floor. Two bottles of water on the nightstand.

Not as messy as I figured he'd be.

He leads me to his bed and turns to me, practically attacking me with another kiss. I submit as he pulls me onto the bed.

This is so much more comfortable than the kitchen chair, which was starting to hurt my ass. Although, maybe it was only warming me up for what I'm curious about.

Zane rolls on top of me as our kisses become gentler, our bodies relaxing now that they know we're surrendering to our urges, unwilling to deprive ourselves of how fucking good this feels.

He finally pulls away and takes a few breaths, gazing down at me with those steel-blue eyes.

"If I'd known it was going to feel like that," he says, "I wouldn't have left these lips alone that first night."

"Me neither."

He grins ear to ear before licking up my lips, until his tongue touches my nose. Even there, I feel a tingle radiating, as though his tongue is charging everything it touches.

"How am I gonna keep away from you long enough to get you out of these fucking clothes?" For the first time since we started kissing, he looks fucking pissed, but just as soon, his lips are back on mine, and now we have a challenge.

We work together, at first nearly fighting each other's hands to get the other's fly, but I finally surrender and let him undo mine first. When he's finished, I grab the hem of his shirt and pull it over him. I've barely tossed it off the bed and he's already tearing my shirt off, and once we've gotten rid of those obstacles, his mouth is on my nipple in no time, his tongue flicking, teasing me.

"Fuck," I moan, relaxing as he takes his time, as though he's got a bone to pick with my nipple. He heads to the other, giving it some love before offering a gentle peck and a lick beside it.

"I'll get a condom and lube," he whispers into my flesh. "And I want you out of these fucking clothes."

He grunts like it's paining him to get off me, then rolls over to the nightstand. I take his words as the order they seem to be, speedily removing and discarding my clothes off the side of the bed.

Zane tosses a condom and lube on the pillow, then starts removing his own clothes.

His movements are slower, more controlled. When he removes his boxers, once again, I'm shocked, and he notices.

"Still surprised that a little guy can be this big?"

"Kinda," I admit, which makes him smile.

God, that smile. Such a relief after how sad and angry he's looked tonight.

He crawls over to me and offers a kiss near my navel, then kisses up my body until his lips are back on mine. He grips my cock and strokes.

"Well," he says, pulling away from my mouth, "since you're my little virgin, we should take things slow. First things first, I want you to get to know my cock better before I bury it in your ass." He wears a wicked smirk as he rolls off me and sits up by his pillows.

"Please," I say, not wanting a repeat rejection. "I want to try. Let me taste you. I need it, Zane."

His smirk twists into his dimples. "That's the kind of begging I expect. Come here. Say hey."

Now I'm smiling as I get to my knees and crawl over to him, studying his girth, the perfect veins along the shaft. I lean down and lick at the base, near his balls, running my tongue up the shaft, tasting his flesh.

"Fuck yeah," he says, "that's right. That's good, Leif."

His encouragement makes me lick even more.

"Don't be mean, Leif. Don't tease me."

With those words, I grab the base of his cock, noticing how fucking stiff the thing is before I slide the head into my mouth.

A rush of sensations radiates in my chest. Why does such a simple act have this effect on me?

Zane moans as I slide him a little farther into my mouth, enjoying the sensation of his soft skin against my lips.

As I relax into it, I bob my head up and down, taking him farther back each time.

Zane's hand settles against the side of my face, his thumb stroking. "That's good. You're doing so good," he tells me, his validation urging me on as I make it my mission to get him to the back of my throat.

But he's too big for me to do that easily, and he notices my struggle. "Hey, hey. You don't have to be so ambitious. Just enjoy yourself."

I relax, running my tongue along the base of his shaft, adjusting to the sensation of having my mouth full. As I pull back to the head, I taste something against my tongue. Precum?

I swallow it, eager to get any part of him in me.

As I move up and down some more, his fingers thread through my hair. "God, that feels good. Wow. That's it."

His dick throbs in my mouth. I can tell it's satisfying him, so I speed up my movements.

"Whoa, whoa," he says. "If you want me in your ass, you can't make me come like this."

His warning is enough to make me release him, letting his wet cock fall against his abs.

"Come here, beautiful," he says as he leans into me, licking my lips before offering another kiss.

He grabs the lube off the pillow beside us, pumping to wet his fingers. "I want you to be nice and open for me," he says before sliding down the bed and reaching between my legs. He pushes between my cheeks, massages my hole with his forefinger and middle finger. "Gonna need that ass to be ready for me, right?"

I close my eyes, enjoying the sensations he stirs as he explores farther with one finger. I'm impressed with how well he reads my body, knowing how to ease me into it before adding another finger. He's like some kind of sex god as he pushes back, teasing at that delicious spot.

My body vibrates, and I gasp.

"Yeah, that's where you want my cock, right? You want it slamming up against it again and again, cum dripping from your cock as you take me?"

The way he's got me worked up, I feel out of control. I love it.

I lean down close to him. "I want to know what it feels like," I whisper against his lips.

I don't know where this is coming from. For a guy who'd never thought twice about this, now I'm pleading for Zane's monster cock. Doesn't even feel like a desire, but a need. I'm so fucking horny that in this moment, it's like my entire existence has been just to discover what he would feel like.

"Please, Zane. Please, I fucking need it."

He gives my prostate another quick stroke that sends a warm sensation rushing through me. Then he leans back, assessing my expression. "Now that's what I call begging," he says with an almost sinister smirk.

When he pulls his fingers out, my body's aching, wondering why I'm depriving it of such intense pleasure, but I remind myself it'll be worth it. I watch as Zane readies himself—so smooth with his movements, how effortlessly he slides the condom on, then pumps some more lube into his palm before generously rubbing it around the condom.

"You're gonna start off riding," he says. "It'll be easier that way."

He scoots forward so he can lie against the pillow, and I straddle his waist, leaning down to take another kiss.

He positions himself between my cheeks, the head against my hole, but leaves it there. Clearly not in the rush I'm in. I push my ass back toward it, the head pushing in.

"Fuck, you really do need it," he says.

"You have no idea."

He can't understand all the fantasies he's activated within me now that I know how good it can feel. And the way he left me hanging the past few days has left my body desperate.

I want him to show me everything.

I close my eyes and sit back farther, but I have to stop when the pressure's too much for me.

Zane rubs his hand against my thigh. "It's okay. We have plenty of time," he assures me, but he doesn't understand this sensation that's pulsing through me. How desperate I am. How it feels like the only way my agony will end is if he's balls-deep in me.

But I know he's right, so I take deep breaths, allowing my ass to relax.

Zane gazes up at me and runs his fingers through my bangs. "Come down here and kiss me. I miss your mouth."

I do what he says, crushing my lips against his, appreciating his playful tongue once again. As we kiss, my body viscerally relaxes, and I feel his cock shift farther back in me.

"Yes, yes. Just like that."

As I moan into his mouth, his hands rest against either ass cheek, pulling them apart as his cock steadily pushes deeper.

The pressure mounts, but as I fear it's about to be too much, his cock halts in place.

"It's okay. You're doing so good, Leif. You have no idea how good you're doing."

I appreciate the compliment. I'm just so fucking nervous, but I can tell he's learned how to ease a man into this, and I'm benefiting from all his experience and wisdom.

"Teach me, Zane."

We kiss again, and he cups my face with his hands, and as I relax, I find my ass sinking, pushing him deeper into me.

A rush of sensation moves through me when his cock hits that spot in me. I pull away from his lips long enough for a moan, grinding my teeth as I try to take him a little faster.

"There's no rush."

"But I *need* it."

"If you're too eager, then that means I might have to wait to fuck you again next time."

A warm sensation swirls in my chest. He's already thinking about a next time?

It's enough to encourage me to take my time. And as I calm down, he feeds me another inch.

The way that thick cock rubs up against my prostate causes a rush of energy, and my cock trembles before I feel precum push out of the head.

"Oh, yeah," Zane says before I feel his hand around my shaft. He runs his thumb across the head, using the precum to lubricate me as he strokes. "That's nice."

I relax farther back still, a moan escaping my lips, the pressure intensifying. Just as soon as I think I might not be able to bear it anymore, my ass hits his pelvis.

I did it.

I fucking did it.

Why does that make me feel like a fucking champion?

"Nice work, Leif," he says, rewarding me with a few generous pumps. "Stay right there. Let your body get used to having me in you like this."

I want my body to get used to this.

I take a few more breaths as the pressure eases up. I lean back farther, trying to sit with the sensation.

"Never figured I'd have a dick in me, let alone one this size."

"Never thought I'd get to have your ass, and oh, fuck, it's better than I imagined."

I love hearing that he was imagining this moment.

I take deep, steady breaths as Zane stares, this cocked smirk on his face suggesting he could lie there all night like that.

As the pressure loses its bite, I enjoy the way his shaft is pushed up against my prostate, and rise up on my knees. My body vibrates as sensation pools through me, urging me back down. Then up again.

It feels so natural, just some animal impulse guiding my rhythm.

With each motion, Zane continues stroking my cock, which leaks across his abdomen. It's like his dick is fucking pushing it out of me.

As my movements become broader and faster, Zane starts to match them with gentle thrusts.

Soon, I'm all sensation, radiating from my ass through my chest and head, to my goddamn fingertips. I jerk and twist, and my eyes roll back as a network of nerves pulses through me.

"That's great," Zane says, thrusting and pumping my cock. "You're doing so good, Leif. I'm so impressed with you."

I maintain my pace, feeling more confident in my movements when I hear him say, "Okay, I think you're ready now."

"Ready?" I ask as his cock hits my prostate again just right, sending another wave of sensation pulsing through me.

"Yeah. Pull off and lie on your back."

"But I just got this thing in me."

"Don't worry. It'll be easier now that you did it.

Trust me."

He's shown me how much I can trust him with my body already.

As I pull off his cock, I marvel at it again. It's laughable to think I ever had doubts.

I lie back against the pillow beside him, and he gets on his knees and moves between my legs. He hooks his arms around my thighs, positioning my body, not even needing to guide his cock in with his hands as he pushes up against my hole and slides right back in.

He was right. It's much easier now that he's loosened me up.

As his cock pushes into me, my back arches as he rubs up against my prostate again. Once he's firmly back in, he offers a series of subtle thrusts, building up.

His mouth's hanging open, his abs contracting as he clasps down on my thighs and works me up. "How does it feel now?"

"Inc-red-ible."

He rests my thighs down and leans close to me, taking another kiss, his tongue forcing its way in as he gives me a few more thrusts in quick succession—broad, sweeping thrusts, each one hitting me just right, taking me higher, making me want so much fucking more.

"Something tells me you don't want a nice, slow fuck," he says, his breath slamming against my lips. "Am I right? Tell me I'm right. You say the word, and I'll give it to you."

"I don't know where this is coming from. I'd never even thought about this before."

But with him so deep in me, my body feels so fucking hungry.

He smiles before offering a kiss against my jawline, then kissing down to my neck.

The warmth of his kiss, combined with what his cock's doing to me, sends another network of nerves tingling through me.

"I want it hard," I say, surprising even myself as I speak the words, and I hear him chuckle before he offers another tender kiss.

"I fucking knew it." He leans back and hooks his arms under my thighs, and this time there's no hesitation, no easing me into it. He offers a series of sharp thrusts so that I can hear the slap of his pelvis against my ass.

As he's deep in me, my head instinctively rolls back, my hands gripping the sheets since my nerves are so excited, I feel like they might burst through my flesh.

The bed trembles with my body, my cock bouncing on my abs with his intense movements as he impales me with that monster cock.

I feel a warmth on me, and as I check to see what it is, I notice beads of sweat drop from his bangs, his expression determined as he gives it to me the way I clearly need it.

I love knowing how he's working himself up for this.

For me.

The pressure in my balls is too much for me, and I grab my cock and stroke.

He hammers away, and he's in just the right spot.

"Like that," I tell him. "Right there, right there."

He doesn't let me down. Doesn't alter his pace.

"Give me that cum so I can lap it up," he orders.

The thought of my cum on his lips is too much, and with one more thrust, it's over for me—ropes of cum shoot out, and I feel some land on my fucking chin as he pushes it right out of me.

I vibrate and twist with sensation as his movements finally slow, and soon, I'm a corpse on the bed, my muscles surrendering to the sparks that still fire off in me as I come down from the high of what we shared.

Zane pulls out slowly, his care reminding me that even though he can drill my ass, he can still be so considerate and careful with me. It's one of the many reasons I'm glad he's the one who showed me what it was like.

He removes the condom and discards it, jerking himself before he buries his face in my load, lapping me up just like he said he would.

"Please don't come yet," I tell him.

He growls into my abs. "Leif, I don't know if I can."

"Please, I'm begging," I say, since I know what that means to him.

And he shoots a look my way, pulling his hand away

from his cock.

I sit up and grab it, stroking. "Please, I really want to."

He starts to smile, but his chin quivers as his hips move back and forth.

I gaze down at that beautiful cock. Damn, how did I never look at a dick and see what I see when I look at Zane's? Why does he make me so needy for it? How has it got me begging to do this?

Whatever the reason, I submit, leaning down and taking him into my mouth.

16

ZANE

WHAT THE HELL are we doing?

I mean, it's obvious *what* we're doing, but how did my fantasies turn into Leif sliding his lips down my cock as I lick off some of his cum from my lips? As fresh as when I lapped it off his abs, the taste sets me at ease despite how on edge my body is.

His ass already took me close, and then when I pulled out, I figured I was just going to shoot on him, when he threw me with his request, and how the hell was I going to say no to that?

As he braves farther down my shaft than the first time he made the attempt, I have to warn him, "Leif, I'm so close, I'm gonna shoot if you…"

He pulls off briefly and whispers, "Shoot in my mouth." Then he's back on my dick, his lips clasping around it.

His warm tongue glides across my flesh, torturing my nerves, which are already at the very edge, waiting for him to flip that trigger. And when he does, my balls and dick throb before a jolt rushes through me, heat building in my face.

"Fuck!" I call out.

As my hips jerk in a quick series of thrusts, Leif grips my ass cheeks. He's not even halfway on my cock before I'm shooting down his throat.

The release is explosive, my mind spinning as I call out, my nerves hypersensitive as Leif bobs his head up and down quickly, then pulls back, and I hear him fucking swallow me before he licks cum off the head.

I don't know what comes over me—hell, I'm hardly in control of my movements—but I reach down and take his chin, guiding him up until we're face-to-face. "Open your mouth," I tell him, and when he does, I lick his tongue for a taste. Then I grab either side of his head, burying my face into his as we're all tongues, saliva, and remnants of us.

I should be sated after everything we did, but I can't get enough of Leif, and I pull him back down onto the bed, making out with him, wanting to stay lost in this experience for as long as we can. Away from the real world and bullshit, the grief of the loss of my brother and the fucking fears I have about Leif's safety.

When I finally manage to pull away, I keep my arm hooked around him, tugging against his back so his torso is tight against my body.

"That was bold," I say as my gaze fixes on his lips.

"I was too curious not to try." He hooks his leg over

mine. "And I figured after taking a dick, what the hell, right?"

I chuckle. "Don't know what I'm laughing about. Nothing about that was funny. Just hot."

"Yeah, that was hot. But you liked it?" He quirks his eyebrow, and my eyes widen. I'm stunned.

"Are you fucking kidding me right now? Or just baiting for a compliment?"

"Maybe baiting a little. Wondering how it compares with the guys you've been with who are more experienced."

"Okay, Leif, you can get those kinds of insecure thoughts out of your head because you're in your own league."

"Whoa, whoa. I wasn't saying I was insecure. But I'm not as practiced as other people my age might be."

"In that case, don't worry about your inexperience because that's part of what makes it hot too."

I lick his lips, and he licks right back.

As my dick gets hard again, he glances down. "Seriously. You're already good to go again. Little thing just packed with cum, aren't you?"

"Maybe being short helps with the circulation, but yeah, doesn't take me long."

"Now I know what they mean by a short king."

"Normally I don't like people commenting on my height," I say, and his smile shifts to a frown. "No, I meant I normally don't, but I like you calling me a short king. That makes it sound kinda hot."

"Oh, it is," he assures me as his smile returns.

"I have to warn you: now that you've spoiled my cock, it's gonna be expecting this kind of naughty fun all the time."

"You could say the same about my ass."

Now he's got me grinning like a dork. Fuck me.

He leans close and licks my chin, and when he pulls away, I steal another kiss.

"See, and if you'd kept ignoring me, you were never going to get that," he says, reminding me of all the tension before he first came over.

That kills my smile, and I settle on my side, resting my head on the pillow; Leif mirrors my position.

"That was supposed to be a fun tease," he says. "I wasn't trying to put you in a mood."

"Sorry. Reminded me of all the bullshit in my head before you came over and sucked it out of me."

I'm trying to lighten the mood because, really, if only it were that easy and it wasn't still rattling around in my brain. But I think about how hard it was to confess what was on my mind to him, and that he didn't judge me for it, just stayed here, holding my hand, wanting to know more.

"Who are you, Leif Anderson?" I meant to say that in my head, but as the words push out of my lips, I don't stop them.

His brow furrows. "All this time watching me, and

you don't already know the answer?"

"No, I don't." And that kind of pisses me off. Shouldn't I?

"Only fair because I'm wondering who you are, Zane Grayson."

Good point.

I think about how I got off the subject earlier when he brought up my father.

It wasn't his fault for imagining Dad was a typical loving dad, like his. How could he know any differently when I keep this so tight to my chest, along with all the other shit I carry?

I should keep it to myself, be grateful he backed off and helped me forget all the bullshit with our messing around.

But maybe it's what we just shared. Or how he's pressed up against me, gazing into my eyes. Or how good it felt to share other shit with him. Whatever the reason, I feel a lump in my throat, as if the words I want to say are pushing to get out. And I surrender. "Do you remember when you asked me where I learned to shoot?"

"Yes."

"My father taught us when we were kids." There's a part of me saying it's not too late to back out, but I ignore it. "Mike and I didn't have a normal childhood. Not that there is such a thing, but from people I've talked to, it sounds like Mike and I had an even less normal childhood than most. Do you know what a survivalist is?"

"Like people who live in the woods?"

"Yeah, but think of that on steroids. There was a show on National Geographic called *Doomsday Preppers*. You ever seen that?"

He shakes his head.

"It's about people who have bizarre ideas about how the world will end—and some maybe not so bizarre. Like, there's someone who thought there would be a water crisis. Or the destruction of our industrial food chain. You name it, someone's got some idea of what it might be and what they needed to do to survive."

"I take it your dad had some idea like that?" Leif's cautious with his wording; I can tell he doesn't want to sound dismissive or judgmental, which I appreciate.

"Yes, but he wasn't always like that—though we always knew something was a bit off. When Mom was alive, he still had his strange days. He'd have days where he'd disappear, which was hard on Mom. She'd act like he had to go somewhere for work. At the time, I bought it, but she always acted weird when he'd come back home. They got into fights at night, so loud we could hear them from our room. After she passed away, Dad got really into conspiracy theories—books, websites, podcasts. Anything he could get his hands on. As an adult, I can look back and see that *surprise!* It's genetic, right?"

That was my attempt at a fucked-up joke, but it's

clearly not amusing to Leif, who just lies there, listening.

"Anyway, Dad sold our house. Took us to a cabin in the woods, taught us how to shoot and survive off the land. He didn't explain the conspiracies. He would talk about them to friends who came by, but I guess he felt we were too young for it. He made out like this was all some great father/son bonding time, a lengthy camping trip. Then one day he took me out for a hunt and told me that all the countries were going to go to war, and I'd needed to know how to survive, and that I had to take care of my brother. He made me promise I'd make sure Mike stayed safe if anything happened to him, and I promised.

"I mean, I was fucking terrified. Even then, I don't know that I believed him, but I knew *he* believed, which had me in a fucked-up headspace for an eleven-year-old. And we stayed in that cabin for, like, a year. And then one day Dad went off into the woods with his shotgun and didn't come back. Mike and I waited…and waited. I was scared Dad was right and what he'd told me was really happening. This end he'd warned me about. After two days, we were running out of food, so I went looking for him, and I found him in the woods."

Suddenly, I'm numb as the scene details flash through my mind.

Dad's camo khakis, shoes, and flannel.

The flies. God, there were so many flies.

I push ahead in the story, hoping if I move past that

point, these haunting images will fade. "Dad had a few friends he trusted and had left numbers for in case of an emergency. So we contacted one, and she came over with the cops."

I study Leif's expression, trying to make out what he's thinking, and I feel his fingers against my cheek.

"Zane, I'm so sorry."

I lean into his hand, enjoying his comforting touch.

It's not only that; carrying that kind of thing…there's a loneliness to it. And it's like now that he sees it, I'm less alone.

"It was a nightmare. Child services told us they'd try to keep Mike and me together, but that didn't happen, and we were put with different families in the foster care system."

I reflect on the days and nights of crying, still grieving the loss of my mom, my dad…and then my brother.

"I hate myself for believing them when they said we'd end up together," I say as fire burns in my chest. "And I fought and tried to get them not to take him away, but I was too small to put up much of a fight. And I remember feeling like I'd let Dad and Mike down."

A warm tear slides down my temple. "Fuck," I say, and as I'm about to move my hand off Leif to get it, he beats me to it, wiping it away with his thumb.

I watch him, wondering how a person could possibly respond to all that, or if he just wants to pry away from the guy with more issues than he could possibly know what to do with, but he hooks his arm around me and pulls me close for a hug.

Just holding me.

I thought, after digging all that shit up, nothing could ease my pain, but I was wrong. So fucking wrong.

Because I feel safe in his hold.

And when the tears start falling, he pulls away and kisses the tears away.

He can't know this, but it's exactly what I need in this moment. Not words or assurances that can't possibly make up for the past, but someone to lie there with me, to know how much it burns and to sit with me in my grief.

While he's kissing my face, I turn my head until my lips find his for another kiss.

And oh…fuck.

It doesn't free me of the searing pain in my chest, but it dulls the burn. And the more we kiss, the easier it feels to endure. After sucking, licking, and nibbling at each other, soon our passion turns into soft pecks, until we're nuzzling our cheeks together. I can't even make sense of what we're doing, but like so much of what we share, it's driven by instincts, and I don't give a fuck how weird we're acting as long as he keeps close to me.

Soon, we pull away and stare into each other's eyes.

It feels different than the other times he's looked at me because in the past, I've had the security of knowing he had no idea whom he was looking at. Not really.

But now he knows far more than he should.

Finally, he breaks the silence. "I'm trying to think of something to say…but I'm at a loss for the right words. And I really don't want to fuck this up and say the wrong thing."

"You've been doing fine without words. This is what I need right now." I tug his body so he's even tighter against me.

"I appreciate you sharing that. It clearly wasn't easy."

"Yeah, *easy* isn't the word for any of that. But can we leave that alone for the rest of the night? I don't want to go back there anymore."

"Of course."

"Sorry for ruining what was otherwise a sexy night."

He flips his hand over and runs his knuckles across my cheek. "That didn't ruin anything. I like getting to know you."

Damn. Once again, he couldn't know what it means to hear him say that.

"Well, if you want to get to know me more, I suggest you get your ass over here more often. I want to kiss you until it hurts. Until our lips burn and our jaws hurt. I want to kiss until it doesn't sting to pull away from your mouth. How does that sound?"

"Sounds like I need to invest in a lot of ChapStick."

I laugh. God, I'm fucking laughing after all that.

Only you have this kind of power over me, Leif.

I take his lips once again, and I relax into him, wishing life could just be this moment. That we never had to deal with the bullshit, and we could simply get so lost in each other, I could forget all past nightmares.

As the tension I'd awakened subsides, I pull away from him. "I guess we should talk about what you need to tell your parents. That's why you came over, right?"

"I mean, we need to figure that out, but you must know I was only using that as an excuse to make you talk to me, right?"

I laugh. "Sorry. I won't do that to you again. If something comes up, I'll talk to you."

"Promise?"

"I promise."

I wish he could know I truly mean it. How much he's assured me that I can trust him with all this dark shit in me.

"Good," he says. "So I've been thinking that they should know they're in danger, but I'm worried if I say something, they'll talk to Detective Roth, who is gonna tell them about you…"

My thoughts exactly. "Yeah. And then it's gonna further complicate things. If Detective Roth finds out I'm here, she's gonna freak them out. They might be able to get a protective order or worse if they find the cameras I set up. And if I have to leave…or spend time in jail, I'm not gonna be able to protect your family. And the cops sure as hell won't be here if something happens."

"That's what I keep thinking."

"I know it's asking a lot to trust me, but, Leif, if you're in danger, I can protect you and your family. And if this is all in my head, then you're not losing anything by my being over here."

He studies my face. "You're right. It's a big ask—"

Fuck. "Then tell them. You should do whatever you think is right. And I'll—"

He kisses me again, silencing me with a sweep of his tongue before he pulls away and looks me in the eyes. "You didn't let me finish. I was going to say that it's a big ask, but that I do trust you."

Being inches from his face, gazing into his eyes, I don't doubt his words. "I won't let you down, Leif." It's my promise as I attack his lips yet again.

It's a significant promise, but I'm more determined than ever. I may not have been able to protect my brother, but I will protect Leif. And this person who's after him will lay a hand on him over my dead body.

17

LEIF

"COME ON, KYRA."

I sit on my bedroom floor, legs crossed, her cage in front of me.

I want some evidence that she can use her wings, but she just hops about, not making any effort that might lead me to think she's healing. I offer words of encouragement, but Kyra goes about her usual business, ignoring me.

"Dammit," I mutter, more than a little disappointed.

I pick my phone up and text Zane: **Short King, Flight 6 is a bust. Think it might be time to take Kyra back to the clinic.**

I return Kyra's cage to the spot by my window and settle at my desk, browsing the vet's online portal, when I get a reply from Zane: **Sorry. :(Why don't you come over tonight and I'll try to make up for it? *devil emoji***

A rush of excitement moves through me.

Something changed in me two weeks ago—the night Zane fucked me.

That initial curiosity for his cock has turned into an obsession, a mission to get him in me as much as possible, something he clearly doesn't mind making time for either. Even sitting here at my desk, my ass cheeks clench in anticipation. It doesn't even have to be in moments like this, when there's at least the promise that we might mess around again. Sometimes I'll be sitting here when I feel that familiar clench, as if my ass is reminding me what we must get back to.

It's not only the fucking, though.

I like Zane. He's not the creeper I believed him to be when I first started seeing him around the neighborhood. Now that I've gotten to know about his past, I get what lies behind his intense gaze. So much pain, and I'm glad he felt he could share it with me.

When I finish booking an appointment through the clinic's online portal, my phone screen switches to a FaceTime from Steven—a welcome surprise.

"Hey, stranger," I answer, placing my phone in my mount.

"Leif, man. How's it going? What've you been up to?"

His typical cheerfulness is charming as ever, but it stirs an awareness that I'm still not totally out of this funk. Back when we started talking at the beginning of our first semester, he was friendly and playful. We could go out to a party for a good time and laughs without me thinking twice about it. But now, that smile and the levity in his voice shine a light on the dissonance with where I'm at now compared to back then.

The fucking around with Zane has helped, but I have to accept that maybe I'll never get back to that place before I crumbled under the weight of intense depression.

"It's going okay," I say. "I had another flight attempt with Kyra. It was a no-go."

"I'm sorry, dude."

"It's okay. I was hoping it was an easy fix and she'd be back to normal, but looks like it's gonna take longer than I figured." As the words escape my lips, I can't help but imagine that's how Mom and Dad must feel about me and this time I've needed to recover from last spring.

"Anyway, I made an appointment with the clinic. I'll keep you posted. How are you doing?"

"Trying to get some papers done, and I have a group project to manage before I start cramming for finals, but it'll all be worth it when we get to winter break."

"Are you gonna see your family?"

"Yeah. Sucks that I'm gonna be here through Thanksgiving, you know?"

Steven's family lives in Michigan, and from things he's mentioned, I can't imagine he or his family have the money to have him fly out for both fall and winter break.

"Hey, my parents are flying back out to see my grandma for Thanksgiving…"

"I thought they hated her."

"I'll have to catch you up. She's been sick, and my aunt is stressed out dealing with her enough as it is, so they offered to help her manage through the holiday. But I'm obviously not going. You're only a thirty-minute drive from Wyachet, so what if you came over here and I threw something together?"

"Really?"

"Are you kidding me? Did you forget my MO?"

He laughs. "Well, if I come…I know it's not a Thanksgiving dish, but I'm gonna want some of those chocolate-chip cookies."

"Consider it done."

He grins as he adjusts his cap. "In that case, I'm all for making an excuse to get some good food."

"Let me check with Mom and Dad, but I can't imagine they'll say no. And once I get the go-ahead, if you run into anyone else who might want to come, I'll be eager to make enough for an army."

"I don't know that I can get an army, but I have these friends Ilsa and Max who are from out of town, and I think they're staying here. I'll let you know."

The thought of having a Thanksgiving dinner excites me in a way that reminds me of how I used to be. It's not the same as it would have been, but it makes me feel more like my old self. A baby step in the right direction.

And I already know who else I want to invite—obviously, Zane.

After Steven and I finish catching up, I hang up, and

I'm already texting my short king fuck buddy: **If you want to see me before tonight, you free to hit up the gym later?**

Since we started fucking around, we've jogged around the neighborhood and hit the gym together; he's becoming my own personal escort. Even though I know it's to make sure I'm safe, it's nice getting to spend time with him outside of messing around at his place.

> **ZANE: I'll be finished up around three, if that works for you. Or I can drop this and get back to it later.**
>
> **ME: 3 works great.**
>
> **ZANE: I'll text you when I'm done.**
>
> **ME: Or you could come over…**
>
> **ZANE: You aren't worried your parents will get the door?**
>
> **ME: That's kind of what I'm hoping for.**

Maybe I'm pushing this too far. What if he's not comfortable with that…or thinks I've become all clingy and needy? Is it weird that I want them to meet him?

> **ME: I just think they might as well meet you since we're spending so much time together. They're starting to get suspicious with me coming over every other night.**

And if they meet him, that could probably change to every night.

Okay, that does sound pretty damn clingy.

That damn ellipsis pops up and then disappears. Fuck. Why do smartphones do this shit? To torture people?

I'm nervous, but then a message comes through.

ZANE: Sure. I'd love to meet your parents. :)

That shouldn't make me grin so big, but I can't help myself. I like the idea of him meeting my family instead of this only being my dirty little secret.

A bit before three, I start listening out for the doorbell as I change into my gym clothes. I'm tying my sneakers when I hear Mom's voice—sounds like it's coming from the foyer, followed by Dad's.

Is he here already?

I finish tying my shoes, then head out. When I reach the top of the stairs, Zane's inside, chatting with Mom and Dad near the front door.

"And how are you liking the area?" Mom asks.

Zane's got his hands tucked in his hoodie pockets, not really looking her in the eyes. He looks all tense and awkward.

"Yeah. It's good," he says.

Fuck, how does he manage to look so fucking sexy just by being uneasy?

"What made you decide to move here?" Dad asks. "When I was your age, I wanted to be near the city to go out and do things with my friends."

Zane's eyes widen.

"Oh, hey, hey!" I call out, hoping to spare him that particular question.

Zane's gaze shifts to me, and the tension in his expression eases up as his lips curl into a smirk—the sort that has my chest swirling with sensation, my dick plumping up, my ass clenching.

How can he get me all worked up with only a look?

"We were getting to know your new friend," Mom says.

"Nice that you're both around the same age," Dad adds. "The gym's a great way to get some exercise."

"He used to go to the gym all the time," Mom says, "but he hasn't been getting as much exercise as he should recently. But he's got his father's genes, and all it seems to do is plump out those muscles of his."

"For now," Dad teases.

My cheeks warm. "Okay, guys. Enough of this. We have to go."

"He thinks we're going to embarrass him," Mom says before Dad chimes in, "But we can do that over dinner sometime soon, right? Maybe get the chef here to whip up something for us?"

"We're going out of town this weekend through next weekend," Mom says, "but maybe when we get back?"

"Oh, about that," I say, figuring this is as good an opportunity as any, "I was wondering if it'd be all right if

I had some people over for Thanksgiving."

Mom's and Dad's eyes widen, their mouths slightly open. They aren't even looking at each other, so I assume this is one of those things they share because they've been together so fucking long.

Mom looks to Dad before blurting out, "Of course. That would be great."

I know they mean well, but the fact that they're making a big deal out of this is a reminder of how fucked up I've been. In the past, they wouldn't have thought twice about it, but now it's like they're about to call the *Gwinnett Daily Post* to see if this can make the front page.

"Yes. That's totally fine with us," Dad adds. "Anyway, we'll get out of your hair, but, Zane, again, we'll make sure to reach out about dinner when we get back."

Zane's expression relaxes, and a warm smile slips across his face. "I'd really like that, Mrs. and Mr. Anderson."

"Oh, please. Ginny and Paul."

Dad offers him a handshake, and Mom tackles him with a hug. After we all say our goodbyes, Zane and I get in my car.

"Your parents are very friendly," he says as I pull out of the driveway.

"Yeah, they're good people, but that seemed like a lot for you."

"You haven't seen me interact with anyone other

than you. I'm not great around people."

"No shit," I tease. "You forget how we met?"

He cringes. "Yeah, but really, my therapist says it might have to do with my childhood. When Mike and I first went into foster care, at the new school, I was kind of out of it, and kids were nasty. Not that they knew what was going on, but they could tell I was off, and I guess like kids sometimes will do, when someone's different, they came for me. And that only made me even more closed off, and I learned how to skate under the radar."

I imagine a younger version of Zane, after all that horrifying shit he endured, with kids teasing him, adding to his misery.

"Sorry," he says quickly. "Wow. Made that a downer real fast. That might be some kind of record."

"It's fine. It's your life. I hope you don't expect me to be happy-go-lucky all the time. And really, I like that you're just you. Like when I saw you talking to Mom and Dad, you weren't pretending to be charming or trying to be someone you're not. You were the sexy, awkward-as-fuck guy I met a few weeks ago."

"I think you'll say anything to get more of this dick," he says in that familiar, playful way he has.

"Would you blame me?"

He laughs. "No, I definitely would not. But back to the whole not-pretending shit, sometimes in moments like those with your parents, I wish I could summon some super-cool, chill guy who could effortlessly navigate his way through that kind of thing, you know?"

"Eh, well, having been that guy for plenty of my life, I can tell you it's not all it's cracked up to be. There's a lot of fake smiles and small talk that goes nowhere."

"Yeah, neither sounds like my thing."

I chuckle. "I agree. Those don't sound like the Zane I'm getting to know at all."

But now that we're talking about this, it brings to mind something else I wanted to ask him about.

"What is it?" he asks.

Can this guy really read me that well?

Regardless, there's no point keeping it from him. "That Thanksgiving dinner, I invited a friend from college, said if he knew of anyone else who needed a dinner to go to, he should invite them. Obviously, I want to invite you, but if that would make you uncomfortable..."

"Leif, of course I'm coming. I can get over my fucking bullshit to spend more time with you."

I do a double take.

"Oh, you like knowing that, don't you?" he asks, and my cheeks warm. "Why is that making you fucking blush? You know I enjoy spending time with you, right?"

"You haven't said it like that before. I know we do a lot of bedroom stuff, but..."

"Bedroom stuff?" He chuckles. "I don't know that you're old enough to mess around with me if that's what you're calling me fucking you."

I laugh. "That's obviously what I meant. I don't even know why I said it like that."

"I assumed you noticed I enjoyed spending time with you beyond fucking. Don't get me wrong, I like that too, but if there's any question in your pretty head about what we're doing, let me be very direct and reiterate that I do. It would make you uncomfortable knowing *how much* I enjoy spending time with you."

I sneak a glance, and he wears that familiar determined, deadly serious expression.

God, why did he have to go and say the Zane-iest thing he could say?

It only makes him that much more adorable.

And makes me realize I'm really crushing on this guy.

Me, Leif Anderson, crushing on a dude. That's not something I ever imagined.

"I enjoy spending time with you too," I confess.

"Good. Now we should stop talking about this unless you want everyone eyeing me in my gym shorts."

I reach over to the passenger seat and place my hand on his crotch. "It's like you got a steel rod in there," I say, gripping it firmly.

"Okay, that's definitely not gonna make it better."

After enjoying a good laugh, I give his cock space, and fortunately, he's only got a semi when we head into LA Fitness. While I pump weights downstairs, Zane hops on one of the treadmills upstairs, by a rail that gives him a view of the first floor. I'm sure he knows he doesn't need to keep an eye on me while I'm working out. No one's gonna abduct me in broad daylight in the middle of a busy gym, but maybe he can't kick the habit so easily. Or maybe he just likes watching me. Either way, I don't have any complaints.

When I finish my workout, Zane hops off his machine, and we hit the showers, selecting neighboring stalls like we have the past few times we've done this. Not for the first time since we started coming to the gym together, with the stone privacy walls, I think about how easy it'd be for one of us to slip into the other's stall and mess around. But it's a busy day, and there are plenty of guys coming and going. That would be way too bold. But it sure makes me hard.

It seems like I just noticed my erection when the curtain pulls back and a nude Zane comes rushing in, pulling it closed behind him before attacking my mouth and forcing me back against the back wall.

Fuck, his mouth tastes good, and his hand quickly finds my cock, gripping and giving it a few strokes.

But I pull away. "Zane, what the fuck?" I keep my voice low enough that the guys I can hear chatting outside won't hear us.

"I tried to be fucking good, but you make that impossible," he says, still stroking me, displaying a condom and bottle of lube in his free hand.

"Did you plan this?"

"No, but I'm not an idiot; I knew I needed to be prepared if I was gonna be around you while you're all sweaty and huffing and puffing for an hour, and now all these muscles are pumped up. I'm only fucking human, Leif."

The way he ogles my body almost makes me forget that there are people close by who could discover us in here, but only *almost* forget.

"You think you can take my cock without making too much noise?" he whispers, his breath hitting my lips.

That sounds like a challenge.

I should say fuck no. I should push his horny ass away. I should tell him to get back to his fucking stall and leave me the hell alone.

Instead, I say, "Only one way to find out."

18

ZANE

I COULDN'T HELP myself; I'm a greedy fuck.

The past few times we've gone to the gym together, I've had to have the strength of a warrior to restrain myself. I watched him for nearly an hour, getting all worked up and sweaty, having to find ways to distract myself from how hard he was making me, which sure as hell didn't make my jog any easier.

I've thought each time we've showered off that, the way the stone divider at the entrance to the stall is placed, it'd be so easy to get in a fuck without anyone noticing. And as I spin him around, push him up against it, I get to see how right I am.

With his hands up against the wall, his gorgeous ass facing me, my mouth waters. I press my body against his, running my cock up between his ass cheeks. Leaning close to his ear, I whisper, "Stick this ass out for me."

As I roll on the condom, he obeys, though his gaze keeps shifting to the entrance to the stall, like he's expecting someone will catch us.

At this point, I don't give a fuck if someone walks in; Leif's ass is mine.

I lubricate the condom and place the bottle on a cubby in the wall before heading back to him and steadily working the head of my cock inside him.

As his ass devours my shaft, I can't help enjoying how his body welcomes me now. "This isn't like when it was a virgin hole," I whisper against the back of his neck. "Now that your body knows how good it can feel, everything's opening right up for me."

"Jesus, can you keep it the fuck down?" He glances over his shoulder, his expression all worry.

He's right, though. But the idiots laughing outside are too involved in their own shit; I'm sure we could be a lot louder without anyone catching on.

"I'll be good, Leif," I say, sliding in a little farther.

His expression relaxes, his mouth dropping open before his head rolls back.

I keep my movements slow, knowing I'll have to keep this pace throughout; this isn't the place for the kind of ass-clapping sex we usually go for.

As I work up my pace, Leif rests his forearms against the wall. And I speed up as much as I can, carefully ensuring my pelvis doesn't slam against that sexy ass, which is a fucking struggle when I want to give him the kind of pounding he prefers.

I watch as my dick enters him, which has images running through my head that are driving me wild. I lean close to him, whispering, "I keep thinking about what it'd be like to fuck you without this goddamn latex between us." I slide my hand down his back, around to his abs. "I want so bad to come deep inside you. Be the first man to mark you."

He glances over his shoulder again. He looks concerned.

Fuck, great job, you fucking creeper. "Sorry. Not that I would ever want you to do that if you weren't—"

"You think you have to apologize for that?" he asks, a smile sliding across his face.

My dick pulses in him.

His gaze drifts, and I can't tell what he's thinking until he says, "I got tested a few months after my last time, which was a long fucking time ago now. All negatives. And it's only been you after that."

"I'm on PrEP, and I get a full panel regularly. All negative here too."

My thrusts have slowed. Are we really considering this?

I want it so bad, but even though it'd be safe, still feels like we shouldn't.

No. There's no way he'll go for that.

I stop fucking him, waiting for his reply when he walks forward, my dick sliding from him.

Fuck, I ruined it. "We don't have to do anything. I'm sorry I even mentioned—"

He reaches behind him and grabs my shaft, sliding

the condom off my cock, and when I catch the next glance over his shoulder, he wears a mischievous smirk that lets me know I'm a fucking moron.

He places the condom in the nook beside us, then returns to his initial position, even spreading his legs a bit more like he really wants me to get up in there.

Another glance back to me. "What are you waiting for?"

Oh, Leif, you fucking incubus.

I move close to him. This is a bigger conversation than we can easily get away with in a crowded locker room, but still. "We do this," I whisper, "and this ass is mine as long as we're fucking around. That means you don't mess around with other people. I don't mess around with other people. You say the word, and that ends, but I don't fuck around with shit like this."

He leans close and kisses me, then as he pulls back says, "Agreed. Now. Get. Inside. Me."

I chuckle. Nothing's funny, and I can't believe this is happening as I head back behind him.

Despite our serious chat, I'm still stiff as a board, surely because the thought of him taking my load right now is at the forefront of my mind. I put some more lube on before returning to him, pushing my head up against his hole, this time enjoying the sensation of flesh meeting flesh. Once again, his ass welcomes me as I feed it inch by inch until my pelvis is against his ass. I hook my arms around him, tugging his body close to me, and kiss his back gently.

When I was just watching him from next door, this was the kind of experience I would imagine, being buried inside him, our bodies pressed up against each other.

Keeping his body tight against mine, I thrust a few times. He vibrates against me with each greedy thrust as I revel in the sensation of his grip on my cock.

For a moment, the locker room is quiet, and I only hear Leif's heavy breaths.

When the laughter and chatting resume, I whisper, "How does that feel?"

"Shut up. Someone's gonna catch us."

"Tell me how my cock feels in you."

"Amazing," he whispers. "In-fucking-credible."

I snicker against his back as I run my hand down to his cock, stroking. I've still got some lube on my hand, only enough to make him a little slick as I pump him and fuck him.

"Fuck," he says in a low, breathy moan.

"I thought we were supposed to be quiet," I tease. "You thinking about what it'll feel like when I fill you up? Is that what you want?"

"Yes."

"After I come, you want me to keep fucking my cum into you?"

Another low, breathy yes.

I pick up speed, hating how I have to restrain myself to keep from getting that familiar slap from his ass, but knowing the clap of my pelvis hitting the water really won't help right now either.

"You dirty boy," I go on. "Bet you wish someone would come in here just as I'm shooting in you, so they could see how good you are at taking a dick."

His cock pulses in my grip.

"Oh, you like that, don't you? My dirty little Leif."

I notice he hasn't told me to shut the fuck up again, and I'm sure it's because he's enjoying himself too much.

He gasps, louder than he should, before warning me, "I'm close. Faster."

He arches his back, serving me that ass, and I pound him as much as I can manage till I feel his body jerk in a familiar way, his ass gripping my shaft.

He's about to come, and I know how he gets when he climaxes, so as the first sound escapes his lips, I put my free hand over his mouth, letting him call out into it as his cock expands in my hold.

I move my hand around his shaft quickly to catch some of his load, and it's too much for me. The pressure mounts quickly, surging through me, and my body finally slams up against his ass, making a series of claps— I can't help it—as I dump my load inside him.

I pull my cum-soaked hand back and use it to keep from repeatedly slamming against him.

"Did you hear that?" someone says from the locker room.

Fuck.

With my hand still over Leif's mouth, I pull him close, my cock still buried in him. Our bodies are still trembling from our climaxes as we wait in anticipation before the chatting outside continues.

As I sigh, relieved, I pull my hand away from his mouth and he bites my fingers gently, playfully, making me chuckle.

I pull out of him, and he spins around, mouth against mine in no time before he shoves me back against the adjacent wall, his lips offering a series of kisses that feel like a thank-you for the amazing fuck.

My hand gravitates to his ass, and I run my finger down his crack, to his hole, massaging as I feel some of my cum dripping from him.

A smile tugs across my lips. "You are such a good fuck," he whispers against my lips. "I liked it when you had your hand over my mouth like that."

"I bet you did." God, he's fucking naughty. I love it. "But I think you need to finish your shower, you dirty boy. I accomplished my mission."

His forehead creases. "Did you come in here planning to fuck me raw?"

"Nah. I just didn't want you to be able to call it bedroom stuff ever again."

He practically snorts out a laugh, covering his mouth with his hand. Then he presses his forehead against mine, releasing a much softer chuckle.

AFTER I RETURN home from the gym, I can't get that fuck out of my head.

That it was in public.

That he let me fuck him raw.

That he let me breed his tight hole.

As much as I wish I could cling to the experience, it fades too quickly as I start pulling up docs in a folder on my computer desktop. I don't even feel like I chose to pull this shit up, but I was compelled to look at what I've saved on Isaac Tolle.

It's mostly stuff I've collected when I first started looking into him: His online profiles. Photos from his social media accounts. Information from LinkedIn, his professional website, the college website, and various other sources I came across during that period of obsession, including his personal emails.

As I go back through his CV, I'm reading it like there'll be some sort of code embedded into it. Something that will tie everything together, the piece of evidence I'll show Detective Roth and say, *See! I fucking told you!*

By now, I should get that even if this was my 500th time looking at it, it won't be any more fruitful than the 499th. Still, there's a hope that I'm wrong.

Ever since I saw him at the library Leif and Mike

frequented, I've struggled against this gut instinct I have about Isaac's potential involvement in Jason's and my brother's disappearances…and the break-in the night I stopped whoever the hell was in Leif's place.

But as I expected, my brief trek through the information doesn't do anything more than chase away my wonderful afternoon and drag me back into the anxiety-ridden past.

There's no magic *aha!* moment. Nothing clicking into place.

I pull up my browser, heading back to my DMs on Reddit, where I see my last exchanges with Dman281, the mystery guy who posted about the note Mike received before he went missing.

Dman, I need to talk to you.

I just want to have a chat with you about my brother.

Please. You're the only one who knows about this letter, and I have so many questions.

My messages were sent over a series of weeks, but he never responded.

I tell myself that even if he replied, it wouldn't do me any good. Maybe he wouldn't have anything else that could help me. But of course, my imagination has me convinced that he could have that missing piece I need to put it all together. Maybe some damning bit of info about Isaac. Hell, maybe about someone I haven't considered.

Something. *Anything.*

It's a wish, the fantasy of a mind that won't be satisfied, not until I have answers for what happened to Mike.

19

LEIF

Z ANE ARRIVES AT my place early to help me prep for my Thanksgiving Day celebration. As I pull out the oven rack to check the thermometer in the turkey, he stands at the adjacent counter, grating cheese onto a plate for the mac and cheese.

"You think that would disturb Kyra?" he asks, glaring at the turkey. "Seeing a huge-ass bird in the oven?"

"Might make her feel safe since she knows she doesn't have nearly this much meat on her." I push the rack back in and close the oven. "Might cut down on how much she eats, though."

Zane chuckles, and I approach him, inspecting his work. "Yeah, the rest of that'll be plenty. But speed it up. I gotta get you on potato duty after this."

"I like when you boss me around in the kitchen," he says, looking me over.

"Funny because I like when you boss me around in other areas." I squat down and hook my arm around him. As I kiss his neck, my pelvis slides right up against his little ass.

"You're distracting me," he says as I caress his crotch.

"Your cock isn't complaining."

"*You* will be if we start running behind."

"Fair point." I give him a quick lick on his cheek before restraining myself.

"You keep playing dirty like that, and I'm gonna give your ass something to be distracted by."

My cock shifts in my briefs at the promising threat.

"Okay," I say, inspecting the pot of boiling noodles. "We don't have time to fuck around, Z. They're gonna be here in two hours, and we're already running behind."

"I'm making great time for an amateur. You're the temptress trying to lure me into distractions."

"Who the fuck says temptress?" I say with a laugh.

"Sounds like something a temptress might say." He sneaks a glance over his shoulder at me, glaring.

"You better stop being a dork."

"You love when I'm a dork."

"Yeah, but you keep it up, Z, and you're gonna have to stick that dick in me again, and then we'll really be behind." I'd underestimated how long it would take the turkey to cook, and I need the oven for other dishes.

Zane says, "Have I told you you're adorable when you try to act like everything's fine, but you're really stressing out?"

"Honestly, I was thinking you haven't told me how adorable I am today at all."

"I'm saving it for after we stuff ourselves so that you'll let me stuff you." He glances over his shoulder, looking particularly proud of himself for that one.

I don't know why he's in this silly mood, but I fucking can't get enough of it.

As I fetch the potatoes from the pantry, he says, "So you don't know the people your friend Steven invited?"

"No, but he says they're cool. He met them at the rec center. Part of a racquetball group."

"I'm glad you're doing this."

His comment catches me by surprise. "Really? I was thinking, given what you said about small talk and people-ing, this would be a nightmare for you."

"It is, but you aren't like that. Clearly, you're more social. Like how you said you'd make food for a bunch of kids at the dorms. Even just as soon as I came over, I don't know…you seem really excited about having people over and getting to share all this with them."

He's not wrong. "I guess it's making me feel more like my old self, you know?"

"I hear that."

After he finishes up the last bit of the cheese block, I check the thermometer on the turkey again, and we're good to go. So we pull it out and get to work on the other dishes I have lined up before reheating some of the ones I made the night before. When Steven, Ilsa, and Max arrive, we're still a little behind, but they're quick to offer to help set up at the dining room table, and soon, we're enjoying our Thanksgiving meal together.

Since they arrived, I can tell Zane's pushing himself out of his comfort zone as he chats everyone up. I like that he can't stop being himself, fidgeting with his hands or glancing uncomfortably around the room like he's not sure how he's supposed to act. At first, they seem to struggle with his sarcasm, but they catch on fast enough.

As we're sitting, chatting, Ilsa finally asks, "So how long have you and Zane known each other?"

I turn to Zane, who wears a blank expression. Funny because we probably should have considered that we would get asked about how we knew each other.

"Only since last month," I say. "He lives next door, and we hit it off."

"Yeah," Zane adds. "I broke into his house one night, held a gun to him. Pretty much scared the shit out of him, and we haven't been able to stop hanging out ever since."

My mouth hangs open as Max, Ilsa, and Steven burst into laughter.

"Oh my God," Ilsa exclaims. "I love it! Zane, you are too much. Never know what you're gonna come up with next."

"True," I say, "you don't." I turn to him, and he's grinning ear to ear, clearly enjoying the reaction he got by simply stating a truth no one was going to fucking believe.

"So Steven says you were going to GSU," Max says,

"and you took the semester off."

I turn to Zane again, this time for a very different reason.

Steven's eyes widen, and I freeze up before I feel something on my leg. I'm so thrown, it takes me a moment to realize it's Zane's hand. He rubs his thumb along my jeans. Such a simple gesture, but it's like he shot me up with a sedative. "Yeah. I did."

"I'm sorry," Max says, surely because he notices the awkward-ass way I'm answering this. "None of my business really. I'm gonna shut up now." He shoves a forkful of mashed potatoes into his mouth.

"I needed some time off," I say. "Life stuff."

"So what exactly is the goal of racquetball?" Zane pipes up from beside me.

It's a wild transition, but damn, even with everyone's expressions twisting up, I'm appreciative he just saved my ass.

"You don't know how racquetball works?" Ilsa asks.

"I've seen people play it, and like, I know they aren't competing against the wall, but is it like…they're on the same team against the ball? Or are they competing against each other? I've heard of the sport enough you'd think I'd know by this point in my life."

They exchange looks before laughing again.

I'm relieved at how easily that moves the conversation into safer territory as they take turns explaining the rules of racquetball. After my fumble with Max's question, I'm appreciative that Max and Ilsa keep the conversation on lighter topics, since there are certain things in my life I'd rather not get into right now. Fortunately, that doesn't keep us from having a good time. Our guests are generous in their praise for the food, and eventually, they help us clean up before heading out. As soon as I close the door, I turn around, and Zane comes at me, his body forcing me back against the door as his lips smash against mine, tasting of mint.

"Mmm…" he says, "you still taste like that mint chocolate mousse."

I snicker. "Funny. I was thinking the same about you."

He moans as he kisses me again. "I should get a reward for how good I was through that whole thing. Are you proud of me for people-ing?"

"Very proud."

"They helped us clean up, so why don't we head up to bed, and I'll show you how proud I am of the host of the night?" His hands lower to my ass, perking my dick right up.

"I like the sound of that. Then you want to do something really lazy? Maybe watch a movie or something?"

His smile returns. "Yeah, I'd like that."

We head up to my bedroom and don't waste time. Zane grabs the lube, and we get to it. Fuck, the guy knows how to give it to me every damn time. After we come, we shower off together. I brush my teeth, offering him a spare I got at the dentist office on my last visit. I'm already in bed when he finishes up and joins me, wearing only his boxers.

As I scroll through Netflix, I say, "So this is your first night in my room for something other than fucking around. What do you normally watch?"

"Horror. Thrillers."

"Really? Horror? With everything that's going on?"

He shrugs. "I'd rather see someone else's life going to shit than think about my own."

"I guess we deal with stress very differently. I prefer a lighthearted comedy. Will Ferrell. Maybe Seth Rogen."

"Those are such dude movies. Tell me you want to watch *Fast and Furious* movies, and I'll suck you off again right now."

I laugh. "Now you're getting where I'm at."

"Fuck me," he says, tapping the back of his head against the headboard. "You have the most stereotypical straight-man taste ever."

"I like escapist things that'll make me hopeful about the world."

"That shit only makes me feel even worse."

"How didn't I know this about you already?" I ask.

"Like you said earlier tonight, we haven't really known each other that long."

"But I know you pretty well."

He narrows his eyes. "You know my dick pretty well."

I laugh. "Well, I guess I should say I feel like I know a lot about you."

"Don't worry, Leif. We have plenty of time to get to know each other better. Now let's pick a movie. I'm game to try something new tonight. If I get bored, I'll just fall asleep on you."

He cuddles up against me, wrapping his arm around my waist, resting his head on my chest.

A rush of warmth radiates from my chest, pushing out through me. I sling my arm over him, resting my hand on his back.

"Yeah," he says, rubbing his face against my skin, "if I can lie like this, then we can watch whatever the hell you want."

"If you hold me like this, I guess I could try a horror movie."

He angles his head so he's looking up at me. "Aw, that's sweet, Leif. But we don't have to do that. We can watch *Fast 932*."

"Shut up. Those are great movies. But no, no, let's try a horror movie. You know, I never watch that stuff. Could be fun. Let's see…"

I search under Horror and see a familiar title: *It Follows*.

Sounds like it could be kind of safe and dumb, so we watch that. Or I should say, I watch that but Zane falls asleep on me halfway through, not even stirring during the screams, and I realize as he's asleep, with his arms around me, that maybe it's easier for him to get some rest since he doesn't have to be alert from across the street, ready to kick his ass into gear if someone breaks into the house.

He breathes heavily, something that's almost a snore but not quite. I could get used to that sound.

I WAKE WITH Zane's arm and leg still slung over me, securing me in this position on the bed. His body's so warm, like a little heater keeping us cozy under the sheets. I adjust slightly, and it makes him grip me even tighter.

"No," he says. "It's not time to get up yet."

I laugh. "I thought you might have gotten up and left after I fell asleep."

"Someone had to protect you from the scary movie monsters."

"You didn't even watch it."

"Eh, I've seen it already."

"What? Why didn't you say something?"

"I didn't realize until we were like thirty minutes into it. That's why I dozed off." He kisses the back of my neck gently.

"Well, it freaked me out. I actually didn't wake you because I felt like the least you could do was stay."

"You could have just asked. I enjoyed our first

sleepover."

"First? You know my parents will be back."

"And then you can come sleep over at my place. I mean, after all, it does make my job easier. Nobody's gonna touch my Leif if he's in my arms."

"*Your* Leif?"

He offers a gentle tug. "I said it. What are you gonna do about it?"

"Does that make you *my* Zane?"

I feel him smile against my neck, and my cheeks warm. "Depends. Do you want to be my Leif?"

"Yes." I'm surprised by how fast I blurt that out.

"When Ilsa asked if we were friends, I didn't like it when you said yes. Made my chest constrict. And that's when I was like, I don't want to just be friends with this guy."

"So you want to be boyfriends?"

"Nice deduction there." As I chuckle, he says, "You think us being boyfriends is funny?"

I spin toward him, and his hold relaxes so I can face him. His bangs are pressed down against his forehead, his eyes only open slightly.

Zane says, "It'd be easier for me to keep you safe if we were boyfriends."

"Is that why you want to be boyfriends?"

He shakes his head. "Added perk. Looks like I'm gonna need to give you a spare key now."

The warmth in my cheeks practically burns. Why

does something so simple make me feel so damn good?

"I like that," I say, "even if this is the weirdest-ass circumstances for guys to become boyfriends."

He reaches up to my face, strokes his knuckles across my cheek. "Well, we are weird, aren't we?"

"Yeah."

"I'm gonna enjoy getting used to that," he says. "*Oh, I was just talking to my boyfriend. Sorry, I'm busy; I have plans with my boyfriend. Can't do Friday; that's date night with my boyfriend.*"

"My boyfriend's so fucking weird."

"Your boyfriend's so fucking horny." He takes my hand and places it on his crotch.

"Guess your boyfriend's gonna have to do something about that."

And as he grins, I know this is gonna be a fun morning.

20

ZANE

SINCE LEIF'S PARENTS are gone for the week, I wind up staying over more often. It's easy enough since I can bring my laptop and work at his desk. He's got a strict no-guns-in-my-parents'-house rule, which is fair enough, but even without my gun, I'm more relaxed over here than I ever was watching surveillance footage from my place.

I don't think I've ever eaten so much goddamn food in my life, which is an amazing feeling. And we're filling up in other ways too. Lots of BJs, jerking off, and anal that I can get whenever my dick's hard.

Leif sates *all* my appetites.

Then after the final fucks at night, we'll stream something. I'm willing to put up with a few romantic comedies for him, and he's more open to psychological thrillers than straight-up horror, since apparently, I traumatized him with *It Follows*, which he's still got on his mind even after a few days.

Unfortunately, playing house comes to an end when

his parents come back the following week, but Leif doesn't let that stop the sleepovers. Now he's sneaking over to my place for the night.

But during the day, when he's at his parents', all my worries and anxieties are as intense as ever. My life is back to watching footage and cramming in work whenever I can manage. It's the beginning of the second week of December when I get a text from Leif: **So Mom and Dad wanted me to invite you to come over for dinner sometime this week.**

They hadn't mentioned it since they got back, so I was thinking they'd been busy trying to get back to their routine.

LEIF: Does my boyfriend have plans for Wednesday night?

A familiar swirl of warmth in my chest.

I can't help myself—it feels so damn good every time either of us says it.

I've always thought that was such a stupid word: *boyfriend.* Doesn't sound so stupid when Leif calls me it, though. I've never had one, and neither has he. For different reasons, obviously. Him because of the whole thinking he was straight, which is amusing, given the number of times I've come inside him since we started messing around. Me because I'd never met anyone I even considered doing something like that with.

Until Leif.

I was supposed to protect him, not fall for him, but I couldn't help myself. He's too fucking hot. Everything from that sexy-ass smile to those goddamn beanies. And now that I've gotten to know him, I'm greedy for more.

ME: You know damn well your boyfriend doesn't have other plans. I'll be there.

LEIF: Cool. I'll let them know, and see you later tonight. ;)

Of course he's gonna come over again, but hearing him say it excites me. My feelings for him are such a fucking cliché, and I don't give a fuck as long as he's mine.

"So...Zane, tell us about yourself," Leif's dad says as I'm scarfing down Leif's roast.

Eh, not much to know. I'm kind of fucked up, and I've been protecting your son from what I think is a serial abductor, who I'm pretty sure abducted my brother and another guy, but maybe not, because sometimes I have trouble distinguishing between what's real and what's not. Also, I've been fucking your son. A. Lot. Like I don't know if it's normal for a guy to come so many times in one day. And we're now officially an item. Can you pass the brussels sprouts?

I don't say that, of course, but damn if it's not right

on the tip of my tongue.

Something about having so many goddamn secrets has them bubbling up to the surface, and the way I'm stuffing my face like I'm about to go into hibernation makes me think some part of me is trying to keep all those secrets down.

"Not much to know," I say. "Grew up closer to the Snellville area. I'm a freelance IT guy. I do odd jobs here and there."

"It must be expensive renting next door," Ginny says.

"It's pricey, but I do fine. And I cut back on other areas to make it work, you know?"

"Is there a reason you chose this neighborhood? Do you have family nearby?"

"Somewhat. Jill and Todd are about twenty miles from here."

"Are those your parents?" Paul asks, squinting— maybe wondering why I'm using their first names.

"Foster parents. The better ones, so I keep in touch."

"Oh, sorry," Ginny says. "We didn't mean to pry."

"It's all good."

"Well, how have you liked the neighborhood so far?"

"It's great. And Leif's been helping me get to know the area better."

Particularly the area around his ass.

"Can I grab some more of the brussels sprouts real quick?" I ask, and Leif passes them to me.

"So Leif told us you came over when there was that

break-in?" Paul says.

"Yeah. I saw the guy outside, looking around your place, and I called the cops."

True enough.

"We appreciate that. Otherwise they could have taken something or worse."

If only he knew how bad the worse could have been.

"Well, don't worry," I say. "Your son's safe as long as I'm next door." It's like my dumb fucking mouth is desperate to give me away, and as soon as Paul and Ginny react to the odd-ass comment, I say, "I meant, you guys are safe as long as I'm next door. I'll keep an eye on your place, and you guys can keep an eye on mine, right? That's what neighbors are for."

Leif purses his lips.

You find this so fucking funny, don't you?

I'd punish him later by edging him, but I doubt I'll have that kind of self-restraint.

The rest of the dinner goes fine, and I have fewer slips, mainly because I'm wise enough to keep my damned mouth shut.

Afterward, I head back to my place and wait for Leif, who tells his parents he's gonna come over and hang out. We fuck around some before lying in bed. I curl up close to him, his ass gravitating to my pelvis as our bodies lock together like a puzzle.

"Your parents are nice."

"Yeah, I think I'll keep them."

I laugh. "You think they liked me? Or did I come off too weird?"

As he rolls toward me, I pull away to let him face me. "You worried they might not?"

"I don't know. I said some weird shit…"

"You always say weird shit. That's what I like about you."

"You know that makes *you* really weird too, right?"

"I'm getting more comfortable with my weirdness," he says, leaning close and offering a kiss. Gentle, tender. When he pulls away, he adds, "I think they like you."

"I don't think they'd like me if they knew all the bad things I had in mind for you tonight."

"Talk is cheap."

So I show him just how serious I am.

I'M SITTING ON a bench in a long, familiar hallway.

Muffled voices come from nearby—an office along the same wall as the bench.

I look down the hall again, trying to figure out where I am, when suddenly Shelly is standing beside me. She's the social worker who's been working with Mike and me.

She wears an apprehensive expression and makes eye contact as she says, "Zane, I'm sorry, but we won't be able to find a family that can take both you and Mike."

My heart sinks. I knew this would happen; another

social worker had sworn to me we'd already had enough happen to us and that this will work out.

"But we were told we'd be kept together," is all I can think to say.

She bites her lip. "We've done everything we can. We really were hoping, but it's hard to find people to adopt kids your age already. Childcare facilities are packed, so we're lucky if we'll be able to place both of you anyway."

"You won't separate us! No one will separate us!" I shout, pushing to my feet and heading to the office. Somehow I know that's where Mike is. I push it open, but now I'm outside and Shelly is standing in front of me.

Mike's in tears as a man—one of the staff here at the facility—pulls him by his arm. Mike reaches back to me, his eyes wide with terror. "Zane! Zane!"

I start toward him when I feel an arm hook around my waist and pull me back.

"No! Let me go!" I turn to find another staff member. I hit and slap and struggle as he restrains me. "Mike! Mike!"

"I'm so sorry," Shelly says.

In my fit, I realize this is a nightmare.

Because it's already happened.

But even knowing my efforts are in vain, I must give this my all. So that I can, at least in this fantasy, see my brother one more time, talk to him. A desperate part of me will do whatever I need to spend another moment with even a dream version.

"Let me go!" I scream, but I can't break free, and in the

background, I hear Mike crying out, "Zane! Zane!"

As I turn back, expecting to see him being pulled away, he's already gone.

"Let me go!" I plead, but it's like no one hears my screams. No one cares how much I ache. Not even my own mind, which can only be putting me through this to make me suffer once again.

A quick jolt moves through me, and the nightmare is gone.

There's only darkness. My eyelids are heavy as I start to open them. Seeing my desk and computer monitors, my dresser and open closet, I'm reminded I'm not a child anymore. As recollections from the night before filter through, I remember where I am in time—years away from that incident.

Leif and I stayed up later than we should have to watch two movies and part of a series we started a week ago, the night after my dinner with his parents. Usually when I wake, I have my arms securing Leif close, but they're empty, and a surge of fear courses through me.

He's gone.

Someone's taken him.

Adrenaline races through me as I sit up.

I let my guard down, and now he's fucking gone. But as I glance around, I discover him at my side, right where he usually is.

He's here. He's fine. He's safe.

I repeat that mantra as I catch my breath.

My panicked movements weren't subtle, so I'm not surprised when he stirs, his eyes opening. "What is it?"

"Nothing. I scared the shit out of myself. Thought you weren't here."

He smirks. "Was my short king worried about me?"

"Yes," I say without a trace of humor.

He must realize how deadly serious I am because his expression twists into a frown and he props himself up on his elbow. "It's okay. I'm right here."

I relax on my back, and he cuddles up against me, burying his face in my chest.

Between how he's gripping me and his words, my body relaxes. I kiss his head, his hair gently tickling my lips. "Sorry, I had a bad dream, so when I woke up, I was on edge."

"What was it about?"

"It was about when Mike and I were at that children's home. The social worker who promised they'd try to keep us together was there. Even when she first told us, I knew it was bullshit, but I think she was trying to set us at ease after everything that happened. She's the one who let me know about the couple wanting to adopt Mike. I screamed and cried and tried to cause a big fuss, thinking it would make it stop. But crying doesn't stop the world from being shit." It's a fact that weighs heavily on my chest.

"That's horrible." His gentle breath rushes against

my skin.

"It's still rattling me. In the dream, I'm putting up a bigger fight than I did back then. Like really doing what I think I should to keep them from taking him away, but they still do. And there's nothing I can do to stop them."

Leif kisses my chest and gazes up at me, worry in his expression.

"Sorry for waking you," I say. "And good morning."

He kisses near my pec. "You don't have anything to be sorry about," he assures me. "You want me to do something to take the edge off?"

"I don't know how."

I can barely process what he's saying before he crawls down and takes my cock into his mouth.

I figure not even that would do me any good, but Leif knows how to work my dick after all this time we've spent together, and I relax and let him give this to me. It's one of the wonderful perks about our little sleepovers, and it helps distract me from the haunting echoes from the past.

After his quick pre-breakfast swallow, I help him get off, and then we get up, brush our teeth, and take showers. I'm getting a morning shave in when I hear from the bedroom, "Dude, it snowed last night."

"What?" I ask, even though I heard him.

The day before, I'd seen the app on my phone predict snow, but in Georgia, that rarely means snow.

I approach Leif and peek out the blinds. A white

blanket covers my yard, the nearby rooftops suggesting at least half a foot.

"Holy shit," I mutter.

"Mom said we might get an inch, but Jesus."

Despite the heaviness that even Leif's BJ couldn't completely shake, some more of it lifts.

"Looks like we get to have a snow day," I say, drawing him close and kissing his cheek, getting some shaving cream on his face.

21

LEIF

I'M GIDDY LIKE a kid at the prospect of spending a snow day with Zane.

We eat breakfast and brush our teeth again before I head back to my parents'. After I hop into my winter gear, I inflate two pool tubes in the garage and meet Zane in front of his place.

We head to Palamone Park.

A rarity for Wyachet, the snow is nearly as thick over the streets as it is the yards. It's still pretty early, so there are only a few families out building snowmen and engaged in snowball warfare. As we pass the McKendrys' house, their two middle-school-aged boys, Dirk and Cameron, approach their parents' SUV, which their younger brother, Jordan, is hiding behind.

"Help me with this," I say, setting my tube down and scooping up some snow. Zane follows my lead as I pat a ball in my hand, creep up behind the guys, and nail one right in Dirk's coat collar. As he drops his snowball, Zane lands one on Cameron, who spins around and launches his own attack.

"See what happens when you try to sneak up on your brother?" I say.

Zane and I exchange snowballs with them until Jordan is confident enough to come out and join us in our surprise attack.

"This is three against two!" Dirk calls out. "No fair!"

"Now you know how it feels," I reply, and we keep at it until Cameron finally says, "Okay, okay. We get it, Leif."

"Yeah, and if Jordan tells me you try to gang up on him again, we'll be back."

"We'll be good," Dirk says with a guilt-ridden expression that assures me he'll behave. "Now can you help me get this ice off my neck?"

I brush some of it out, and he adjusts his toboggan hat.

Jordan approaches me, eyeing Zane uneasily. "Are you friends with *him*?" Jordan asks, and the way he leans away from Zane and says *him*, it's clear he has some preconceived notions about him, just like I did before I got to know him.

Zane glances at the ground uneasily, and it makes me think of when he was a kid, after all that trauma, and his peers treating him like something was wrong with him because they didn't understand the guy I've come to realize is pretty awesome.

"This is Zane," I tell Jordan. "Zane, this is Dirk,

Cameron, and Jordan. I used to babysit these little troublemakers when I was in high school."

Zane offers a friendly wave and musters as much of a smile as I figure he can manage. I tell the guys to tell their mom hey for me before Zane and I head back to our tubes and continue toward the park.

"So you were a babysitter?" Zane asks once we're out of earshot.

"More like a fill-in for their regular babysitter. I watched them sometimes after their mom divorced their dad. She needed some help, and it's a pretty tight street, so a few of us helped out when we could."

"That's really cool. Although, it's interesting to note that even the kids in this neighborhood think I'm weird."

It reminds me of his reaction to Jordan's remark. "They don't know you like I do," I say, though I can't imagine that helps him much.

"You're sweet, Leif, but it's okay. I didn't get this far in life without being used to people prejudging me."

"Me included," I confess.

"Well, you've more than made up for that." He turns to me, flashing a wry smirk. "I've always told myself most people are shit anyway, so what does it matter? But I must admit, I'm learning that way of thinking gets awfully lonely."

"I feel like I'm supposed to say something supportive and encouraging, but I've still got my own guard up from the way my so-called friends acted when I came back home."

Zane turns to me again, his forehead creasing in that familiar way it does when he's confused.

"Remember when you asked me why I thought anyone would send me that admirer letter as a joke?" I ask, and he nods. "I had a few friends from South Wyachet High...or at least that's what I thought they were. Some went off to other states for college, but we kept up. After I came home, one reached out to see how I was doing. I was vulnerable and needed to talk to someone other than a therapist, so I told them what went down, asking them to keep it between us.

"Shortly after, the group got weird when I messaged. Being short with me. Like I was dead to them, which hey, we're in college now, I figured that was natural. But then I ran into this girl from high school at the mall, outside the Build-A-Bear where she worked. And she randomly started chatting me up about her mental-health issues, which I thought was strange since we didn't know each other that well. Come to find out, she was being so open, she said, because someone from another friend group—not the one I'd told—said I'd lost my mind at GSU."

"That is not cool."

"Right? I don't know what they told her, but she mentioned she was surprised I wasn't doing jail time. So I confronted my so-called friends, and they treated me like I was unhinged because I was pissed about their lies. One of the guys, James, went on Facebook and posted that I was spreading vicious lies about him to people. Tried to act like some kind of hero too. Said he knew I was going through shit, but it didn't excuse bad behavior. It really did a number on me because that was the total opposite of what was going on, and none of the others in our group came to my defense. Then suddenly, I was getting nasty messages from other people from school. Started getting spam, like people were signing me up for shit, and then a few nasty messages from numbers I didn't recognize. It was open season, I guess, since they thought I'd been a dick to their friend. So when I got the letter, I was in a weird headspace. Thought it might be someone who got wind of 'Psycho Leif' and was getting a laugh at my expense to avenge their cool buddy."

As I finish, Zane's quiet before he stops on the side-walk.

I stop too and turn to him. "Do you believe me?"

His head tilts, his forehead tensing. "What?"

I shouldn't have asked that. I should keep my dumb fucking mouth shut, but I can't help myself. Not around him. "I know it's stupid, but even after everything we've shared, part of me fears you heard all that and think I must've been in the wrong. That all those people wouldn't have turned on me otherwise."

He steps toward me, studying my expression. "Get that out of your pretty head. The only thing I was thinking is that maybe I made the right choice by not letting people in." My knee-jerk response is to agree with him, when he adds, "But had I done that, I never would have met you."

As we gaze into each other's eyes, I feel like I can see all the hurt and torment in his soul reflecting the dark times he's shared with me and even those he hasn't. All those things he's put up walls to protect and guard, the very walls he's broken through to share with me.

He reaches out and takes my hand, stroking the back gently, reminding me of the walls I've broken through to share with him, including that story about my ex-friends.

He pries his hand away, glancing at the houses around us. "Guess I shouldn't give the neighborhood gossip mill something to talk about."

"No, I guess you shouldn't," I say, then lurch forward, taking a kiss.

His lips feel better than ever, offering much-needed warmth, and my tongue takes a quick sweep across his before I pull away.

He grins. "This could get back to your parents."

"Maybe it's about time it did," I say, taking his hand and starting down the street.

We've never held hands on a walk like this before, but I like it. Hell, if I'd known it would feel this good, I would've done it sooner.

The park is less than half a mile from our homes, and when we arrive, Zane asks, "Where are all the people? I figured it'd be packed."

"Most everyone around here has their own yards. And there's a huge slope on the other side, near Graham Drive, but there's another hill I like to come to."

I lead him through the entrance, along a path through the trees, across a wooden bridge, to a wide field of untouched snow, carved out from the woods.

It's like something out of another world.

"See what I mean? Come on."

I race across the snow to a hill on the far side of the field. We take turns on our tubes, creating a path to slide down. The grass and weeds under the snow are iced over, which makes it perfect for sledding. Zane and I enjoy a few solo turns before we start getting adventurous and sharing one tube, with Zane sitting in my lap.

Definitely the date-iest thing Zane and I have done since we became boyfriends—wild to think how close we've gotten without ever having an actual fucking date.

On one of our descents, as I'm considering possible dates, we hit a bump in the hill, which lifts us off the ground before the tube slams back down. Something about the reckless play has us both laughing, and I can hardly detect that pain I saw in Zane's expression earlier. It's just a broad grin.

And as he looks back to me, his ass pressed firmly against my crotch, I find myself becoming intrigued.

"What? Why are you looking at me like that?"

I grab his hip, pulling him tighter against me. "This

position has me thinking about something we haven't tried yet."

"Oh really?"

"Seems like you prefer to top, so we don't have to."

"What? Who said that?"

I'm shocked. "I figured if you wanted to bottom for me, you would've mentioned it by now."

"Leif, I would like getting off with you however we did it."

I laugh; it's nice to hear. "I guess I was greedy because I was adjusting to knowing what it felt like, but I'd be curious to try the other way too."

"Just know that I'm not gonna let you make up for lost time all in one night. I think that might kill us both."

I burst into a laugh.

"You can fuck me anytime you want," Zane says, draping his arms around me and planting another kiss.

I wrap my arms around him, pulling him to me. My lips and face welcome his hot breath, my tongue trying to soak up as much of his heat as I can get. Of course, I know it's not only body heat I'm interested in.

I want him.

All of him.

My fucked-up short king.

My Zane.

Here in the snow, it's one of those moments I want to freeze in my mind, hold on to and never let go of. But my desperate wish only reminds me that moments like these are fleeting, and that most of life can't be these magical moments.

22

ZANE

WE SPEND ANOTHER half hour tubing before heading back to my place.

I don't know what's gotten into us—we've spent the day together, but we can't keep our hands to ourselves. Even in the shower, our arms are hooked around one another, our bodies locked together as our lips smack, our tongues teasing.

"Someone's frisky," Leif whispers against my lips.

"Not my fault. I was just chilling on our snow day, and then you said you wanted to fuck me."

Leif grins.

"This position has me thinking about something we haven't tried yet."

He's been so greedy for my cock, and I was so eager to please his ass, I hadn't thought much about it until he said those words. I was totally fine with doing whatever he wanted, but now that he's expressed this desire, it's like my ass can't wait to get my boyfriend inside me.

His hard cock pushes up against my torso, and I grab

it and stroke. Clearly, the idea of fucking me gets him as excited.

"We're never gonna finish this shower like this." I turn off the water and snatch my towel off the rack.

We work together to dry each other off, but it's such a fucking mess, and we're only half dry as we step out of the shower.

"Fuck," I say as desire courses through me, so overwhelming I think I might explode if I don't get Leif inside me.

He glances around. "I should get some lube."

"Jesus fucking Christ," I say, opening the cabinet under the sink and pulling out a bottle of aloe vera gel. I rub a glop on his cock and then give myself some before setting down the bottle and positioning myself with my hands on the counter, facing the mirror.

"Come on, Leif. I wanna see you fuck me like this."

His eyes are wide, his expression locked in a smirk. He runs his hand through his wet bangs, moving behind me. I feel him lining up the head of his dick with my ass.

"Yeah, ease right in there," I tell him, and he pushes.

I curse as he steadily enters, opening me.

Leif's hands gravitate to my hips, one of his hands still wet with the aloe. Some water drips from my bangs and down my face as he slides farther in. He wedges right up against my prostate, like flipping a damn trigger that sends sensation rippling through me.

His gaze meets mine in the mirror. "How's that?" he

asks with an adorable-ass smile.

"Very, very nice." I tremble as the words escape my lips, and Leif takes it as an invitation to push in farther.

I tighten my grip on the counter and push my ass back till I feel my cheeks against his pelvis, enjoying knowing that my man is filling me. I want to satisfy his curiosity. Want to be the best ass he'll ever fucking get. Selfishly want to ruin him for any man who comes after me.

I take deep breaths, allowing myself a moment to relax, but even before I'm fully there, I rock my hips, back and forth, feeling the smooth motion against that sweet spot. As my eyes roll back, I catch him gawking at my expression.

"You like seeing what you're doing to me?" I ask him, making a broader thrust. There's a bit of a bite to it, but I don't mind it.

"It's fucking hot," he says, starting to move with me.

We work together, creating a smooth rhythm between our push and pull. It takes some work to get my ass ready for him, but once we do, he picks up the pace so that with each thrust, a clap echoes through the bathroom.

I revel in the stimulation each time he pounds in, absorbing the shockwave of pleasure that surges through me as I get lost in the sound of those claps and our steadily intensifying breaths.

Leif leans down until his chest's against my back. He

kisses the side of my face, taking my cock in his hand and stroking as he shoves that dick back sharply.

"Fuck, Leif," I call out.

He hits that spot just right again.

And again. And again.

I release the counter and lean back. Leif moves with me so that soon I'm standing. Behind me, he squats down, jerking me while kissing my neck and thrusting deep.

I watch in the mirror as my abs tremble with each thrust, my body a fit of sweet pressure and electric pulses.

"Bet you didn't know I'd be as good a bottom as I am a top," I say, which makes him snicker.

"So conceited," he says right into my ear, the flash of heat tingling at my nerves.

"Damn right," I say. "Here."

He stops thrusting, and I pull off him. He looks surprised, disappointed even. I spin around, lifting myself so I rest my ass on the edge of the counter. Leaning back, I prop myself up so my elbows are on either side of the sink. I raise my legs, displaying myself for him.

"Get that cock over here," I say, and he obeys.

As I figured, he's the right height; this counter was made for us to fuck on.

When he's all the way in, I hook my legs around him. It's not intentional, just like my body isn't willing to let that dick get away. Not now that it's had a taste.

"Give it to me, Leif. Don't hold back."

His eyebrows jump up, like he's fucking impressed. He drills into me, our gazes locked as heat surges through me, rushing to my face. He hooks his arms around my legs, keeping them in place as he fucks me. Each thrust sends me soaring higher and higher. My body buzzes with excitement, and I'm shifting so much that my elbow slips into the sink.

"Fuck," I say, but Leif must've noticed because his arms are under me in no time. He pulls me up, lifts me off the sink and pushes me up against the wall beside the towel rack.

I hook my legs around him for support as he keeps fucking me.

Something about this angle makes him feel like he's getting in even deeper, and each thrust is like he's hitting the trigger to a web of nerves radiating out through my body.

Leif's kisses are wild, a frenzy of licks, sucks, and nibbles. He's out of control, and I fucking love it. As he pants, beads of cool water mixed with warm sweat drip onto my face and chest.

"You gotta come. I'm about to shoot," he warns before nibbling at my neck.

The pressure's so intense. With every slap of our flesh against each other, the urgency becomes that much more unbearable.

"I'm about to blow. Do it," I say, which has Leif

pistoning his hips like he was just waiting for permission. The intensity of his movements, how they strike that spot, is too much for me. I reach for my cock to end my agony, but before I can grab hold of it, my ass grips Leif's cock as white streaks soar from the head, striking my abs. I throw my head back and redirect the hand I was going to jerk off with to his nipple, offering the subtlest of pinches.

Leif delivers a final thrust before I feel him swell inside me.

"That's right," I say, chuckling. "Come inside me, Leif. Come inside your short king."

He gasps for air before snickering with me. I'm not sure if it's from my comment or if it's because he's so stunned by what we just did…and how much he clearly enjoyed it.

He kisses me again, and we cling to each other, thanking one another for the experience with our lips and tongues.

When our mouths part, I rub my nose against his, loving how he's still buried in me. "I think I needed that more than I realized."

With that out of the way, we get back to cleaning off in the shower, and then we turn on a movie. As we lie in bed, with my arms and legs locked around him, his hands gravitate to my ass.

"That was lovely earlier," he says. "Didn't realize my power top would be such a power bottom."

"Now that you opened Pandora's box, you're not gonna be able to stop." I'm not playing either. It's like my prostate was lying dormant, and now that he's woken it, I'm already feeling like I want another go as soon as we recover from that first session.

He beams like he's thinking the same thing. "And I noticed you just took a shower, and you cleaned that hole real good, but you didn't go to the restroom."

"Go to the restroom?" I laugh. "Is that you being discreet?"

"You have me inside you still." His grin expands.

"I wanted to keep it a little longer."

He scoots closer until his leg presses up against mine, then slides his hand down my inner thigh, back behind my balls. His fingers find my hole, which he massages gently.

"And you think *I'm* a pervert?" I say.

He pulls his fingers back to his face and gives a lick before returning them to the same spot. My ass clenches, my cock stiffening.

"Maybe that's one of the things I'm attracted to," he says, his voice lower than usual.

He slides his fingers away and grips my ass cheek, then offers a soft peck against my throat.

Despite the pleasurable experience we just shared, now so far from the afterglow of our fuck, reality creeps back in.

"So," I say, "what you said earlier... Are you really

ready for your parents to find out about us?"

He pulls away, tilting his head. "Why are you asking?"

"It was hot in the moment when we kissed in the neighborhood, but I don't want you to do anything that'll put you on bad terms with your folks. Especially right now."

"I don't think they'll think twice about me going out with a guy."

I chuckle; it's a relief to hear. "But how about when they find out that guy is me?"

"But they like you. I can't imagine they'll have any issues with us seeing each other. Even if they did, they don't get to decide who my boyfriend is."

A vibrating sensation in my belly—that word still has an effect on me.

"Speaking of my boyfriend," he adds, "there was something I was thinking about while we were sledding. You and I never really had a date."

"We've spent plenty of time together."

"No. Like a real, live, I-take-you-out-and-show-the-world-you're-my-man kind of date."

Again with that feeling in my belly.

"I like the sound of that."

"Good, because I was thinking, if the snow clears up enough that they're open, we could hit up the Wyachet Nights of Lights tomorrow night."

"I haven't been."

"Good. We can see the lights, grab some hot chocolate, maybe hop on the Ferris wheel."

"I'd like that," I say, gazing into his beautiful brown eyes.

We make out some more before taking a much-needed nap. About an hour later he returns home, and I start catching up on work, still reveling in the beautiful day we shared, and thinking about tomorrow night.

Throughout the day, it was easy enough to let go and enjoy my time with Leif, but as soon as he leaves, once again, I'm checking out the surveillance feed on the computer monitor, dragged back to the real world, one that isn't only about Leif and me.

One where he's still in harm's way.

I take a sip of coffee, trying to cling to our day, but it seems the more I try to hold on, the faster it escapes.

Guilt courses through me. How can I allow myself to enjoy my time with Leif while my brother's still missing?

He'd want me to be happy, I tell myself, but he'd also want to be found.

23

LEIF

"THE PAELLA IS particularly good tonight," Dad says before taking another bite.

"Thank you. I changed up my saffron-to-paprika ratio."

"Tastes like a success," Mom adds as she blows on a forkful of her paella.

Since I returned home after my day with Zane, I've been trying to create the perfect coming-out opportunity, rehearsing those first words that will come out of my mouth:

Quick question: did either of you ever consider I might be bi?

So...what are your thoughts if I started messing around with guys?

Oh, by the way, I've been fucking around with the neighbor for the past couple of months.

"I know you said you didn't want to go," Mom says,

"but there are still tickets on that cruise, and your dad and I don't mind buying an extra one last minute."

They've booked a Caribbean cruise for Christmas—something Linda will pry them away from over their dead bodies—and I'm glad, but I think they could use some alone time…and really, for the first time in a while, I'm enjoying what I have here.

"I'm good, but I appreciate it."

There's a stretch of silence.

Just get it over with.

"So Zane and I had a good time at the park today," I throw out, gauging their reactions.

"That's good," Dad says. "Were there a lot of people over there?"

"Nah. Pretty much had it to ourselves. Then we went over to his place after."

Mom blows on another forkful of paella. "It's nice you've found someone you can hang out with. And he seems like a very nice guy."

"He is. He's an awesome guy. So awesome, in fact, we're kind of not just friends anymore." That's a weird way of saying that, so I spit it out. "We're boyfriends."

Dad's eyes widen, and Mom swallows her food so quickly, I'm worried she might start choking.

"You're surprised by this?" I ask.

"Well, yes, I'm definitely surprised," Dad says. "Not about you being attracted to guys, but the neighbor?"

"Yeah, you both seem so different," Mom adds.

Their first comments throw me. "Wait, so neither of you is surprised that I'm attracted to men?"

"It's not exactly outside the realm of possibility," Dad replies. "Even when you were little, we had to consider, at least, that you might eventually be attracted to guys and we'd have to help you navigate that."

"Yes, but Zane?" Mom can't seem to let that go.

"He's a really cool guy."

"So you're not going over there to play video games?" Mom asks. "That makes more sense. I guess I was just happy you were getting out and doing something with people again."

"I did suggest that this is what could have been going on," Dad tells Mom.

"What?" she asks. "When?"

"The other night, when I said, *So Leif's going over to play video games with Zane again.*"

"How was that suggesting anything?"

Dad repeats the way he said it; Mom rolls her eyes and says, "Maybe you should be clearer when you're insinuating things."

"Or you could put down your Kindle for five seconds to listen to how I say it." He glares playfully.

Mom chuckles. "I'm sorry, Leif. We're making this about us. Thank you for sharing that."

"Yes, we're glad you felt comfortable saying that. And Zane seems like a nice kid."

"I'm glad you feel that way because I plan on spending more time over at his place."

I'm waiting for them to object, since they must know what Zane and I will be up to, but Dad nods and Mom offers a subtle shrug.

"Is that it?" I ask.

Mom tilts her head. "What do you mean?"

"You're not going to object or ask me if we're being safe?"

"You're living here, but you're not in high school anymore," Dad says. "And we already had those talks with you, so we trust your judgment safety-wise. Unless you had any specific questions we didn't cover."

It's not that I thought they would be dicks about it. Maybe more surprised, given that I, sure as hell, hadn't known this about myself. I guess no one ever knows what to expect with stuff like this.

"You covered everything fine."

"If anything comes up, we're always here," Mom says. "We love you."

"Yes, and we'll always love you, no matter what."

Mom's gaze wavers. "Unless we find out you're a serial murderer or something."

"Or that you're part of some secret hate group," Dad adds. "Or you run for office and try to take rights away from those less privileged than yourself. But other than that, our love is unconditional...with those conditions." He winks, and Mom and I laugh.

I appreciate that they didn't make it this big, heavy

thing. And after dinner, they hug me and tell me again they love me.

I know they do.

And I know I'm lucky to have such cool parents.

JUST AS I'D hoped, the Wyachet Nights of Lights is open the following day, so Zane and I get tickets online before driving over. We get our wristbands and head inside the festival grounds, where they've set up with carnival rides, food trucks, and drink stands.

Zane glances around uneasily, his jaw tense. I know he's not thrilled to be around a bunch of people, but I have a feeling his uneasiness isn't about our date. He's been on edge since I met him last night, after coming out to my parents. He was thrilled about the news, and so damn supportive, but I could tell he was off.

I've tried not to push. Despite what a good time we had yesterday, a good day can't wash away all the bad. But I tell myself we don't have to work that all out right now, and I do the best I can to enjoy our first official date.

We hit some of the rides—classics like the Gravitron, the drop tower, and the bumper cars. Then we grab hot chocolate and head through the Lights Walk.

"Everything okay?" I ask him after he glances over his shoulder.

He finally makes eye contact. "Yeah. Sorry. I keep having this feeling we're being watched. That sounds stupid, doesn't it?"

"It's not stupid," I try to reassure him, and he takes a breath, as if hearing me say that has set him at ease.

"I'm sorry I'm being like this. This is great. Just…I don't know, all that shit with my brother really got on my mind yesterday, after we went to the park. At first it started as a little guilt, but then it got bigger throughout the night. Like it was wrong of me to enjoy myself when he could be…" He stops himself, like he doesn't dare speculate what could be happening to his brother right now.

"Hey, come over here," I say, guiding him off the walk to an empty bench beside an illuminated, human-sized nutcracker decoration.

I take his hand, interlocking our fingers, and his gaze meets mine again.

"I don't want you to be miserable tonight, thinking you have to act cool or together for me. I've felt that with my parents, and it sucks and only makes things worse. It's okay to have a bad night or week. I want you to feel comfortable being yourself, in whatever form that may take."

He studies my expression, then snickers. "It's hard for me to imagine I ever did anything good enough to deserve a boyfriend like you."

I lean toward him. "Maybe you're just that lucky," I

tease before stealing a kiss. He doesn't resist, accepting my lips, then my tongue. I expected it to be quick, but soon, our faces are pushed up against each other's, my cheeks appreciating the much-needed heat.

When I pull away, I'm practically humming with pleasure, when I hear, "Leif?"

The hairs on my neck and arms stand on end. I turn to see James in jeans and a leather jacket approaching with Avi, Lex, and Steph. The old gang, all back together, without me. It shouldn't surprise me. They're all home from college for winter break, and this is a big event around town.

James approaches until he's about a yard from me, sizing me up.

In one hand, I'm still gripping Zane's; in the other, I tighten my hold on my hot chocolate, trying to keep from crushing it as I think about the fucked-up way James turned his social media followers against me.

While James looks me in the eyes, everyone else is searching around, like they want to enjoy their night out, not confront an ex-friend.

"Good to see you again," he says.

"Is it?" I ask.

He winces. "Wow. Here I was coming to give you a chance to apologize, but—"

"Apologize? *Me?*"

"You accused me of talking shit to everyone about what happened to you."

"I didn't accuse you specifically, James, but based on how you're acting, I guess I should have." My cheeks are on fire as my rage intensifies.

James releases a nervous chuckle, the sort that confirms what I already know. "Figured not much has changed. You know, if you were trying to figure things out with your sexuality or whatever, I get it, but that's not a reason to take it out on all of us."

"What?" I ask.

Zane's grip tenses against mine, like he's as pissed as I am…or maybe trying to keep himself next to me rather than going after James for being such a fucking asshole.

"I get it," James says. "My cousin got all weird and went a little crazy when he was struggling with being gay."

Now my chest is hot. Although, it shouldn't surprise me that James would thoughtlessly throw around the word *crazy* without considering how offensive it is to others around him.

How was I ever friends with this guy?

"I was struggling with shit, and you knew that, but it didn't have anything to do with my sexuality, and clearly, none of you were my friends to begin with because at least one of you knows I'm not the asshole here." I try to make eye contact with Avi, but he avoids my gaze.

James releases another nervous chuckle. "Fine. Be a dick." He spins around and starts off, the others following him. Steph and Avi glance over their shoulders. I can read the guilt all over their expressions.

I take a breath before turning to Zane, whose jaw is clenched as he stares forward, like he's about to chase after them and hunt them down one by one.

"Hey," I say. He shakes out of his state and turns to me.

"They were your fucking friends?"

"Yup."

"Well, at least you made it clear they needed to fuck off."

"Yeah. But it does make me sad. I mean, there was some problematic shit before, but friends have issues and hit rough patches. At least that's what I thought it was, but now that I saw Steph and Avi…they looked like they didn't want to go along with James, but they knew he'd be a dick if they didn't. He used to say dumb shit, and I'd let him get away with it, but if he'd tried back then to turn all of us on a friend like that, I would've spoken up. I would have told everyone what they were doing was wrong."

"Those guys who hang with him are cowards," he says through his teeth.

"Only wish I'd known that sooner, you know?"

His grip on my hand relaxes, but then he firms it slightly. "I'm sorry you had to run into them tonight."

"It was bound to happen sooner or later. Not that big of a city. Now can we pretend that didn't happen and enjoy the rest of our night? As much as we can, at least."

"Hey," he says. "Keep in mind what you told me before those assholes showed up. We don't have to pretend to be okay with each other. We don't have to pretend we're fine tonight. Let's be not-fine together."

A smile tugs at my lips.

He moves toward me, and I eagerly accept another kiss before we continue our stroll along the Lights Walk. Neither of us pretends things are fine. We don't act like nothing's wrong. Like we're not hurting. We go through the walk, holding each other's hand, carrying our pain and hurt.

There's relief in not feeling the need to pretend that allows me to enjoy the walk and the Ferris wheel more than I would have if I'd needed to perform, to appear like I was having a fine time.

We don't talk much. We don't need to.

It's nice to feel like this and know I'm not as alone as I once was.

When we finish, we head back to my car, and as I slide into the driver's seat, Zane reaches over and takes my hand. "Thanks for tonight. It was nice."

"It wasn't what I was expecting, for sure, but I enjoyed spending it with you."

He offers a warm, soothing smile. "Now how about we get back to my place and fuck away some of this bullshit?" he asks, leaning toward me.

"I like the sound of that."

As I'm about to kiss him, a buzzing sound catches me by surprise. It comes again and again as he pulls his phone out of his pocket.

He looks at the name on the screen before eyeing me strangely. "It's my foster mom. Do you mind if I—"

"No, please. Take it."

"Hey, Jill?" he says, not disguising his confusion. "Everything okay?"

"Have you seen the news?" I hear her say.

"No, I haven't."

"I think you should check. It's about Mike…"

Tension rises within me as his gaze catches mine. An adrenaline kick, a surge of hope. But from what I can make of Jill's voice, I know it's misguided. If he was found alive, she'd have told him. The hope turns to fear, anticipating the news she's about to share.

24

ZANE

BODY DISCOVERED NEAR WYACHET DAM LINKED
TO RECENT DISAPPEARANCES

A source close to the Wyachet Police Department
revealed to the Gwinnett Daily Post *that a body
discovered not far from Wyachet Dam is believed to
be one of the missing local men from the past year.*

*Though the department refuses to discuss details
of the case until a DNA test confirms their suspicions, the* Post's *source says the remains are believed
to be Michael Grayson, who went missing last
March.*

*Lead Detective Clarissa Roth is expected to give
a press conference about the DNA test results at 10
a.m. tomorrow morning when she will discuss the
department's investigation further.*

Here I was worried about this paranoia I was experiencing—feeling as though eyes were boring into me from
behind on our walk. But now it's not some imagined

phantom I have to fear, but reality.

A series of scenes play through my mind.

I try to imagine the state Mike's body was in when they found him.

Was he rotting away, or was his body intact, having been disposed of recently?

The images in my head aren't helped by all the horror movies I've watched. Vivid, graphic depictions of Mike plague my thoughts until my mind shifts focus back to when we were kids. We're in the family room, laughing and playing video games together. He's eating Cap'n Crunch, flashing a smile after getting a taste. Then there's one much later, as I hold him and tears slide down our faces. *"Don't worry. I'll take care of you,"* I say.

I'm a fucking liar.

I expect I'm about to explode into a fit of rage, grief, agony, but I don't even feel connected to my body. There's a numbness, like after Mom and Dad died.

Like I can't accept this is true.

"Zane? Zane?" Leif's voice sounds distant, like I'm not sitting beside him in the car but like I'm standing outside it.

After Jill alerted me to the news, I got off the phone with her to look up the headlines on my phone. Said I'd call her back, then frantically googled and found that article.

"What is it? Talk to me," Leif says, but I can't tell him this. How could I even get the words out?

I pass him my phone, and as he reads the article, I'm transported back to the day when Shelly and those fuckers from the CPS tore us apart.

My mind leaps forward again, to an image my mind's crafted of a body shoved back into a sewer line. Discarded like my brother wasn't even human.

He didn't do this to himself. I fucking knew it.

But there's no relief in the thought, and it's as though all the pain finally catches up with me.

My chest constricts, my body trembles.

"Detective Roth hasn't reached out to you?" Leif asks.

"No." With all that's on my mind, it wasn't something I'd even considered, but now that he's mentioned it, I can name the emotion that overtakes me: rage.

Considering how much we talked early in the investigation, she should have given me a heads-up. And if she fucking knows it's my brother and hasn't told me, fuck her!

"It doesn't say it's him for sure," Leif says. "It sounds like a guess."

"It's not a guess," I snap. "A source from inside the department leaked that, so they know more than is even on the damn page."

I didn't mean to practically shout the words at him.

"Fuck, I'm so sorry, Leif."

"Zane, you don't owe me an apology for that," he says, looking far more disturbed by my apology than when I shouted. "I can't imagine what reading this is like."

I press my hand against the window and grip the seat with my other.

Why's the car fucking spinning?

Tears push to my eyes.

All those images seizing my mind have stopped, but it's like I'm holding them behind a wall that's about to burst. I open the car door and lean out, my body going through the motions like I'm about to hurl, but I only manage to dry heave.

I don't know what happens next—it's like a fucking blackout, and soon I'm on the ground, shaking, light-headed.

"Zane! Zane, don't leave me!" I hear Mike call out, but I know it's too late.

When I finally shake free of the memory, I find Leif at my side; he must've gotten out of the car at some point.

"Zane, are you okay? Please talk to me."

His words reorient me, and I glance around, trying to make sense of everything that happened, when there's a familiar buzzing sound. Leif pulls out my phone.

Jill must be calling back, but I can't talk to her now.

Not about this.

Leif says, "It's Detective Roth. Do you want to take it?"

As it buzzes in his hand again, I can't...I don't want

to hear. Don't want to know.

But I reach forward and take the phone, answering it.

Just get it over with.

"Why the hell didn't you tell me?" I ask.

Getting my anger out is cathartic, feels like the only thing that's keeping me from losing my goddamn mind.

"Zane, I'm so sorry. It's not Mike, though. We know that."

My hand trembles so much, I nearly drop the phone, but instead, I fall back against the asphalt.

Thank. Fucking. God.

As tears well in my eyes, I finally manage, "Roth, what the fuck is going on?"

LEIF AND I sit in the reception area at the station.

I'm still reeling in emotion.

My grief has flared up along with my anger, but it's all muddled in a confusing mix after my chat over the phone with Detective Roth.

"Come to the station. I'll explain everything. It's not Mike."

Even after hearing those words, it's not enough to console me, and I can tell Leif's on edge as he sits, scrolling through his phone.

Along with the other emotions that have taken over my body, there's the guilt that I just ruined what was a lovely date with my boyfriend.

"I'm sorry," I tell him.

He looks up from his phone. "You don't have to keep apologizing."

Do I keep apologizing? I barely remember how we even got to the station, so maybe I have.

"This is a big deal," he adds. "It's okay to be worked up."

There's a *click* of heels, and Roth rounds the corner, running her hand through her bangs before catching my eye. Her gaze shifts, and she notices Leif.

A part of me is like, *Fuck*, but with what I went through at the Nights of Lights, I don't really give a damn.

"I'm gonna see if I can bring you with us," I tell Leif, then approach her and ask.

Her gaze wavers. "Zane, no. Not for this. And I think we need to have a chat."

I turn back to Leif, shaking my head, and he nods.

Roth doesn't say more. She guides me through the building until we're in her office. But the moment she shuts the door, she lays into me, "What the hell is going on, Zane?"

"I'm freaking the fuck out right now, that's what's going on."

She paces toward her desk, then spins back around to me.

"I need to know what makes you so confident that

body isn't my brother."

"Do you think I'm an idiot? I've met that kid. And I know why you really reached out to him, so what is he doing in my office?"

"That kid is my boyfriend."

She puts her hand to her forehead. "Why do I feel a migraine coming on?"

Fine by me after the stress she put me through.

"Roth, my brother," I press.

She searches around the room, like she's sifting through so many thoughts that she doesn't know what to address first.

"Couldn't have given me a heads-up?" I ask, hoping she'll focus on why I'm here.

"I was told it wasn't going to print until tomorrow. I thought I had time. But apparently, someone in the department wanted this information out, for whatever messed-up reason, and now here we are."

"But there's still a body you thought at some point might be Mike, which for all I know right now *is* Mike."

She closes her eyes and takes a measured breath. "When we found the body, there were identifying features that lined up with Jason Kilbourne, not your brother, which is why I didn't reach out. We've been waiting for confirmation."

"Then why the hell didn't you let me know right then? I told you that case was connected."

"Can you just sit down? You standing there is stressing me out."

I don't feel like fucking sitting, but I accept that making her comfortable is the best way of getting more details from her. After my ass hits the cushion of the chair in front of her desk, she says, "I want to remind you before I tell you what happened that I never had an obligation to tell you anything. Everything I shared with you before was because I saw a grieving kid who was trying to find his missing brother. And I sympathized. I knew I should have had more boundaries. I shouldn't have entertained your visits as much as I did, but I cared, and I realized that I enabled you."

"Do we have to get into what you and your therapist have been chatting about?"

"I'm only trying to let you know that even right now, what I'm about to tell you, I tell you because I under-stand why you're distressed."

"You don't understand."

"You're not the only one who's ever lost someone, Zane," she snaps, and that shuts me up. "There's a reason I chose this job, and just because I don't talk about it doesn't mean I haven't had my own shit to deal with."

I quiet.

In all the times I've spoken with her, she's never mentioned this.

She shakes her head. "Over the weekend, a hunter's dog came across the body along the shore of a creek not far from the dam. It was weighted with rope and cinder blocks. From what the coroner has been able to make out, the state of the body suggests it was submerged for at least a couple of months. There was a storm last week that we think caused enough of a stir in the creek to shift part of the body out of the rope so that it surfaced.

"Because of how much of the body had decomposed by this point, we knew it'd be hard to get a positive ID off just that. A skeletal and dental examination suggested the age we were looking at was right for Jason Kilbourne and Mike."

"That couldn't have been enough for you to think it might be them, though."

Her gaze wavers. "While searching the area, we discovered ashes nearby. Among them, there was a bit of plastic, and one of the officers on the scene recognized the style because it reminded him of his son's WCC student ID."

Fuck.

"The body didn't have any wisdom teeth," she says quickly, as if trying to chase away my concern. But that's not fucking happening. "Kilbourne's records show he'd already had his removed, but Mike didn't, which ruled out Mike to my satisfaction. I didn't broadcast this information around the department because in the past we've had an issue with leaks from people with political motivations. Given the nature of the crime, we didn't want anything out until we knew what we were looking at."

It's hard to miss how she said that last part. "What do you mean by *nature of the crime?*"

She breaks eye contact. "I'm not getting into those details with you, Zane. You can follow the news, same as everyone else. The only reason I mentioned any of this is because our attempts at discretion around this are what caused the confusion. Inadvertently done by one of my colleagues, in an effort to obfuscate the truth and keep anything from being made public early. That's how this mess came about. And I'm sorry for that."

Her apology sounds sincere, but... "I know you mean that, but it doesn't change how it felt to see that article pop up on my phone."

She gulps. "I know. But because of the nature of the crime, and the fact that we knew we were on the verge of a media frenzy, we managed to rush the genetic testing, and they confirmed what we already knew. It's Kilbourne, not Mike. And the moment I was notified about the post, I called you. I really thought we only had to keep it together for another day."

In some ways, it's easier to breathe knowing the *Gwinnett Daily Post* got it wrong. But now I have very different worries.

That maybe they just haven't found his body yet.

Or maybe he's being held captive by a man who plans to kill him.

Nothing good.

"Well, I appreciate you telling me now," I say, since I owe her that much. "Do you have any leads?" I press.

"That's not your concern."

"What do you mean that's not my concern?" Now I'm back to being pissed.

"I'm not letting you Hardy Boy your way around this again."

"Have you checked if Isaac Tolle has a connection to the place where the body was found? Maybe he used to work around there? He'd need to know the area to feel like he could dump a body without getting caught."

"As I already said, I'm not getting into this with you." She steps around her desk, as if using it as a physical boundary to make a point. As she settles in her chair, she says, "Now that we've gotten all that out of the way, there's something else I'm interested in discussing. Something you've avoided since you stepped in here. Why are you dating the kid who was in my office a couple of months back, who told me you approached him about your brother's case and a letter he'd received?"

"Well, look at where we are now. There's a body. Someone did something with it. Doesn't this mean there's a possible serial killer who also took Mike, who's maybe keeping him alive somewhere so that they can do this to him?" As soon as the words escape my lips, I feel like shit. Because a part of me can't believe he's being held anywhere. A part of me knows that he's—

No, I can't think that! I have to have hope. For him.

"Zane," Roth says, her tone much gentler than when she brought up Leif. "I know a lot of civilians have this impression that there are serial killers running the country because of this obsession with true crime, but really, serial killers are so rare. You know how many people go missing? You know how many non-white people have gone missing in this town without making the news? Children being abducted by parents who can't get custody. Senior citizens with dementia wandering off. People with drug problems who wind up in other states but can't bring themselves to reach out to their families. Right now, we have two disappearances of guys around the same age, who happened to attend the same community college."

"That sounds like more than chance."

"It's a college. If it were more than five thousand students, no one would think twice about it. The reality is, this likely got started on campus by kids who grew up on a diet of YouTube and podcasts and who have nothing better to do with their time. And not to belabor the point, but Leif doesn't go to WCC. And so far, only one body has shown up. Even if we had another, we don't jump to the conclusion that there's a serial killer without evidence linking the crimes. Even with what you claimed before, there's nothing to suggest that in a world where I believed a note was sent to your brother by the same person who sent something to Leif, that this in any way connects to Jason. You get that, right?"

The way she says it, she's like a teacher trying to see if I grasped the content of her lesson, which is like a poker stirring my rage.

"Are you asking because you think I'm seeing some pattern that isn't there? That maybe I'm predisposed to see that because of my mental-health issues?"

She raises her hands. "I didn't say anything about that. I was talking to you, one reasonable person to another, asking you to draw a reasonable conclusion. Put yourself in my shoes. Even if I wanted to, at this point, now that the case has been elevated to a homicide investigation, I'm not calling the shots on my own. If I have a lead, it's gotta be compelling. I have to justify every action I take to a team, and also to the politicians we rely on for funding."

For the first time since this chat began, I can appreciate that she's not trying to make my life difficult. She has her own series of obstacles and politics to navigate.

Sucks, but I get it.

"Zane, I know you can only see this system from your perspective, but do you know how many people come in here with theories about how a loved one died? I've had people accuse their parents, siblings, the neighbor, the guy who works at the deli… Sometimes they don't even have a suspect, only leads they think are relevant from five years ago. You'd think with how long I've been doing this work, I would've known better than to follow your leads back when you first came into my office, but you know what? Maybe I have the same biases as other people. Maybe I thought it'd be like a movie where we cracked the case and I brought some relief to a guy who'd gone through a horrible tragedy."

"Because you felt sorry for me."

She hesitates before responding. "I *sympathized* with you, and I wanted to believe you were right. So remember that I'm the one who felt betrayed by what went down. I went out on a limb for you once already. I'm not making that mistake again."

I imagine it'd sting less if she wasn't right.

"As for you and Mr. Anderson," she says, "if you are boyfriends, I hope it's for the right reasons and not—"

"What is that supposed to mean?" I practically bark out.

Her eyes widen and her head jerks back. "I think you know what I meant. I hope you actually have feelings for him and aren't trying to use being near him to play amateur sleuth."

"I care about him. A lot."

"Good. I'm glad to hear that, Zane. I think we've discussed everything we needed to, unless you have any questions."

"No, you've been perfectly clear." I push to my feet. "Thanks for the heads-up." I can't help my sarcastic remark as I start for the door, but I'm seething. And not just because of my panic earlier, but because even with a body on her hands, Roth doesn't buy my story.

Even worse, I hate that I understand why.

As I reach the door, Roth says, "Oh, and, Zane."

I stop and glance over my shoulder.

"A lot will come out in the next few days about Jason Kilbourne's death. I hope you can focus on your new relationship and not get hung up on the details."

"Meaning?"

"I don't think it would be a good time to let your imagination get carried away."

"Thanks for the hot tip," I spit out as I grab the door handle and pull.

Locked.

Fuck. So much for my grand exit.

"You know I have to escort you out of here, right?" She pushes to her feet.

"Yeah. I remember."

Although clearly, in my fury, I forgot.

25

LEIF

"A s the media reported," Detective Roth begins—

Zane asked me if I would stay at his place through her press conference the morning after we went to the police station, so we sit in bed with the omelets I fixed for breakfast.

Detective Roth stands at a podium with several uniformed officers and people in suits as she addresses the crowd of reporters. "…a body, later identified as Jason Kilbourne, was found yesterday around seven thirty a.m. on a property approximately five miles from the Wyachet Dam. When our team arrived on the scene, we discovered a body submerged in a creek with ropes and cinder blocks attached, clearly a deliberate attempt to conceal the body. That said, what was a missing-persons case has become a homicide investigation. Some of the inquiries I've received recently have pertained to who will oversee the case. After several internal meetings, it was agreed that homicide lieutenant Malcom Berkley and I will collaborate from this point forward. As some of you already know, I have experience in the homicide unit, and with our expertise, we hope our joint efforts will help us find justice for Jason Kilbourne and his family."

"It's all such bullshit," Zane snaps at the TV.

He's been pissed since talking to Roth. There's been so much shit for him to process, I can't imagine what's going on in his head.

He fucking thought his brother's body had been found. And though he was relieved that wasn't the case, after his meeting with Roth, he was on edge. And I'm on edge too. If he's right about the connection between Jason, Mike, and me, and that the guy who was in my parents' house is a serial killer, that could have been my fate too.

I remind myself we don't know who was at the house that night, but it's a thought I can't help but entertain.

When Detective Roth finishes speaking, Detective Berkley takes to the podium, offering assurances about his new role on the case. Zane hangs on his every word.

"At this time," Detective Berkley says, "given the condition of the body when it was discovered, forensics is continuing to search for viable DNA samples to help identify persons of interest, but it's still early days on that front, and we are eager to provide the public with answers as they become available to us. If anyone has any information, please don't hesitate to call the local department number..."

"Should I give them a call?" Zane huffs.

There's humor in his tone, but pain too.

I set my hand on his thigh, rubbing gently. He places his on top of mine.

When the press conference comes to an end, we set our plates on the nightstand, and he curls up against me, nestling his face into my chest. I just hold my Zane, hating that I can't do more.

"When I saw that article last night," he says, "I really thought it had to be him. As excruciating as it was to believe, it was a relief to have an answer. And to know that meant he wasn't suffering. But then when I found out that wasn't the case, God, I felt so damn guilty. Like I was wishing my brother dead."

It's a haunting statement, a glimpse into another way Zane can turn the blame on himself for his brother's disappearance.

"Please tell me you know that's not what you were doing," I say.

"Death just seems preferable to some of the other thoughts I have about what might have happened to Jason before his death."

His arm tightens around me, and he pulls me close. There's warmth against my chest, and it takes me a moment to realize it's a tear.

Oh, my poor Zane.

I slide my hand over the back of his head, running my fingers through his soft hair.

"Why is the world so fucked up?" he asks.

"I don't know, Zane."

He offers a gentle peck against my chest.

His words make me think about his dark childhood. His and his brother's lives. Everything he's had to deal with around his mental health.

How much is a person supposed to bear in this life?

"What do you have going on today?" he asks.

"I need to get home and check on Kyra. And I was gonna take her to the animal rescue clinic. She's still not even attempting to fly."

"Maybe it's too cold out. She doesn't want you to set her loose so she can freeze to death."

I laugh. "The vet said she'll be fine unless it's below freezing. And I won't just kick her out. I need to know that her wings are getting better. I can't imagine she wants to spend her life all cooped up in that cage."

"You're a good bird daddy. But ask your parents if they'll check on her, and go to the animal rescue center tomorrow. Stay in bed with me today. I'll keep you safe right here."

He tightens his hold even more, and though I know this has more to do with his brother than me, I can't deny how safe I feel in his arms.

After half an hour, he finally relaxes his hold, and while he checks on the news articles about Jason, I get out of bed and take our dishes downstairs.

Zane brushes his teeth and showers up first, and then

I do the same. When I finish washing shampoo out of my hair, I hear, "Leif, Leif!" coming from the bedroom.

Tension rises within me.

Did he read something about Jason? No, he doesn't sound upset. Almost…excited? What the fuck is that about?

He draws the shower curtain. His eyes are wide, and he looks me over as though it's the first time he's seen me naked.

"Fuck, I'm feeling guilty for not violating you this morning."

He's changed. This isn't the guy who was so full of melancholy all morning. He's more like his usual self, but I can't make out why.

"What's up?" I ask.

"I got a message from Dman281."

I remember the name from when he was explaining how he'd wound up in my parents' place, but it hasn't come up since.

"The guy who was on that subreddit. He reached out this morning." He turns to his phone and reads: "'Hey, man. Sorry I didn't see these. Just caught the news about Kilbourne, which made me check this account. If you want to talk some more, maybe we could meet up.'"

"What are you gonna tell him?"

"Hell yes I want to meet up with him." He must read the concern in my expression because he says, "I'm not assuming this is magically going to solve all my problems, Leif. But I must do fucking *something*. I can't lie around this place and sulk. And who knows? He could know something the police don't yet. They never followed up with him since Roth thought I made up the damn account myself. I'm gonna see if he's free today."

"I get that. I'm more concerned about you meeting a stranger from some online forum. But as long as I'm invited to tag along, I'm fine with that."

He smirks. "My boyfriend coming along to keep me safe?"

"You've worked so hard to protect me; it's time I return the favor."

Despite being playful about it, I'm dead serious. I'm not letting my boyfriend meet some online rando who might be more of a psycho than Jason Kilbourne's killer.

Zane's smirk expands into a grin, and he leans over the side of the tub. "I think that sweet comment deserves a kiss."

I lean toward him, and he takes my lips. He jerks away briefly, setting his phone on top of the toilet before seizing my lips once again.

I feel him pushing forward as he takes steps toward me. "Zane, what the hell?" I ask as he steps into the shower with me, water racing down his body, soaking his sweatpants. But he doesn't stop kissing.

I welcome the fresh taste of Listerine on his tongue as his hands probe my body, gravitating to my ass.

It's clear this news has cheered him up. And I'm

happy to see him so frisky, but I'm worried too. This Dman guy might not have any answers for Zane, and it's entirely possible that after we chat with him, Zane will be just as sad as he was this morning.

But I accept it's not something I can control; the best I can do is take advantage of this moment with him.

He urges me to spin around and pushes me up against the wall. In no time, his cock is sliding between my ass cheeks. As he nibbles and bites at my shoulder blades, I enjoy the way he humps my ass with his fat cock.

"I want to fuck you right now," he says. "Can I fuck you, Leif?"

"At this point, I'll be pissed if you get out of this shower without fucking me."

He snickers as he grabs a bottle of lube off the caddy, which we've used for a few fucks since we started messing around at his place.

AFTER WE FUCK around, Zane coordinates with Dman.

"He wants to meet at Caribou Coffee by campus," he tells me as I'm throwing some clothes on.

"That works. And it gives us time to swing Kyra by the animal rescue clinic."

Zane fucking beams before throwing his phone on the mattress. He tackles me with another kiss again. He's so fucking frisky all the way to the clinic, probably even having a hard time keeping his hands to himself when we're with the vet.

"She looks healthy," Dr. Minh says, "so you've done an excellent job caring for her."

She has Kyra in a towel as she moves one wing about carefully, then the other. "She has good range of motion, but there could be a soft-tissue injury from the initial attack. Or it could have hurt for a while, and now she's nervous about moving it and feeling the same pain. But I'll run an X-ray to see if we're missing something. It won't detect soft-tissue damage, but it'll let me know if there's anything mechanical that's gone wrong."

"Thank you."

"Maybe she needs some more time. If you broke your leg, you might be done for a bit and be reluctant to move around on it, even after it's better. I personally don't believe in rushing these things. Nature has a way of doing everything it needs to on its own time."

"I get that."

"But you've done an incredible job. Maybe hold on to her for a few more weeks. If she's still not showing any interest in flying, bring her back in for another checkup."

Dr. Minh heads off to do the X-ray, leaving Zane and me in the examination room. I take a seat in a chair along the wall.

"You feel better?" Zane asks.

"What?"

"About Kyra? I can tell it's been stressing you out that she hasn't taken off yet."

"I guess I'm impatient."

"Well, you heard what the doc said. She just needs some time." He rests his hand on my shoulder, rubbing with his thumb. "I think you of all people would know what that's like."

I know what he's getting at. Maybe it's one of the reasons I've taken to Kyra. Because we have that in common—still wounded in our own ways. Seem fine, but not quite ready to throw ourselves into the real world.

He plops down in the chair beside mine.

"Thank you for coming with me."

"Of course. If you'd told me you wanted me to come sooner, you know I would've been here. That's what boyfriends are for."

He leans close and offers a kiss. I accept it, but I'm tense, on edge, and he must notice because when he pulls away, he says, "What's wrong?"

We haven't been together long enough for him to read me this well.

"Just nervous about meeting Dman."

"You don't have to come."

"That's not what I meant. We don't know who this guy is. Have you considered that he could be connected to all this and trying to see if anyone was suspicious?"

"I have. But it'd be stupid to leave a digital trail.

Still…yeah. We're gonna be cautious. That's why we're meeting him at Caribou Coffee, not in some dark alley. He already knows who we both are, since I mentioned I'm Mike's brother when I first reached out, and when he replied, he already said he'd seen your post. So it's not like we're safe just by not meeting up with him. And if anything feels weird or off, we bail. Deal?"

"Deal," I say.

It doesn't shake all my worries, but the only thing I know for sure is that, no matter what happens, I'm here for Zane.

26

ZANE

AFTER OUR VISIT to animal rescue, Leif and I take Kyra to his parents' place before heading out to meet with Dman.

Leif said he's nervous about meeting with a stranger, which fair enough, but I know there's more to it than that. I'm sure he's worried for the same reason I am—that this guy won't have the answers I'm so desperate for.

I tell myself I'll be fine if that's the case, but it's a lie.

When we get to the coffeehouse, we enter through push doors. The place isn't far from campus, and it's fairly busy. For the most part, the patrons are kids in their late teens, early twenties. There's a large, decorated tree, and snowflake ornaments and other seasonal paraphernalia are strung about the place as a pop Christmas song plays overhead. Dman said he'd come to us, so he must know what I look like—from my brother's social media accounts, I'm guessing.

No one's looking up or moving from their seats, so he's probably not here yet. We order our drinks. I go for

289

a black coffee, and Leif adorably orders a hot chocolate with whipped cream. Then we head to the other end, where the pickup counter is.

"A hot chocolate?" I say, quirking my brow.

"Don't give me shit about that. It's all Christmasy right now. I couldn't help myself."

"It's adorable, so I wouldn't dare give you shit."

He scans the room, something he's done a few times since we arrived. "What do you think he looks like?"

"My brother was quiet and distant. Played a lot of video games, so I'm thinking he'll be a gamer with hair down to his shoulders because he's too busy playing *Call of Duty* to get to a barber. Maybe a beard with crumbs in it."

Leif laughs. "Okay, I was being serious."

"We'll know soon enough. Although, if he's as introverted as my bro, he might be a no-show."

It's a thought I've tried to push to the back of my mind. If he doesn't come, that might be the thing to break me.

When the barista sets our drinks down, we grab them before I hear, "Zane? Leif?"

I turn to see a six-foot-something man approaching. High cheekbones, a jawline that looks chiseled from stone, his biceps and chest filling out the thermal he wears. The fluorescent lights shine on his hair, which I would call dirty blond, but seems like a crime to say there's anything dirty about this man who looks like a model.

His face twists up, and he glances between us. "It's me. Dman." As he says it, I realize I'm staring as he looks at me with bright, baby-blue eyes.

"*You're* Dman?" I ask.

"It's Wes," he says with a charming-ass wink before looking between Leif and me. "Aren't you two a pair of cuties? Will you grab us a booth while I order? Think we need privacy for this."

"Sure, totally," Leif says.

As Wes heads to the register, I sneak a glance at Leif, whose lips are pressed together like he's trying to suppress a smile.

"Yeah, the guy's a real introvert," he says. "Surprised he made it out, for sure."

"Shut it," I say through my teeth.

Leif and I grab a booth.

I was nervous before, but now my hands are shaking, and surely this caffeine won't help in that department.

I try some of Leif's hot chocolate and regret giving him hell about the whipped cream because that's some good shit. When Wes slides into the seat across from us, I scoot closer to Leif. I'm sure it's because I feel threatened by this hunk across from us.

"What?" Wes asks. "Why are you looking at me like that?"

"I think because of how we met, I was figuring you'd be this dorky internet geek. Not that there would have been anything wrong with that, but—"

"You weren't expecting me to be this hot?" he asks, his smile distracting from the cocky remark.

"Um…maybe," I confess.

"Fair enough. First off, I want to say I'm so sorry about everything that's going on around Mike. I can't imagine what you're going through. And sorry I didn't get back to you before. That wasn't my usual Reddit account. Wasn't something I wanted linked to my other shit, you know? And it kept getting inundated with requests from podcasters and TikTokers, so I stopped looking at it after a while. Wasn't until I saw the press conference being tweeted about that I checked again. Even more requests, but then I see this one from a guy claiming to be Mike's bro, and I was like, the hell?"

"I appreciate you got to it at all."

He glances between us. "You guys are a lot cuter than the pics I've seen of you online."

"You looked at Leif's?"

"I checked out his profile when I got that reply on the subreddit, so I already knew what he looked like, but I pulled it back up when you said he'd be coming with you. And obviously, I've seen you on Mike's Insta."

So I was right.

"We didn't have that same advantage," Leif points out.

"Probably for the best. All my socials link to my OnlyFans, so you'd have gotten to know me way better than I would've gotten to know you."

Wes just gets more and more interesting by the second.

"But if y'all want to see…" he goes on.

"We're good," I say.

Leif turns to me, not even attempting to disguise his smile as he rests his hand on my thigh. I'm waiting for him to call out my jealous streak, but he offers a gentle rub of his thumb, and damned if that doesn't offer the reassurance I need.

"But enough about me," Wes says. "We should get to the point of why you wanted to meet up."

"You said you were friendly with my brother."

His gaze wavers. "Eh, he'd come over and we'd smoke a joint or take an edible…and stuff."

And stuff?

Holy fuck. Not that I'd never considered my brother might have been queer too, but is this how I'm going to find out?

"Wait. You and my bro were hooking up?"

"What the hell?" Wes asks. "That's what you thought I meant when I said *stuff*? No. We played *Fortnite* together. You know your bro's straight, right? But trust me, if he'd let me, I would have let that guy do whatever the hell he wanted to me. But speaking of…you guys are sitting awfully close. I figured when you said you were bringing Leif that it was only because of the note on the subreddit, and maybe my instincts are totally off, but is there more here?"

"We're boyfriends," Leif says. It's nice hearing him claim me like this in front of a stranger, especially one that, frankly, I'm intimidated by. This guy is way more in Leif's league, and I'm enough of a creeper without sitting near fucking Adonis.

Wes's eyes widen, a smile sweeping across his face. "Wait. Okay, there's a story here. So I assume you didn't know each other before any of this?"

"No," I say. "We met…" As the details come to mind, I realize this is going to distract from what I actually want to get. "You know, maybe we can get to the stuff about my bro and then tell you about our fucked-up meet-cute."

"He held me up at gunpoint," Leif pipes up.

Wes winces. "That a joke?"

"It wasn't funny at the time."

Wes cringes, like he's not sure what to think, before his smile returns. "You guys are weird. I like it. Are you exclusive, or are you open to—"

"Closed as closed can be," I spit out, surprising my-self. Some knee-jerk response to make it clear Leif is mine.

And *only* mine.

"Ooh, a challenge?" Wes says with a wink, making something flare deep within me, before he adds, "I'm teasing you, man. Sorry. I forget you guys don't really know me, so it's hard to get my sense of humor."

"Trust me. I know the feeling."

Leif chuckles, which makes me think of that first discussion, when he was still adjusting to my sarcasm.

"So you hung out with Mike some," Leif says, "but you weren't friends?"

"We were both taking what was supposed to be a basic graphic-design class, and the teacher was kicking our ass. Nothing brings people together like a crappy teacher. So we'd study a little. Then chill and drink, get high, play video games. He was easy to talk to. We both had weird stuff in our childhood. Oh shit. Maybe that's not stuff I should be bringing up." He glances between Leif and me again.

"It's fine," I say. "I've talked to Leif about how we grew up."

"I was raised in a New Agey religious group," Wes continues. "I figure most people would call it a cult. Didn't get out until I was in my teens and went to live with my mom, so both Mike and I had daddy issues to bond over. Long story short, even though we didn't get into the details much about our experiences, he felt like a kindred spirit."

"And he told you about a note he received?" Leif asks.

"One day, after we ate some brownies and were play-ing *Fortnite*, he mentioned this weird-ass letter he got. He thought it might have been from me, but I don't write weird-ass notes when I'm into someone. But when we were talking about all this, it was just a funny thing. I didn't think much of it.

"Then he went missing like a month later, and that rattled around in my brain. And people were already talking on campus about how Jason Kilbourne had disappeared a year before that, so I thought there might be a connection. The cops didn't seem all that interested in my vague recollection about a note. I told them what I remembered, but they didn't, like, document it or ask me to write it down."

"Why did you go to a Reddit forum to post about the note?" I ask. "You could have reached out to me."

"That was before Leif's note popped up, so at the time, I assumed if there had been anything to what I told the cops, they would've told you. And if it was nothing, I would have felt like an ass for planting this wild theory in your head when you must've been worried enough as it was."

That makes sense.

"What about after you saw my note?" Leif asks.

"After the Reddit account got inundated with requests for interviews from around the country, I let it go. I didn't know there was another note until I got a call from Detective Roth. She mentioned the possibility that the note in the response was a copycat trying to get some attention online."

Meanwhile, she'd led me to believe she hadn't followed up on his post, but now I figure she was trying to keep me out of it because of my bad behavior.

"I think it's my fault she didn't take you seriously," I confess.

"Why would that be your fault?"

"I fucked up, and I think she probably followed up on what you said about the note initially because of me. But afterward, she might have thought I'd talked you into writing it."

"That would be a strange thing for someone to do."

"I did a strange thing," I say. "But that's a separate, long-ass story."

"Whatever happened, after talking with that detective about my post, I tried to move on with my life and forget about it. Then I saw the news, and it got my head back in it. And when I checked my account, I was shocked to see a PM from someone claiming to be Mike's brother. Now I wish I'd reached out to you, that I'd trusted my gut about there being some connection."

His comment reflects my feelings around my gut instinct about Isaac Tolle. And how much time I've spent trying to talk myself out of something that feels like it's burned into my fucking soul.

"So once you told Mike the note wasn't from you, did he say anything about who else it might have been from?"

Wes shakes his head. "At first when he brought it up, I didn't even think he was being serious. And then he just changed the subject."

"Did he ever mention a teacher helping him with his essays?"

Wes's gaze drifts, and he bites his bottom lip. "That's not ringing any bells."

"Isaac Tolle?"

His eyes widen, and a rush of adrenaline shoots through me.

There it is!

A flare of hope.

But as quickly as Wes's expression came to life, it twists up. "Oh, wait. No. I'm thinking of Isaac Clarke from the *Dead Space* series. Sorry."

Fuck.

An emotional sucker punch.

Nearly as quickly as my hope returned, it vanishes, and I'm left with a hollow feeling in my chest.

I sneak a glance at Leif. The way he's looking at me, he knows how disappointed I am.

"He's a teacher at the community college," Leif explains. "Maybe Mike didn't say the name, but did he mention anything about an English professor he met up with on campus? Or maybe at the Chelsby Hill Library?"

I can tell Leif's grasping at straws.

Wes takes another moment, but this time, his expression doesn't change. He shakes his head. "I take it you think this Tolle guy is involved, but what's the library got to do with anything?"

"Just somewhere I've seen him, and it's a library

Mike frequented," I explain, leaving it there.

"None of that rings any bells. A lot of teachers at that school. I barely know mine. And like I told you before, we didn't hang out too much, and besides the crap we talked about for that graphic-design class, school wasn't exactly at the top of our list of things to talk about."

Maybe Mike never mentioned him, but they went to the same school, so Wes might recognize him. I pull up Isaac's picture, the one I showed Leif. After I pass it to Wes, he studies it for a few moments before shrugging. "Maybe I've seen him around campus. He looks like an average, fortysomething white guy, you know?"

"Yeah." I can't disguise the disappointment in my tone.

"You think this guy might have had something to do with his disappearance?"

I tell him what I found in my brother's planner, and my subsequent interest in him. How I had suspicions when I joined him at Habitat for Humanity, and that led to my unhealthy obsession. I don't get into the details of just how bad it got, but I make it clear that Roth didn't find anything down that path.

"Yeah, you're right," he says, "that doesn't sound like much."

After everything we've discussed, I'm starting to lose hope that I'm going to get anything out of this exchange, but I try to hold on a little longer. "Any chance you noticed if Mike was acting strange or different before he went missing?"

He shakes his head. I'm really losing hope.

"Is there anything else you might have found note-worthy?"

"Nah, man. I wish I did, but that note was really the only thing that stood out to me."

"What about Jason?" Leif asks. "Did you have any interactions with him?"

"You don't miss a face like that, but we never had any classes together or talked. I saw him on Grindr, messaged him once, but he didn't message back. I took some screenshots of his profile pics because he's a hot motherfucker. I think I still have those… Haven't even looked because I took them not too long before he went missing."

And with those words, he's deflated the last of my hope.

AFTER WE FINISH our chat, Wes says he plans to stick around a bit longer to see what he can find on Grindr. Leif heads to the restroom, and I take our drinks to the trash bin near the front of the coffeehouse, where a line has gathered along the lengthy stretch of counter between me and the entrance. The place was busy when we arrived, but now it's packed.

My disappointment is starting to settle in, a hollowness in my gut.

Although I'm glad we chatted with Wes, I'd hoped for some clue that might illuminate something about Mike, something that would help me figure out what happened to him. But I don't know much more than before we came here.

While Leif's in the restroom, I figure I'll check the news on my phone, and as I'm about to retrieve it from my back pocket, something draws my gaze. Through a gap in the line at the counter, I notice a man in a hoodie leaving the coffeehouse, and as he turns, I catch his profile.

I'm sure I recognize the nose and jawline.

Isaac Tolle?

But it's only a flash of part of his face before one of the patrons in line moves slightly, obscuring my view.

By the time I reposition, he's gone. Only the door swinging closed.

It was so fucking quick, I couldn't get a good look. Was that him?

I'm all instinct as I head toward the entrance, frustrated with every person I have to say "Excuse me" to.

Isaac works around here; he could have just been swinging by, like the day I found him at the library. But wouldn't that be a hell of a coincidence for him to be here the day I chat with Wes about Mike? He sure as fuck never came here when I was following him.

Outside, I search around, first for Isaac, then, when I

don't see him, for his Toyota Corolla. No sign of either.

I notice a guy in a hoodie getting into his car. He pulls off his hood before he gets in, and it's definitely not Isaac.

Was this the guy I saw?

No, it was Isaac. It had to be.

I rush to either side of the building, checking the lot, but still no sign. At the pace he was moving, he wouldn't have been able to get away fast enough to evade me. Although, he could have seen me too and bolted. But he had to have parked somewhere.

Unless he was here to spy on us.

The image of his face is burned into my fucking brain. It reminds me of when I was in my manic state, seeing his face in places where I knew he couldn't have been.

This felt different, though. Real.

It felt real then too…didn't it?

Fuck. I'm shaking, and I know it's because I fear the worst.

"Zane?" I hear, and I turn to see Leif jogging toward me.

"There you are. I wondered where you went." As he approaches, he stops in place, studying my face. "What's wrong?"

"Wrong? Nothing," I say, still searching around.

Wouldn't he be out here if I'd really seen him? Or is he hiding somewhere?

Or is that what I'd tell myself even if it was just in my head, to justify the delusion?

"You look so pale," Leif says. "Let's get in the car and get you warmed up."

"Yeah, that sounds good."

I try to act normal, but that's fucking useless since my mind's playing on loop that moment when I could've sworn I saw Isaac.

But what if I didn't? What if I'm having another episode?

27

LEIF

THAT WAS SO surreal, sitting in a coffeehouse, talking to a guy about Zane's missing brother. Like what happened the night we first met, it resembled something out of a movie, not the kind of thing I'd ever expected to deal with in real life.

Just as I feared, Wes didn't add any clarity around what happened with Mike, and it's not something Zane can magically recover from.

But that doesn't explain his bizarre behavior in the coffeehouse parking lot.

He wasn't himself. And he kept looking around, like he'd seen someone or something, but when I pressed, he wouldn't explain. It's what's on my mind all the way back to his place, as we sit in silence, listening to Christmas songs.

I won't push. Give him some time to digest everything. He'll let me know when he's ready to talk about whatever's on his mind.

He finishes up some work at his desk while I get

ready for bed. Then he moves through his nighttime routine before joining me in only his boxers. Wrapping an arm around me, he pulls me close.

I'm still worried about pressing, but I want him to know I'm here for him. "How you holding up?"

"I'm so fucking stupid," he whispers, his breath rushing against my chest. He angles his head so he can look up at me. "I really thought we were gonna head in there and hear something that would make everything click into place. Then I'd be off with another lead that would help me piece it all together. But life doesn't fucking work like that."

Tears glisten in his eyes, and he turns away. Breaks my heart to see him like this.

"Zane, there's nothing wrong with wishing you had answers."

He takes my hand and places it on my abs, interlocking our fingers.

"As disappointed as I am, I'm glad you were there. Thank you for coming. It would have been a lot harder without you. Even some of those questions, I was like, *Damn, I should have thought of that sooner.*"

"Happy to help."

"You do more than that," he says so softly, I'm not even sure he meant to say it out loud. "I didn't love that he was so fucking hot, though," he adds. "I thought you might backtrack and go home with him."

I laugh.

Even though I sensed some jealousy in my short king at the coffeehouse, I don't imagine this is his biggest concern. Figure he just wants to lighten the mood from all the heaviness we had to work through with Wes.

"He's definitely a pretty man," I say, which earns a glare. "But he's no Zane."

His expression softens again.

"Anyway," I say, "you like guys too. I could be just as jealous."

"But you're not." He says that with such certainty.

"What makes you say that?"

He releases my hand and repositions so he's on his knees, straddling my leg, his hands pressed down on either side of me. He leans close, staring directly into my eyes. "Because you know I'm all yours," he whispers, his breath slamming into my lips, the familiar scent of mint from his mouthwash tingling at my nose.

I didn't even realize how tense I was until his words and expression send a rush of relief through me. It's like someone just pumped me with a sedative as a swirl of sensation radiates from my chest outward.

"If you don't fucking know it, then you should." He leans even closer, tilting his head and licking across my lips. Instinctively, I open my mouth, and his tongue enters before I feel his lips crush down against mine.

My arms hook around him as I pull him so he's pressed up against me. He's right here, his body tight against mine, his tongue as far back as it can get, but it's not close enough; it never fucking is.

As we keep kissing, I don't even feel human anymore. We're a series of breaths, wet kisses, and gentle nibbles.

Zane finally breaks away from my lips, his mouth igniting sparks in each spot he kisses as he trails across my cheek to my ear. "I want you to fuck me tonight, Leif," he whispers into my ear before kissing right beside it. The sensation shoots right through me. "It's all too much for me, Leif. Fuck me until I forget about everything but how much I need your cock in me. Fuck me so that even when my mind tries to wander, it'll keep coming back to the pleasure you're giving me. Fuck me until we don't even remember who we are." His lips return to mine.

"I...don't know...if that will work," I say between kisses, and he pulls away, frowning. "But no harm in trying."

His familiar smirk returns, something mischievous in his expression before he attacks me with another kiss.

These kisses remind me of those early fucks, when we were clawing at each other's bodies, rushing toward the end so that nothing could take it from us, as though the experience were water and we were dying of thirst.

We're a bit of a mess as we work together to get him out of his boxers and me out of a pair of pajama bottoms. Then he scrambles to get lube from the nightstand before straddling my waist again.

He lubes me up, my cock hardening in his grip.

There's an intensity in his expression as he lines my cock up with his hole, navigating me inside.

He's tighter than usual; I'm certain it's the stress of our conversation with Wes. It's been weighing so heavily on him since we left the coffeehouse.

He rests his ass on my cock, his expression straining. "Fuck," he mutters.

I rub my hand against his thigh. "Hey, I'm right here. No rush, Zane."

"No, I need this," he says, urging himself back farther, cursing again before taking deep, steady breaths.

"Jesus Christ, is it this hard to take me?" he asks, which makes me chuckle.

"Come on. You're just stressed. Come down here and give your boyfriend a kiss."

I'm far enough in that I stay lodged inside him as he leans down, hooking his arms under mine so we can exchange a series of sloppy, wet kisses. As his body relaxes against me, his ass opens up.

"Fuck," he moans into my mouth as he takes me farther back, though this time I hear the satisfaction in his curse.

"You make me feel as big as you."

As he laughs, he opens up even more.

"Yeah, right there," he says, assuring me I've hit the spot.

He leans back up, his eyes sealed shut as he takes me

in fully, till his ass is resting on my pelvis. He settles into his position, opening his eyes again and gazing down at me with a crooked smile. He pushes up from his knees, then steadily lowers himself.

I start to thrust, and he sets his hand on my abs. "No, not yet. Let me do this for you." He rocks his hips, sliding up and down my shaft. Between how tight he already is and the way he's clenching his ass as he moves, he's fucking driving my dick wild.

He rests his palms against the mattress, on either side of my legs, and leans back. "Let me know if it's uncomfortable," he says. He's got my cock angled toward him slightly as he continues rocking his hips.

Now I'm the one cursing as I watch his ass work me.

"That's perfect," I tell him, and he grins, rolling his eyes as he keeps up his movements.

Just enjoying himself.

And he's torturing my cock, the pressure building each time his ass clamps down against my hips.

"Fuck me now," he whispers.

I prop myself up on my elbows and offer a thrust, then another.

He mirrors each thrust, pushing with me, and soon we're in sync, working ourselves into a frenzied heat.

I can't stand being this far from him, so I sit up and hook my arms around him. He leans forward, and I pull him down with me and roll so he's beneath me.

"Yes, Leif. This ass is all yours. *I'm* all yours."

I give him my everything, thrusting like a fucking machine, staring at his face as he rolls his head side to side. I revel in it, enjoying the steady climb my own body is going through as his ass works my shaft. I love knowing I'm responsible for his relief, that I've taken him from all the darkness that crept up on him from our meeting with Wes.

As we fuck, I feel Zane relaxing as I serve him the pleasure he doesn't even realize he deserves. We're a collision of pulsing bodies, breath, and emotion, every change of position a part of some dance, our rhythm so coordinated that it's like this moment is fated.

I'm lost in full appreciation of his body, and soon, I'm fucking him from behind, Zane on his knees, my arms wrapped around him as I watch his ass tremble with each thrust.

"Kiss me," I demand, and he turns his head toward me, giving it to me.

As much as I love how he usually takes charge, I equally enjoy calling the shots, especially when I know he wants to let go.

As I continue fucking him, he arches his back farther, surrendering himself to me.

He lowers his arm; we're so in tune that I know he's going to jerk himself off, so I say, "No."

His eyes open, his expression full of worry. "I don't know how much longer I can keep from—"

I take his cock in my hand. "Let me."

His eyes seal back shut, and I drill him, stroking his shaft.

He reaches his hand up, rests it against my head as I bury my face against his neck, licking and nibbling as he calls out.

His eyes pop open, his mouth agape, and I see the moment, a flash, like he's lost in pleasure, the sort of moment where he looks free from the darkness of the past, from pain. Caught up as he rolls his head back. My hips piston, the urgency in me seizing control, the pressure climbing, and I feel his cock stiffen in that familiar way, sliding my palm up to feel his warm cum as he shoots.

Staring at his expression as he's caught up in the moment is too much for me, and it's only a few more thrusts before I'm finished. It's explosive as my body crashes against his, my hips urging me to persist, as though my body wants to make sure every drop gets inside.

Zane grips the back of my head and pulls me in for another kiss.

I press my cum-filled hand against his waist and tug him close with the other.

I want to stay like this, lost in this moment, buried within him.

And as we pull away, catching our breath, I realize that for an instant, I forgot.

About all the bullshit.

All the pain.

The relief in Zane's tone as he whispers, "Thank you," assures me he did too.

That for even the briefest amount of time, we could escape it all and have this moment with each other.

We recover from the experience and wipe up before returning to bed. We curl up together, interlocking our legs, arms around each other for a few more kisses.

When we pull away, Zane strokes my arm gently. "That was exactly what I needed. Thank you for giving me that."

"I should be thanking you."

His gaze lowers to the sheets. "Leif, I need to tell you something."

Between his body language and the way he says it, I'm sure this is what he's been keeping from me since our chat with Wes.

"At the coffeehouse, when you were in the restroom, I headed to the front area by the register. I noticed someone leaving… I don't even know that it was a full second that I saw them, but…it was Isaac. I saw him. At least, I feel like I did."

"Did you?"

"I don't know. That's why I was outside when you came out. I tried to follow him, but when I went out there, I looked for him, for his car, and nothing."

As his body trembles against mine, tension rises within me. I think about what he told me—about experiencing mania while he was trying to make sense of his brother's disappearance. About how he kept seeing Isaac in places he couldn't have been.

"Are you okay?" I ask.

He tears up. "It doesn't feel like it did when it was like that before, but I don't know what I'm gonna do if that's happening again. I'm scared, Leif." He pulls me close for a hug, burying his face against me, and I feel a tear against my shoulder. "What if I'm losing it again?"

It wrecks my heart, reminds me of my own darkness. "If that's what's happening, then we'll figure it out, Zane," I say without even thinking. "You and me. Together."

"I don't want to do that to you. I don't want to put you through my bullshit."

"If I was having a hard time, what if I told you I didn't want to put you through that?"

He chuckles. "I wouldn't let you out of my fucking sight."

Is it messed up how safe his words make me feel? Probably, but I don't give a fuck.

"Then now you know how I feel," I say.

He pulls away, his eyes red, a little wet underneath. I kiss right under one of his eyes, then the other.

"What if I need to go to the ER?" he asks.

"Then I'll drive you. Visit you. Be there to pick you up. And be here to bug you when your health insurance fucks up and you have to call to get them to cover your meds. And to give you a BJ every time you get too stressed."

His smile returns, but another tear streaks from his eyes. "Fuck it," he says, wiping at it.

Then there's another tear.

I'm waiting for him to hide them from me, out of pride, but he doesn't. He studies my face for a moment before his gaze meets mine. "Leif, I lost the people I cared about most. And losing Mike…I thought that was going to kill me. Makes me think it's a stupid idea to get close to anyone. And like, the dumbest thing I've ever done was get close to you."

He sounds almost angry with himself as he says that last bit, and an uneasy sensation stirs in my chest. Why would he say that? Did I go too far? Is he about to push me away?

"Zane…"

He kisses me again, and between the kiss and how he's holding me, I assure myself my fears are irrational.

When he pulls away, he goes on. "What I'm saying is, I don't think I should have gotten this close to you, but now it's too fucking late. I've lost enough people in my life to know that you can't wait around to say the things you have to say, so I'm just going to say it."

He looks me dead in the eyes. The last time he looked this serious was the night we met. "I love you, Leif."

That sensation, like I've been pumped with a sedative, comes again. Those words make me feel so at ease, so at peace, as though I've been waiting to hear them all my life.

From him.

He rushes on. "I don't need you to feel it yet. In fact, it's probably best if you don't feel that way about me. I'd never ask you to pretend you do when you don't, but I need you to know…" He takes my hand and sets it on his chest. "My heart belongs to you. *I* belong to you."

Considering how guarded Zane was from the moment I met him, it's shocking to hear these confessions.

With one hand still on his chest, I place the other against his cheek. "Zane, of all the things I could have expected to come into my life, you definitely weren't it. My little creeper next door."

His expression finally relaxes, his lips curling into a smirk.

"But whatever brought you here, I'm glad you're here now. And I do love—"

"I don't want you to say it because I said it," Zane blurts out.

"I'm not saying it because you said it. I'm saying it because after the past months, I can't imagine not having your creeper face in my life." I take his hand and place it on my chest. "I love you too. And I'm not accepting your heart unless you take mine."

"That sounds like a threat."

"It is."

He leans close for a kiss. As he pulls away, he says, "Now who's being the bossy one?"

We're both smiling, but then his expression turns serious again. "Leif, what am I gonna do?"

It reminds me of how quiet he was on the trip home. How much he's being tortured by what happened at Caribou Coffee.

"You don't have to figure it all out tonight," I say. "That I know for sure."

He trails his hand down my chest, to my navel, and as I follow it, I notice he's hard again. His hand travels around my hip to my ass.

"I have an idea what I could do instead," he says. "Now that I know, I think there's something else I'd like to belong to me right now. If you're ready again, that is."

I snicker as I roll onto my stomach, displaying my ass for him. "That's yours too," I say.

A wide grin overtakes his face.

And he doesn't hesitate to claim what belongs to him.

28

ZANE

LEIF SETTLES AT my kitchen table in the chair adjacent to mine. He's shirtless, his beanie on as he pours syrup over his waffles.

"I love you too."

I replay that moment over and over again in my mind, as Leif gazed into my eyes, not hesitating or holding back. I didn't need him to feel the same for me as I do for him, but it sure feels fucking good.

I cut another section out of my waffles, already doused in butter and syrup, and fork them into my mouth. Damn, that feels fucking good too.

"How are you feeling this morning?" he asks, setting the dispenser between us.

There's worry in his expression. Understandably so.

Amazing as last night was—being able to forget about all the bullshit for a few sweet moments— eventually we had to come back to reality.

To a world without my brother.

A world where, for all I know, he's being tortured

and about to endure the same fate as Jason Kilbourne…if he hasn't already.

A world where I might be slipping again.

"Before you woke up this morning, I pulled up my files on Isaac Tolle," I confess. "And on Jason and Mike. It's like I'm waiting for something to click…some instinct to connect dots a part of me is trying to put together, that my conscious mind hasn't sorted through yet. But…" I hesitate, but I remind myself of what he told me last night: *If that's what's happening, then we'll figure it out, Zane. You and me. Together.*

I haven't let people in; I tell myself it's for a good reason, but for the first time in so long, I'm not on my own. Even if it's true and I didn't really see Isaac last night. Even if I need help, I don't have to be so scared. That doesn't make the anxiety or fear vanish, but it takes some of the weight off. Rather than being lost in panic, as I was last night, I can think this through.

"It's the kind of thing I would have done when I was having a manic episode." I won't lie to him; I trust him to help me know what's real and what's not.

"Okay," he says with a nod. "That makes sense. It's understandable, given what you thought you saw last night."

"*Thought* being the operative word."

That memory of seeing Isaac at the entrance has played so much in my head that I even see details I couldn't have noticed before. The dark hoodie was one

I'd seen him in before. A familiar lock of his dark hair.

My phone buzzes, and it's a text from Wes.

Then another.

And another.

"The hell?" I reach over and open the messages. They're images of Jason Kilbourne. In cute poses in a tee and jeans, sitting on his bed.

"What is it?" Leif asks.

"Some of the screenshots Wes took of Jason's Grindr profile."

Wes sends a follow-up message:

It didn't hit me until I was looking at these after our chat, but Leif had mentioned something about a library where Mike and that teacher would go. I noticed these books in Jason's photos. Don't know if that's where they're from, but figured you'd want to see.

I look at the images, noticing the books on his nightstand, which look like they have library tags on the corners.

Nice catch, Wes.

I show Leif the messages, which he assesses. "Aren't those from Chelsby Hill?"

I shrug. "Any library, I guess. I would assume the one on campus, though."

"Could be from a public library in some other part of town, but Chelsby has yellow tags on fiction books.

WCC's tags are different."

"How would you know that?"

"I mean, you don't have to be a student to check out books there. Even at Georgia State, you only have to show an ID to get in. I was over there when I was going through a hard time, checked out books for reading. I remember they had cream-colored tags."

So Jason went to that same library too?

"Isn't that *The Brothers Karamazov?*" Leif asks, his expression curious.

"What?"

"That's Dostoevsky. That quote you borrowed from Tolle's professional website? I recognized the author when you said *Crime and Punishment.*"

I zoom in, confirming the author and title on the book.

"Zane, he said he took these screenshots right before Jason disappeared."

"I remember."

He hesitates. "Are you sure you didn't see Tolle last night?"

"You think I haven't been trying to work that out all night?" I say through my teeth, but then take a breath. "Sorry. That's not directed at you."

He takes my wrist. Instinctively, I raise it to my face and gently kiss the back of his hand.

This only makes last night even more confusing. "If it was Isaac, when I went outside the coffeehouse, he should have been there."

"But you said he was turning to you, so it's not impossible he might have seen you and run off."

"Not impossible, no. And though I didn't see his car there, what if he'd parked at one of the other stores around?"

"That's possible."

"I followed him enough before, when things got bad… Caribou Coffee was not one of his usual spots. That could have changed, but if that's true, why was he leaving right after we finished up with Wes? And why would he need to run? To leave right after…that's awfully coincidental. I keep thinking maybe he was there to see if Wes was gonna tell us something that would expose him."

"That makes sense. He wouldn't have known what Wes knew," Leif says, "just like we didn't, so maybe he was worried since Wes was the guy who posted on Reddit. Thought something might have come up that you could take to the cops."

"That's right," I say as Leif's words sink in. "He wouldn't have known what Wes knew. Only that we were meeting someone who might have information that could implicate him."

"But how would he have known we were meeting with Wes?"

I have an idea, but I hesitate. Now I'm going a bridge too far.

"What is it?" Leif presses.

"It's wild. I can't—"

"Zane, come on. Tell me."

Fuck, just say it. "What if he'd somehow accessed my messages with Dman? Like me, he wouldn't have known what Wes knew, or even who he was, so maybe he wanted to find out for himself, to see if he was in danger of being discovered. No, that doesn't make any sense. He would have needed access to my messages…"

My thoughts return to the night when I saw someone on the surveillance footage, breaking in through the back door of Leif's parents' place.

"Fuck," I say.

"What?"

"The night I went to your place, after the cops left, when I came back here, I realized I'd left the door unlocked. I wasn't really thinking about that since I figured I was going to nail Isaac then, but I had to check the house because I was freaked out he might have been hiding there. What if, at some point between when I grabbed you and the cops left, he came in and hacked my computer? Put spyware in so he could access my account?"

All my doubts surface.

This is ridiculous! You're losing it again, Zane.

But this image of Jason…

And if that was Isaac, how did he fucking know we'd be at Caribou Coffee?

"That would definitely prove you really saw him last night," Leif says.

"I love your waffles, but—"

"Get your ass upstairs and tell me what you find."

I hop to my feet and plant a fat kiss on him before dashing up to my room. Sitting at my computer, I do a quick scan for any programs I don't recognize. I'm on a mission. But during my search, another thought springs to mind: spyware isn't the only way he could have found out about our plans that night.

"Dman messaged me back…"

I initially told Leif about the message in the shower, but we were in the bedroom when I told him Dman wanted to meet us at Caribou Coffee near campus. What if he'd planted a recording device in here?

As soon as the thought crosses my mind, I'm back to doubting myself. But another thought quickly follows: *"We should go to the Nights of Lights."* We had that conversation in the bedroom as well, and the night we went, I believed someone was watching us. At the time, I'd talked myself out of it. But what if I'd been right?

I jump up from my desk, searching around the monitor for an attachment…anything. Where the fuck could he have planted a mic?

As I begin a hunt around my room, I'm obsessed with my mission, trying to set aside that voice in me that whispers, *This proves you're losing it. You need help. There's something wrong with you.* But I persist in my search.

After checking behind my TV, under the bed, and in the closet, I stop. *Think, Zane.* If I were bugging someone, what would I need to consider?

It'd have to be wireless to transmit somewhere. It'd need to be voice activated so that I only picked up when people were talking. A battery wouldn't be reliable, not for how long it'd have to function for him to have heard us talking about Dman, which means he would either need a way to get back in…or…leach off my electricity. The ceiling fan would take too long, but maybe the electric sockets?

I open my desk drawer, retrieve a screwdriver, and soon I'm unscrewing my outlets, and if that doesn't make me feel like I'm losing my goddamn mind, I don't know what will.

I've removed five before I get to the last one—at the nightstand on Leif's side of the bed.

I'm all tension and suspense as I unscrew the frame.

Maybe once I've torn my room the fuck apart and seen there's nothing here, maybe then I'll have the confirmation I need that I'm fucking wrong and that all these connections in my head are just part of some manic state. I'll be forced to face the truth.

As the screw comes loose, I hesitate to take the frame off.

Even before I pull it off, I accept that all this nonsense can only lead to an ER visit.

So I take that final step, and I see, tucked beside the socket, a mini green circuit board. The wiring from the socket has been rerouted to the device.

Tears well in my eyes as my jaw drops.

It wasn't only in my head.

I was right. I was fucking right.

The relief is palpable as I put my hand to my chest, fighting back tears.

The bastard's been listening in on our conversations. He knew we were meeting with Wes because he heard us making plans to meet up with him. And it's very possible he knew about the Nights of Lights and followed us there.

The relief sweeping through me is so powerful, but nearly as fast as it came, it's replaced by a new tension. Because he hasn't only been listening in on what we were doing, but every fuck. Every sweet moment we shared in my bedroom, even last night when we exchanged I-love-yous.

Chills rush across my body as this sick feeling settles in my gut.

I feel so fucking violated.

So fucking pissed.

And so fucking right.

It was that bastard!

I've got you now, motherfucker.

29

LEIF

Y MOUTH HANGS open as I stare at the image on Zane's phone.

When he headed upstairs, I hoped he might find something on his computer. Not a mic in the goddamn walls.

After our discussion at breakfast, he wasn't even gone ten minutes before rushing downstairs. He wouldn't explain what had him so worked up, but I knew it must've been something as he rushed me over to my parents' place, hurrying with me to my bedroom. Despite my attempts to get him to reveal what he was excited about, he put his finger to his lips and searched my room, plugging a battery charger into every outlet before catching his breath.

Now that I'm looking at what he found in his room, his reaction makes perfect sense.

"He's been recording us? Since the night he broke in?" He already explained that bit, but I'm still trying to wrap my head around it.

"Yes."

I take a seat on the edge of my bed, studying the picture of the device. "How do you even know that's what this is?"

"I ran a Google search on some of the key pieces in the design and searched for spycam. There's a guy on TikTok showing people how to make these things. It can be synced up to Bluetooth, so all Isaac would have to do is come by the house, close enough to download whatever's stored on the hard drive. When I was looking, I suspected it would have to be voice activated to save storage space, and I was right."

He paces, his gaze scanning my room. Looks like he's already trying to figure out what we're supposed to do now that he's found this. Fair enough, since I'm barely able to process it.

After we saw the photos of Jason Kilbourne from Wes, I was confident Zane had really seen Isaac, but I hadn't expected this.

"Are you gonna call Detective Roth?" I ask.

"You kidding me? There's not gonna be any way for her to prove this shit."

"You said it has Bluetooth connectivity, and he could upload it to his phone. If they check that—"

"He's not a moron. He won't use his regular phone. I'm sure he has a burner. No, if I tell Roth now, what if there's no way to trace it back to him? I could have just as easily put that thing in my room. She'll think this is like what happened before."

He's not wrong.

I run my hand around to the back of my neck, giving myself a gentle massage as I try to think this through.

"Where is this now?" I ask.

"Right where I found it."

"You left it in the outlet?"

"Yeah. Right now, this is our upper hand. Isaac doesn't know I found it. So we can plant whatever the hell we want in his head. Use it against him."

"That was smart. If I'd found it, I would have just ripped it out of the wall. But what do you mean, use it against him?"

"That's what I've been trying to think of. Like if he believed we were close to proving it was him. Had a conversation in my room about it, maybe he would realize he has to intervene, and then he'd come for us."

"Like a trap?"

His gaze finally meets mine, and he smiles. "Exactly."

"That sounds dangerous."

"He could have my fucking brother somewhere, Leif. I have to do what I have to do." He's all tensed up, defending this as though I'm not on his side.

"You're right. I just...don't want you to get hurt in the process."

But if his brother is still alive, if he could prevent him from winding up like Jason Kilbourne, he has to do something.

We're both quiet again.

I'm sure he's trying to sort out what we could say to lure Isaac to him, but I'm searching for any solution that doesn't involve putting our lives in danger.

"If we'd known about this before talking to Wes," he says, "when we got back, we could have pretended he told us something useful and then said we were gonna go to the cops with it. Bet that would have brought him running."

"It wouldn't really be believable that we would know something and not go to the cops."

Zane runs his fingers over his chin, nodding. "True. Good thinking."

And unfortunately, the stress of the moment has sharpened my thinking a little too much.

Because I do have an idea.

A really crappy, terrible idea.

"If there was a way we could convince him we were onto something," Zane goes on, "that we're getting close enough that we would go to the cops after we found it…"

Not bad, but… "I have a better idea." I have to force the words out.

Zane stops pacing and turns to me, panic in his expression. I wonder if he's already considered this option but hasn't been willing to say it.

"He tried to get me once before," I say. "He's obviously still watching us; otherwise, he wouldn't have followed us to Caribou Coffee. Maybe he's waiting for his chance, but he hasn't come for me because you've been by my side this whole time."

"No," he says. "No. Fuck that. This isn't an option."

I study the image on his phone. "Zane, this guy's not giving up. And we've been lucky we've lasted this long, but it can't go on forever. I have to rebuild my fucking life. And you're not gonna be able to protect me from everything. You said yourself you have to do what you have to do for Mike, and this might be it."

"I'm not using you as bait to save him."

I tried to avoid using that word, but of course that's what we'd be doing.

"You don't get to make that call on your own," I say. "That's not how this works."

"Well, you don't get to decide to put your life at risk on your own."

"That doesn't make any sense."

"Yeah, I know," he says, flustered. "I'm just trying to think of a way to get this shit idea out of your pretty head."

But with every second that passes, I become even more confident it's the only way. "The last thing Isaac heard us talking about last night was how we were worried about your mental health. All we need to do is have a plausible conversation about checking you in at the ER. My parents are on a cruise Christmas through New Year's."

"Stop. We're not talking about this."

"It's actually perfect if you think about it. We stage taking you to the ER, and then I bring you back. You hide in the basement for a few days. When he comes back, he tries to take me, you pop out and grab him."

"You're speeding through the most important bit."

"We'll figure it out. You have a fucking gun."

"He might too. And when he's got it on you, what the hell am I supposed to do then?"

"You were willing to take that risk before," I say.

His jaw tenses up, and he approaches. "I was not using you as fucking bait, Leif. I wasn't even sure anything was going to happen. I was working off intuition and blind determination. How else was I supposed to handle it? Abduct you myself to protect you from this psycho?"

He sounds irate, like he's furious that I'm even entertaining this idea. But I know I'm right.

"Zane, we have to do this. You know this is the only way."

"I refuse to believe that. We just have to think."

"Fine. Let's say that's the plan until we think of something better."

He glares at me. "I'm not agreeing to that."

"You would if you thought there was even a possibility we'd think of a better plan."

"Stop being so right for one second."

A gentle *chirp* comes from nearby.

"Could you stop upsetting Kyra?"

He huffs. "I can't believe you're trying to crack jokes right now."

"I don't know how the fuck else to get through talking about potentially sacrificing myself to bait a psychopath."

He's quiet.

"You have to do this, Zane. For Mike."

His chin quivers, his eyes watering. "Why would you say that?" He doesn't sound angry anymore; he's hurt.

It was a low blow, but he needs a better reason to disregard my plan than the fact that he doesn't like it.

He shakes his head. "If anything happened to you, I wouldn't be able to live with myself."

"And I can't live needing you at my side every waking moment of my day because he might be around the next corner. I wouldn't be able to live with myself if six months from now there's a news story about a new guy going missing. And then another after that. And another after that. Especially knowing there might have been a way for me to stop it."

I wouldn't be able to live with myself if I saw his brother's body in the news, knowing we might have been able to save him.

"This is too much. I refuse." Zane tears up. He shakes his head.

But I know why he's reacting this way—he knows what I've already realized; this is the way we can end this once and for all.

He approaches me. "I hate this. I hate this with every fiber of my being. I hate that this is one of the reasons I fucking love you. And I hate you for being right." He places his hand against my cheek. "I can't lose you."

"Then you'd better make sure this plan works," I say, and now I'm tearing up, overwhelmed with emotion.

He lurches toward me and takes a kiss, and I let myself have this. It's a welcome distraction from this fucked-up conversation.

He pushes me back onto the bed and crawls on top of me.

We're already kissing like it might be the last time. When our lips finally part, he rubs his nose against mine before pulling back, his gaze shifting away from me.

I imagine he's doing what I'm doing, trying to run through every possible scenario. Trying to think of some solution that doesn't involve putting my life at risk.

But when his gaze returns to me, he looks resigned.

Fuck. What the hell are we doing?

30

ZANE

"How's my short king doing?" Leif asks as he enters my bedroom, where I'm getting all my things together.

"Almost packed for tomorrow morning." I shove a plastic bag of toiletries into my backpack. The plan is to head to the ER in another hour.

"They'll figure out what's wrong," Leif says. "And we'll figure this out. Like I said, together."

Leif was a better actor than I was when we were working through the script we'd prepped for Isaac's benefit. But all that matters is he buys this shit.

Since I found the mic in the wall outlet, I've despised every moment in my room. It's like Isaac is violating us. And it's not only that he's listening, but that we've had to perform like everything's fine, even messing around because we agreed if we don't, he might realize we're up to something.

Fortunately, I don't have to make up bullshit to talk about so we can sound "normal" since Leif's catching me up about his last chat with his parents, who just docked in Antigua. I finish packing my things, including my gun. We've already been moving clothes and my computer monitors to his parents' basement over the past few days, getting everything set up gradually so that if Isaac was watching from nearby, he wouldn't notice.

The plan is: we head out like we're going to the ER. Figure he could have surveillance nearby, so we'll leave for a couple of hours, then circle back to the house. Leif will drop me off at the old church outside the neighborhood. I'll walk through the woods and meet him in his backyard, where he'll let me in the basement.

My whole system is set up in his basement so I can watch outside over the next few days. It's gonna be a long-ass week of waiting for our plan to work, tucked away in a basement with an air mattress, but it's worth it knowing Leif will be safe.

"Well, get your ass over to mine tonight so we can enjoy the time we have left. I'm making lasagna."

I growl. "I fucking love your lasagna."

That's probably the most believable thing I can say as I play nice, to give Isaac false confidence that everything is as he would expect.

"Now let me finish up, and I'll be over in like ten," I say.

"Sounds good. Love you."

"I love you too."

Okay, this is also one of the more believable things.

Leif heads over to his place, and after I hear the front door close, I reach into my backpack and grab the case with my handgun, inspecting it. The reality is starting to hit me, like it did that night when I first met Leif.

I might have to use this thing soon.

"Great shot, kid," Dad says, resting his hand on my shoulder. *"You got an eye for this, my little soldier."*

I set the case back in my backpack and zip it shut, taking a last glance around my room. I'm gonna miss this comfy mattress.

I head into the hall, and as I start down it, I stop. The hairs on my neck stand on end. Something's wrong.

I turn toward the guest bedroom across the hall from mine when I see someone bolt out.

I recognize the face immediately.

Isaac fucking Tolle.

I jump back, spin my backpack around, knocking him in the head with it so he goes flying against the wall, but he grabs it and pulls. I go with it and I'm all fists, slamming them against him, when he hits me in my gut.

Fuck.

My body trembles violently, and I realize he's fucking got a stun gun to my shirt.

He throws me back against the opposite wall, and I try to get up, but my trembling legs send me back to the ground.

Fuck my goddamn fucking body.

When I regain my senses, I feel another jolt against

my neck. Then another.

I'm a fit of spasms.

I'M STILL TREMBLING from the shock of Isaac's repeated assaults.

I think I lost consciousness for a minute there. As my vision unblurs, I notice I'm lying facedown on my bedroom floor. My arms are behind my back, and I attempt to move them, noticing the strain against my wrists.

I feel movement at my legs and glance over my shoulder. Isaac wraps a zip tie around my ankles, and by the time I'm able to struggle, it's too late.

Fuck me.

Isaac feels around my ankles and yanks the hem of my jeans up. "Ah, what do we have here?" He slides my knife out of its holster.

Dammit.

"Guess that's one down. Now you just have to tell me where your gun's at."

"Fuck off."

He snickers as he crawls over to face me. He runs the blade across my cheek.

"Zane, you're gonna learn real fast that I love when they pick the hard way."

"What did you do to my brother, asshole?"

"You tell me where your gun is, and I'll tell you that. And don't try to pretend you don't have one. I've been listening in on you and your boyfriend's little conversations."

The way he says that, it sounds like he fell for our ruse, but then why did he come here now? Did he realize he needed to take me out first to get to Leif?

"Where is your gun, Zane?" He presses the blade harder against my flesh, and when I don't reply for a few moments, his nostrils flare. His eyes widen. And then he smiles.

The expressions are disturbingly erratic, impossible to read.

As he continues applying pressure with the blade, I'm waiting for him to draw blood, but he restrains himself, pulling back.

"It's too early to damage this beautiful body," he whispers as though it's not even intended for me. "Fuck it, I'll find it myself."

He's placed my backpack on the bed; that's where he goes first.

Of fucking course.

He rifles through and pulls out the case. "Well, they weren't gonna let you take this where you were going anyway."

Is he gonna realize it's strange that I would have taken that over to Leif's, even after I'd assured him there wasn't any real danger?

"Where the fuck is my brother?" I ask, trying to get his attention off what might cast doubt in his mind about our real plan.

I struggle with my restraints, but it's for show since I know better than to waste my energy on what would be a futile attempt at escaping. At least while he's got his eyes on me.

"You should be more concerned about your fate than Michael's. It's already been two months since he passed, so you're wasting your tears."

Passed?

He might as well have decked me in the gut.

My body curls toward the floor, a rush of adrenaline from all the excitement colliding with the blow of grief.

No, fucking no.

"You're lying!" I call out as tears spring from my eyes.

He kneels beside me, placing his hand on the back of my head. I struggle against his hold, but he pins my head down, stroking his thumb across my flesh, stirring goose bumps. "Oh, Zane, I really wish I were lying. He was so ripe and beautiful. It was a waste, but he was getting tired. All that beauty was rotting away. Beauty is such a fragile thing. You'll see that for yourself."

It's not true. It can't be true. "Fuck you!" I call out, trying not to show emotion, but that only makes me cringe as more tears burst from my eyes. "You piece of shit!"

I tell myself it's a vicious lie to terrorize me, but in my heart, I already know the truth. I've known the truth for a while now.

He studies my gun. "Oh, these things have safeties, don't they? There it is. Can't make a rookie mistake like that, right?"

Said like a man who's never managed a gun before.

"I was right about you all this fucking time," I spit out.

"You proud of yourself for that one? Enjoy the victory while you can."

"You were pretty fucking obvious when I went to talk to you at that Habitat build."

"I was surprised and, I must admit, impressed with you, Zane. Although, that's when I really figured out your weakness."

He's poking, and I don't mind taking the bait if it'll buy me time.

"What?" I ask.

"How easy it would be to play this game with you."

Game?

He lies down beside me so that we're face-to-face.

"Oh, my sweet Zane," he says, reaching out to me, but stops short of my face before licking his lips. "You were so easy to play. And it was so much fun too."

"What are you on about?"

"You're smart, Zane. That's something I've noticed about you. But you weren't smart enough for me.

Because you guessed wrong. I wasn't after Leif. I was after you."

"The hell?"

"You didn't think it was convenient that you ran into that post on a Reddit forum, displaying Leif's note?"

"You did that?"

"I found Leif at the library I frequent, which I'm assuming you already pieced together. A beautiful specimen to catch your attention. I sent him that note, knowing there was already a post about the one I sent Mike.

"I thought I might have to spread a rumor on that forum to lead you to Leif. Say that a friend of his mentioned it, but he made it even easier when he posted to social media. Then I just posted that to the Reddit forum. As I expected, you gravitated right to it because you weren't going to let it go. My hope was to keep you obsessed, have you going through your own little investigation again—the cops would just assume you were having another mental-health crisis. I must admit, I underestimated you. I didn't realize you'd go as far as renting a place next to Leif to watch him. I had to get creative with my plan, but I love a challenge."

A plan? Fuck.

"That's why I didn't find you at Leif's place," I say. "You weren't there for him. You were there to distract me."

"Very good. You left your door open, so I came in

and set up a mic in here."

Which I already know, you fucking moron.

"Then I looked on your computer and saw where you had the security cameras set up, and I noticed you were so focused on protecting him that your weakness was you hadn't thought nearly enough about how to defend yourself. There's a blind spot right from your neighbors to your basement door. Maybe if you'd given more thought to that, we wouldn't be in this mess now. Clearly, you didn't consider that because that's how I skirted around your little security to break in today."

"What did you do to Mike?" I ask, my tears warm against my cheeks.

"You'll find out. I like that you're a crier. He cried too."

He reaches for my face again, and I pull away.

"You two are such a beautiful couple. What a beautiful way for two people to meet. Something poetic about it, really. It was an honor to listen to you enjoying each other's bodies. I would have come much sooner if I didn't get so much pleasure out of every fuck, every time I heard you call out his name. Speaking of your boyfriend, I don't think it's right to do this without him." He pushes to his feet and grabs my cellphone from the bed.

"You motherfucker!" I call out.

"We'll text him to come on over. How does that sound?"

"This is between you and me. You said it yourself. Leave him out of it!"

"Oh, no, no. You're wrong. It *was* between you and me. But since I've started this, oh, I've fallen in love with both of you. So young. So beautiful. So special. But I only have room to play with one of you. So we'll have a short time with him today."

Room? So he keeps his victims somewhere.

My wrists strain in the zip tie. Feels like I'm gonna slice my skin off from the pressure.

"You fucking hurt Leif, and I'll kill you."

"That's the spirit I want to see, Zane. Keep that up as long as you can. That's what keeps you alive. It's what makes you beautiful. When that fight dies, so do you."

There's no misunderstanding his twisted insinuation.

"Roth is already onto you. You think if you kill the one guy I warned her about already, she's not gonna be looking at you again?"

He chuckles. "Oh, my precious. I told you: I've been listening in all this time, so I know she didn't believe you. And that she was worried about the obsessed kid who started stalking, then dating Leif. And knowing about Leif's mental-health challenges, I mean, it made it hard for me to decide how he should go. It'd be easy to kill a depressed man and make it look like a suicide. But the real challenge, wouldn't that be to make it look like you killed him before disappearing?"

Just hearing him talk about killing Leif is enough to

make rage flare in me.

"So I guess you can tell I made up my mind already. And don't worry, it will be beautiful." He sits on the edge of my bed, keying away on my phone.

"Leif! Leif!" I shout desperately, hoping my cry can reach him, if not physically, then in some wild-ass psychic way.

"I think you know nobody's gonna hear you in here." I continue calling out as he scrolls through my phone. "I should review some of your old messages before I send something. Want it to sound convincing."

I finally stop screaming, knowing this is energy I need to conserve because when this fucker gives me a few moments alone, he's a goner.

He heads to my dresser and opens the top drawer, retrieving a pair of boxers before pulling a roll of black tape from his pocket.

My mind's racing through my options.

I have to fucking figure a way out of this.

I have to save Leif.

And tear this motherfucker apart.

31

LEIF

I HAVEN'T NEEDED my key to Zane's before this plan. He'd usually met me outside even on my short trek to his place, and it's a surprise to be using it for the first time as I enter Zane's place.

Could you come over real quick and help me with a few things?

I thought he was only bringing a bag tonight so we wouldn't look like we were up to something, but maybe he forgot something he needed to put in the basement.

As I close the door, I notice the place is eerily quiet before I hear a sound coming from upstairs. It's strained, muffled.

Something's wrong. Get out. Call the cops.

I whirl around and grab the doorknob when I hear behind me, "You walk out that door, and your boyfriend's dead."

I freeze in place; the strained cry from upstairs is even louder.

I spin around, looking up the stairs.

It's him: the dark-haired man from the photo Zane showed me.

Isaac Tolle.

He has a gun in his hand, aimed at Zane, who has his arms behind his back and a gag in his mouth. The way Isaac's gripping the back of his shirt, it's clear he dragged him to the top of the stairs.

The text was a trick to lure me here, and now he's got us both right where he wants us.

"Hello, Leif." Isaac's voice is a whisper. There's something unsettling to how calm he seems in a situation that has my adrenaline spiking. His lips curl into a smile, something wicked in his gaze.

Zane continues crying out behind his gag, his eyes wide, as though he's trying to plant a message in my head. I'm sure it's something simple like, "Get the fuck out of here!" He'd want me to leave so at least one of us could turn Isaac in.

Or maybe a part of me knows that's more reasonable than taking on an armed man.

Heartbeat racing, breaths hastening, my thoughts are running through scenarios, like shit out of a *Fast and Furious* movie, where I'm able to use quick thinking and strategy to disarm him and save the day. Like the night Zane dragged me into the closet, I figure I could have taken some goddamn self-defense classes to be prepared for this.

If only…

"Get your phone out," Isaac says. "Throw it up here."

My gaze meets Zane's; I can tell with every fiber of my being he wants me to get the hell out of here, but knowing what will happen if I leave, I can't risk that. I obey Isaac's instruction, aiming for his head, but he moves aside so the phone goes flying down the upstairs hall.

He chuckles. "Like the fight. Now come on up. We have things to discuss. I don't think I need to tell you that if you leave, I have no reason to keep Zane alive." He drags Zane toward his bedroom.

Zane continues pleading with me from behind his gag.

I'm running through my options. How easy it would be to spare myself right now.

I could get help.

But the thought of leaving Zane here to meet his end is too unbearable to consider, and before I know it, I find myself mounting the stairs, heading toward my fate, whatever that may be.

I consider my mom's pepper spray, which I have in my jeans pocket. I think about reaching in for it now, but Isaac will be suspicious if I get to the top of the stairs with my hand in my pocket. No, I need to wait for the right moment.

When I reach the top of the stairs, I turn toward

Zane's room. Isaac stands inside, aiming the gun at Zane.

"In here," Isaac says.

"I'm fine out here."

"I could shoot Zane right now. Is that what you want?"

But he could have shot him already.

If he wanted to kill us both, he could aim and have a chance of offing me before I got away.

That's not what he wants. He has other plans for us…

"You killed Jason Kilbourne," I say. "And you took Mike. If I come in there, you'll just kill us both."

He snickers. It's a disturbing reaction.

"Leif," he says. I cringe at him speaking my name. "I hope you don't assume I want this. That I'm some kind of monster. I'm not."

I'm expecting him to have a wild look in his eyes, but he seems subdued. There's something disarming about his presence, even with everything happening before me. I can imagine how easy it was for a guy like this to lure Mike or Jason with that sort of calm demeanor.

"I didn't plan to kill Jason. I enjoyed seeing him around campus. I think a lot of people enjoyed seeing that beautiful man. And he was so kind and curious about the world. I thought I was attracted to him, but as time went on, I knew it was something else. I wanted power over him. Not just once either. I wanted to make him wholly and totally mine. And so I did. But every time I was with him, I felt guilty afterward. I knew it was wrong. Monsters don't know that, do they? I swore I would never hurt another soul. Promised it to God. And then I saw Mike…and the impulse came again. I fought it. I know you have no reason to believe me, but I did. I don't want to hurt anyone, Leif. I'd think you and Zane of all people would understand that this is something in me, like your depression or Zane's bipolar disorder. A switch flips, and then I'm stuck having to act on these urges."

"You could get help for that; you don't have to hurt anybody."

He chuckles. "But both of you know how hard it is to get help once you snap. No, this thing has me. But I'm as much of a victim as Mike or Jason. Or you or Zane."

The way he says it, it's clear he's already made up his mind. We're his next victims. But there's a plea in his expression, like he wants understanding, sympathy even, for what he plans to do to us.

"Outside of this," he adds, "I really am a very good man."

Although, he must know, even if this were his only fault, it disqualifies him from being that.

Isaac stares me down for a few moments longer. "I said come on in."

Again, his words are so gentle, so contradictory to what's happening. Almost lulls me into a false sense of security—but only *almost* as a series of hellish imaginings from true-crime TV shows flash through my mind.

I could still run.

I can still make that choice.

Leave Zane and call the cops.

But what if he kills Zane? Or what if he tries to take him somewhere? I could follow him, but what if I lost them? What if I was left wondering where he was, the way Zane was left wondering about Mike? I might as well be fucking dead. And this isn't just about Zane and me. If I stay, Zane and I can die together. At least then the cops might have a chance of finding our bodies and seeing who did this to us before he finds his next victim.

I take a breath, then step over the threshold. I've made my decision.

Maybe it's not the right one. Maybe this is the dumbest fucking thing I could do right now.

But I don't give a fuck.

I can't leave Zane here with this psycho. I *won't* leave him.

I know he disagrees. I can tell as he continues pleading with me from behind his gag.

Isaac licks his lips and glances me over, like he's sizing me up. He orders me to step away from him, move farther into the room, to the foot of Zane's bed. I obey, and when I'm where he wants me, he says, "Take off your shirt."

"What?"

"You heard me."

I look to Zane, whose eyes are shooting daggers at Isaac.

Maybe this will buy us some time. Or get him to let his guard down enough that I can at least make a go at him.

Or it will just end as it's most likely to end.

I remove my shirt and toss it on the bed.

Isaac's gaze travels over me; it's as though it's burning into my goddamn flesh.

Goose bumps prick across my arms as the hairs on the back of my neck stand on end.

He licks his lips again and approaches.

"Now your pants."

I can't do this and look at Zane.

This can't lead anywhere good, but I remind myself that if he approaches me, this might give me the opportunity to gain the upper hand.

I unfasten my belt, unbutton my fly, and pull my pants down. Once I remove them, I pull them up to my waist, sliding my hand in my front pocket for my pepper spray.

Isaac walks toward me. "You think I don't know what you're doing?"

A chill runs up and down my spine, my fingers tickle the end of the bottle, but I remain still to keep from rousing further suspicion.

"You know I meant your briefs too—which I like, by

the way." He snatches the pants from me and tosses them in the nook beside the bed.

There goes my pepper spray.

Fuck.

My stomach churns.

"Sorry, I'm shy," I say.

He steps even closer, and I notice Zane in my periphery.

He's moving. What's he doing?

I refuse to look since I don't want to draw Isaac's attention to whatever he's attempting.

Isaac presses the gun between my pecs, runs it down my torso.

My stomach clenches. I feel fucking sick, and I'm sure the only reason I'm not vomiting right now is because some part of me realizes that could be the difference between life and death.

As the head of the gun touches my belly, near my navel, I'm shaking.

"Take. Them. Off," he says softly.

I feel a rush of determination. I'm probably about to die, but that was probably how this was going to end anyway. I take my chance, moving fast, seizing his armed hand and dragging him to the floor with me. I'll keep the gun out of his reach if it fucking kills me, but suddenly I feel something press against my shoulder blade, followed by a jolt of energy rushing through me, my body vibrating.

As I lose sensation in my limbs, I barely have a chance to process what's wrong before I'm releasing the very thing I shouldn't have let go of under any circumstances.

I collapse on my back, my muscles twitching and spasming as I see Isaac with the gun in one hand and a stun gun in the other.

"Feisty," he says, his lips curling into a smirk before he turns the gun on me again.

A growl comes from behind him, and Zane jumps up, throwing his arms, still locked together, over Isaac's head, clamping them back quickly as he puts Isaac into a chokehold.

Zane must've shimmied his wrists down and pulled them to the front.

Isaac pulls the gun back, aiming it at Zane's head.

"No!" I call out just as I hear a *click*.

I wait for the explosive sound of a bullet firing and anticipate the horror of having to watch my Zane endure the brunt of it.

But there's only that *click*.

Isaac's eyes widen as he pulls the gun back and fires again. Still without success.

Is it empty? Is the safety on?

Whatever the hell is wrong, I struggle to my feet to help Zane, fighting against the echoes of Isaac's attack that still reverberate through me.

By the time I'm up, Isaac's thrown the gun to the

floor and raises the stun gun, pressing it against Zane's neck.

Zane rears his head back, releasing another muffled scream as I reach Isaac, seizing his arm and pulling the stun gun away from Zane, who still seems to have a good grip on our attacker, Isaac struggling for air.

I manage to pry the stun gun from his grip, and he collapses on top of Zane, crushing him beneath his weight.

Zane still has his arms locked around Isaac's throat, choking him. Isaac's face is bright red as he struggles in the hold, thrashing about. By now it's apparent he's not fighting anymore; these movements are his body's last incoherent attempts at surviving before he goes limp.

His eyes roll back before closing. His limbs relax beside him as Zane studies him, checking to ensure the deed is done.

A rush of visceral relief moves through me.

It's done.

Isaac's unconscious.

And Zane is safe.

That's all that fucking matters.

32

ZANE

A FTER ISAAC PASSES out, Leif helps me out of my restraints with my knife, which he'd discovered in Isaac's jacket pocket with the zip ties. He helps me remove my gag, and then we restrain Isaac.

"The gun?" Leif says, securing a second set of ties around Isaac's ankles. "Why didn't it go off?"

I'm on a third zip tie around Isaac's wrists. "It wasn't gonna fire. Isaac turned the thumb safety off, like any idiot would think to do. But that was a modification from the guy I bought it from. Isaac didn't notice the trigger was locked down."

"What do you mean?"

"I keep the trigger locked down and the safety on so the gun has to be reset before you can fire a round. Guess Dad was right. Only two kinds of men in the world: those who know guns and those who don't."

That was an attempt at making light of this wild-ass situation, but Leif doesn't look amused. Hell, after what just happened, I don't blame him.

If Isaac had known, we'd both likely—I shouldn't even think it.

After we call the cops, I tell Leif about the conversation I had with Isaac: How all this was a trap for me. How he bought our ruse, and he'd shown up because he needed to grab me before I checked myself into the psych unit. How he'd planned to kill Leif and frame me for the murder before abducting me. How he killed my brother.

That last part is pure hell.

Adrenaline courses through my veins, my body clearly unconvinced the threat is gone. Or maybe just realizing there's a different threat now—that the grief of knowing the truth will be too much for me. That I'll fall into a dark despair knowing that Mike is gone.

The only thing keeping me from losing myself is knowing that I haven't lost everything, not as long as I still have Leif.

WHEN THE EMT finishes checking us out, I adjust the blanket around Leif, making sure it's tight against him.

Between the cops and the paramedics, there's a lot of business going on around us. We've both been interviewed by uniformed officers, some of them asking the same questions, and I'm not sure I've answered them the same way each time. The further we get from the incident, the harder it is to hold on to the details.

Placing my arm around Leif, I kiss his cheek.

"How are you feeling?" he asks.

"Overwhelmed and numb. You?"

"About the same."

He turns to me, inspecting my expression before he reaches over and rests his hand on my cheek.

"What?" I ask.

"Your face. It's still all red on the sides."

"It's fine. It was only tape. At least I'm still alive. And you're still alive. Those are the only things that matter."

But judging by his apprehensive expression, I suspect he knows better.

Since now I know Mike isn't here.

"I'm so sorry, Zane," he says, not for the first time.

If anyone else said that to me after what I just found out, I'd tell them to go fuck themselves, but I know Leif. Can see how much he cares. How much he wishes he could make this better.

But nothing can.

A tear escapes my eye.

Fuck.

"I'm fine," I say.

"You don't have to be."

"Let's not talk about it now. There'll be plenty of time for that later."

He nods.

I glance around uneasily at all the traffic and sit in the back of the ambulance, then rest my head against his shoulder.

The front door of the house opens, and Detective Roth steps out.

We already spoke to her briefly. She and Detective Berkley arrived during all the commotion. I could see the guilt in her expression straight away, but she kept things professional. Didn't get into our past.

She approaches the ambulance, and I'm kind of wishing we didn't have to have this conversation. Not now.

"Hi again, Zane. Do you want me to say you told me so, or would you rather be the one to say it?"

"You kind of already took it from me."

She smirks, but for less than a second. "I'm sorry about Mike."

My chin quivers as I fight back the tears. "Did you get anything from him about that?"

She bites her lip and glances around. She can't share details about the case with me, but she knows she fucking owes me.

"Zane, he's saying you framed him for this. So we'll have to wait and see how long that holds up. Berkley did get a warrant to search his home. That's where he is now, and they discovered a room in his basement. A room where we believe he may have kept...people. But other than that, we're still trying to sort through this mess."

That's where he kept Mike. That's where he planned to keep me.

I nod. "I hope you'll keep me posted. If you need to talk to Dman, I found him. He still remembers that note, like the one Leif got."

She glances between us. "I'm so sorry for what you've both been through tonight. I hope you know there are mental-health options for this kind of trauma."

"Please don't give us a fucking mental-health lecture right now. We already got it from two cops."

"Three," Leif interjects.

"I'll definitely keep you both posted," she says, "though at this level, I'm sure it won't take long for the media to get a hold of any developments."

"We look forward to them," I say. "I don't want to be rude, but can you leave me and my boyfriend alone now?"

Her gaze settles on the ground. "Yeah. That's fair. I'll probably have to follow up—"

"Bye, Detective Roth."

She heads off, and I rest my head back on Leif's shoulder.

The EMT suggests that, given how many times I was stunned by Isaac, it might be a good idea to head to the hospital for observation, but since all the vitals they took are fine, I refuse.

I'm just tired. Want to go to bed in my boyfriend's arms. So Leif and I head back to his place. I know where I need to be right now.

When we get into his bedroom, we collapse on the

bed together, and I throw my arms around him, pulling him close.

"I'm so fucking exhausted," I whisper.

"Me too."

"But there's no fucking way I'm gonna be able to sleep after all that."

"Then maybe we can stay up feeling like this for the rest of the night."

I kiss the back of his neck. Once. Twice.

The third time, a tear streaks down my face.

It's like I've been holding in all this emotion, especially with all the people we were around, and now it all comes flooding out. My body trembles, now not from shock, but from the weight of it all crashing down on me in an instant.

"He's gone."

"I'm so sorry, Zane. I wish there was something I could say to make it better."

The tears roll down my cheek, onto his neck, and I surrender, sobbing against him, clinging to him desperately, as though if I held him tight enough, I could make sure nothing bad ever happened to my Leif.

He rolls toward me, and I release him enough so he can face me. I bury my face into his chest, a mess of tears and desperate groans that don't even sound human. "Don't ever leave me," I say into his shirt. "Please don't ever leave me." I can't even control the words that come out. I'm so grief-stricken, so desperate for some assurance.

"I'm right here. I'm here, Zane, and I love you. Let it all out. Don't be afraid. Let me take anything that's too much for you."

What little I've been holding back, I release, and the sobbing intensifies as I surrender to it completely, knowing I'm safe in his arms.

This grief is just the beginning of the journey; I know that.

As my body works through a primal response, whimpers and screams, tears and trembling, he holds me tighter, assuring me that as long as I have Leif at my side, it's a journey I can bear.

EPILOGUE

LEIF

One month later…

AS I STIR in bed, I feel a tight grip around my waist.

"Shh. No. It's the weekend," Zane says. "We can sleep in."

I chuckle. "Is my short king tired?"

He nods against the back of my neck.

"If I stay in bed, how am I gonna make us waffles?"

His arm pops up, and I burst into a laugh.

"Oh, that easy, huh?" I roll toward him.

His arm drops back down on me, and he pulls my body close to his. "I'm only kidding. Although, I wouldn't mind a few waffles after that workout you gave me last night."

I reach down and grip his ass. "Yeah, this ass gave me a good workout too."

"Now that I've trapped you, I figure I'm just gonna be a total bottom. And you're gonna have to come home and drill me with that thing every afternoon."

We share a laugh, and as it settles, I assess his expression.

That spark in his eyes has returned, but I can still see the pain. It hasn't been an easy month, between our encounter with Tolle and the subsequent revelations.

Tolle took a plea deal. Confessed to every detail of his crimes.

How he met Jason and Mike at the Chelsby Hill library. How he talked with them about books a few times before he caught them while they were walking around town, offering rides. He used his stun gun to keep them from fighting, then bound them in zip ties and tucked them away in the trunk of his car, taking them to his place, where he did the sorts of things monsters do. And once he didn't see that light in their eyes anymore—as he saw it, at least—he disposed of the bodies. Jason's was in the creek by the dam, and Mike's was in another creek on the other side of town.

Since Mike's body was recovered, Roth has met up with Zane a few times. She's apologized for their difficulties throughout the investigation and offered him private insights about the case, which has become a high-profile media circus, capturing not only the attention of Wyachet, but the nation.

Zane's had to process it all through the media frenzy while managing the investigation and Mike's service. Despite how wild it's all been, my parents have been amazing, not only to me, but to Zane. They wished I'd felt comfortable sharing sooner, but given the circumstances, they're not surprised we handled it the way we did. Just glad we're both alive.

The past week has really been the first time Zane's had some peace, so long as he doesn't check the news on his phone or see a paper on a newsstand around town.

All that aside, the way he's smiling this morning gives me reason to hope.

A *chirp* comes from the other side of Zane's room, and we turn our attention to Kyra's cage, where she flies from the bottom to her little wooden perch. Since I started staying with Zane after our confrontation with Tolle, we moved Kyra over to his place.

Zane says, "Guess she's trying to remind me that we have to start waffles because we have our big picnic today."

Despite how little interest she'd shown in flying since I rescued her, last week we caught her flying around her cage. At first, she seemed to struggle, but a few days ago, it became clear my friend's back to her old self, ready to take flight, so we planned a big release celebration at the park.

As Zane turns back to me, he rests his hand on my arm, caressing my triceps. "How you feeling about that?"

"Glad she's better, but sad too. I'll miss her."

He frowns. "You were very good to her. You've been very good to both of us."

"You've been good to me too," I tell him. I know he values what I've brought into his life since we first met, and particularly this past month. But I won't let him dismiss how much better I've been with him too.

He smirks and leans close, planting a kiss on my forehead. "Come on. Let's get some waffles in our bellies and then jerk off in the shower."

My kind of morning.

We force ourselves out of bed. Go through our morning routine, getting through waffles before he helps me with prepping food for the picnic. We put on the downstairs TV, cuddling up to watch some of our shows.

I could get used to this routine.

When the afternoon arrives, we head to Palamone Park and settle on a blanket in a spot not far from where we went sledding before Christmas. Kyra starts flapping about wildly in her cage, like she wants to get out.

"Oh, no," I say after I swallow a bite of my sandwich.

"Oh no? That's a good sign. Maybe she knows she's ready."

"I'm just so worried about her."

"Worried? She's been in the wild before. She knows how to survive."

Zane's right, but it still plays on my mind. "What if her wing isn't healed up enough?"

"Is that what the doctor said?"

"No," I reply, reminding myself that she should be all right.

He sets his sandwich on his plate and scoots over, setting his hand on my leg. "I think our baby's ready."

Tension rises within me.

I can't deny there are a thousand scenarios playing through my mind: She's unable to fly far. Some hawk swoops down and snatches her. She falls over in the dog park and becomes their next chew toy.

Zane squeezes my thigh gently, offering me the support I need right now.

"Okay, Kyra, here we go," I say, taking that hard step, unlatching her door and opening it.

It takes her a moment to realize it's open. She perches on the door, glancing between Zane and me.

"It's okay," I say. "You can do it."

And as I'm saying the words to her, I'm also trying to remind myself. My own nerves about what the future holds.

Kyra glances at me for a moment, then flies from her cage and comes to rest on my shoulder. She stays there for a few moments.

"What are you doing?" I ask, turning to her. She tilts her head either way, chirping. In my mind, she's thanking me for the help before she pushes off. I figure her first will be a short test flight, but she soars through the air, heading for the woods without hesitation, her flight looking as effortless as that of any of the other birds I've seen today. A wave of relief moves through me, but there's grief there too.

Zane rubs my back, and I turn to him. "Nice to see that my wildest fears weren't realized, but I'll miss her. It was nice having her around."

"Yeah, well, now you're really stuck with just me."

I chuckle. "Not such a horrible fate. Although, you might only have me until this summer."

"Oh, really?" he asks, a smile playing across his lips.

I've been talking to him about attending WCC for Maymester and summer semester. It kind of surprises me that I'm already talking about it, but my meds have really helped. I'm glad I'm taking them, and I'll continue to, along with seeing my therapist and psych, but Zane took me beyond stability—he's given me a reason to hope. I'm not ready to go back to Georgia State, not just yet. But I feel like I could knock out some core courses at WCC, then maybe transfer those once I'm ready.

Zane takes my hand, rubs his thumb across the back, massaging gently. "Then I'd better take advantage of every moment while we have the chance."

"If I did end up going back to Georgia State at some point, how would we—"

He moves in fast, taking a kiss, silencing me. I relax into it, and when he pulls away, his gaze locks with mine. "Don't think for a fucking second you're getting away that easily." He winces. "Okay, that sounded creepy. Obviously, if you wanted to leave me, I would let you, but if you think that moving to Atlanta is enough to discourage me, then you really are just a pretty face."

I laugh, and as I smile, his gaze settles on my lips.

"Maybe we could get an apartment close to campus,"

Zane says. "When you're ready, that is."

"You'd do that?"

"Leif, you really don't get how fucking head over heels I am for you, do you?"

"You make it hard for me to miss that," I confess.

He shows it every day—in his looks, his words, his actions. And neither of us can keep from showing the other how much we love each other on any given day. Maybe because we've both come to realize how precious each day is, and that another isn't always a given.

"Let's finish up here," Zane says, "so we can get back to the house and I can remind you one more time."

He offers another kiss, and we enjoy the afternoon, though I have to admit, I'm eager to get back to the house with him. When we finally get home, we're on each other before we can even make it to the bedroom.

We strip down, a bit of a fumbling mess, chuckling as we try to get out of these damn clothes so we can get to what we really want.

We wind up naked on the bed, Zane on top of me. He smells of the Altoids we popped after our picnic, his tongue pushing into my mouth, my tongue welcoming the visitor as he rubs that fat cock against my thigh.

After some messy kisses, he manages to pry his lips away. "Fuck, this is like that first time we messed around. Me showing you how good it could feel."

Just him mentioning that day sends a rush through me.

He smirks before crawling off me.

"What are you doing?" I ask. I get a good view of his ass before he grabs his desk chair and rolls it over.

Another jolt of excitement pulses through me. After he's placed the chair, he fishes through the nightstand, fetching the lube and my little toy.

"Oh, really?" I ask.

"You've never even used it after that one sexy call," he says. "Or have you?"

He glares at me like a jealous boyfriend, making me laugh. "I mean, I clearly brought it over in case we wanted to have some fun, but I haven't had any reason to yet."

His smile returns as he sits in the chair. "Get your ass over here."

I position myself as I was that first time, close along the side of the bed, while he lubes up the toy. I spread my legs, gazing at him as he rests it against my hole, massaging gently. I close my eyes, relax as he plays with me, opening me up the way he has plenty of times with his fingers or cock. He takes his time getting it in, and as it hits my prostate, I feel a warm bead of precum spill from the head of my cock.

"Fuck," he mutters before I feel his lips along the bottom of my shaft. He licks along it, creating that pressure like he did the first time he fingered me, now using the toy to tease my prostate as he works me up.

My hips rock as he keeps building me up, and soon I

feel his finger and thumb against my nipple. Yet again, he's playing me like a goddamn instrument. I'm lost in sensation, reveling in the way it radiates from so many different parts of my body.

"Jesus, Zane. Oh, oh."

Another push of the toy, and I arch my back, moaning.

His lips pull away from my cock. "Okay, now it's too fucking much for me." He hurries back onto the bed, on his knees between my legs, readying his cock with the lube.

He's worked me up so much, I'm all desire and need as he hooks an arm around my thigh, positioning me for him before sliding in. My body welcomes him—I'm sure because of how he's already worked me up, but also because he's trained me to take that thing.

"Jesus Christ, Leif. I've bottomed too much for you. I forgot how good it feels to be inside you."

Heat rushes up my body, pooling in my cheeks as he builds into a stride.

He licks his palm before gripping my cock. Then he licks the thumb and finger of his free hand and teases my nipple. Once he's set up his system, he gets busy fucking me.

It's too much, I'm fucking calling out, my moans encouraging him along as he picks up the pace.

I love filling him up, but right now, I just want him shooting into me.

As Zane fucks me, the bed shakes, and he built me up so much with that initial tease that this is too fucking much for me.

"Zane, you have to come. I'm about to—"

"Oh, don't you fucking worry about it, my pretty man."

His hips slam against me, and the way his body shifts and jerks, I know he's shooting into me.

Knowing that, and feeling these sensations with how he's stroking my cock and toying with my nipples, is too much, and it's like a wave comes over me before I blow, calling out, desperate to break that pressure, when the warm sensation shoots across my abs.

I'm lost in the pleasure, reveling in everything he's stimulated as he steadily pulls out before burying his face against my abs, licking and sucking me up. When he's finished, he nibbles at the flesh by my navel, before crawling up my body and resting against me, his elbows on either side of me to support his weight.

As I gaze up into his eyes, he's grinning, clearly thrilled with the experience himself and what he's done to me once again.

"Hot," he says before licking my lips.

I reach up, resting my hand against the side of his face. He closes his eyes, leaning into it, before he turns and kisses my palm.

"You know I'm all yours," he says. "Right?"

"Yeah. And I'm all yours."

He smiles, opening his eyes, leaning down to take another kiss, letting me taste myself.

We've been through some shit—Zane especially—but after what we've survived, feels like together, we can sort out whatever else comes our way.

Wild to think that when I first saw him around the neighborhood, he was just some creepy guy next door.

Now he's my sexy-ass creep.

And so long as I have any say in it, he always will be.

THE END

Receive New Release Alerts from Devon
eepurl.com/gi1Zzn

Find Devon on Social Media
linktr.ee/devonmccormack

ABOUT THE AUTHOR

Devon McCormack

Devon McCormack grew up in the Georgia suburbs with his two younger brothers and an older sister. At a very young age, he spun tales the old-fashioned way, lying to anyone and everyone he encountered. He claimed he was an orphan. He claimed to be a king from another planet. He claimed to have supernatural powers. He has since harnessed this penchant for tall tales by crafting worlds and characters that allow him to live out whatever fantasy he chooses. Devon is an out and proud queer man living in Atlanta, Georgia.

Find Devon:

www.devonmccormack.com